YOU

LOVED

ME

ONCE

You Loved Me Once
Copyright © 2021 Corinne Michaels
All rights reserved.

ISBN—paperback: 978-1-942834-65-6

Cover Design: Sommer Stein, Perfect Pear Creative

Editing: Nancy Smay

Proofreading: & Julia Griffis

Formatting: Alyssa Garcia, Uplifting Author Services

Cover photo © Regina Wamba

YOU LOVED ME ONCE

NEW YORK TIMES BESTSELLING AUTHOR
CORINNE MICHAELS

The women who make brave choices each day.

Today has been a remarkable day. It's the kind that every doctor lives for. I kicked *ass* today. All of my surgeries went perfectly, no big surprises or complications. Two chemo patients got to ring the bell, indicating they're done with treatment, and I only had to deliver bad news to one person.

That is a good day. Being a gynecological oncologist doesn't grant me many of them, but this . . . this was one.

"We have another surgery lined up in about an hour. I'm going to check on another patient and then I'll see you back down here," I explain.

Martina gives me the look that says I'm micromanaging again. "We're prepping the room now. Don't worry, we're on top of it."

"Good. I would hate to have to find a new nurse."

She laughs. "You will never get rid of me."

"Lucky me."

"I agree, you're lucky I love you enough to deal with your

crazy!" Martina yells as I'm walking away.

"Feeling is mutual!" I reply over my shoulder.

She is truly the best nurse I've ever worked with. Her patients come first, and she isn't afraid to piss people off to get things done. Which is pretty much how I live. My patients are my world. There's nothing I wouldn't do to help a patient fight this horrible disease.

I enter my favorite patient, Mrs. Whitley's, room.

"Well, I thought you weren't going to stop by this morning." Her smile is bright and warm.

Mrs. Whitley has become almost like a second mother to me in the last four years. Since she moved to inpatient care this month, I have begun coming here each morning to catch up with her and tell her more than I should. Today, though, I couldn't get here as early as I normally do.

"I had an emergency."

She scoffs. "Oh, please. I know you're a busy doctor and don't have time to sit with a dying woman."

"You're not dying today. You're too ornery to drift off peacefully."

She's the patient that med school professors warn you about—the ones you grow attached to and start to look at as something more than just a number.

I've done my best to keep her at a distance, but she's warm, funny, kind, and very alone. I see myself in her more than I care to admit most days. The way she's pushed her family and friends away when she lost the love of her life. How she struggles with forgiving herself for not doing enough.

But most of all, she reminds me of my mother. Which is really the worst part. "Now, tell me about your doctor beau."

I roll my eyes because most patients want to talk about

themselves, but not her. She got wind of the gossip a few months ago and hasn't let up since.

"Westin is good."

"Just good? Then the boy isn't doing it right."

I laugh. "He's wonderful, but you know I'm not going to get serious about anyone, least of all another doctor who is far too busy for a relationship. Whether he thinks he is or not."

This earns me a pointed finger. "Now, you listen, Serenity, you are not immune to love because you have a career. My Leo was a great businessman, but he had room for me and our son."

She is also the only patient I allow to call me by my first name.

I never correct her and I can't help but smile at how just the mention of her beloved husband causes her eyes to go soft. Leo died of a heart attack about five years ago. All the signs were there, but he pretended everything was fine, like my mother.

I knew better and if I had pushed her harder, maybe she would've lived.

I shake that off because I can't get wrapped up in nostalgia today, I have surgeries, and then tomorrow . . .

"I know that look . . ."

"What look?" I ask.

"The one where you're thinking about what tomorrow is and not the man we were discussing. Don't think I don't hear the gossip, missy. I know it's your big day and you're refusing to talk about it to anyone. Superstitions aren't a good thing."

"I'm not superstitious, I'm being cautious. Big difference, and aren't you supposed to be on my side?"

She shakes her head. "I wouldn't be doing my part if I agreed with you. Besides, you have a handsome doctor who

I'm sure does that."

Back to Westin again. She's nothing if not persistent. "I assure you, he loves to argue with me."

"All men do, but do let him win once in a while, it helps the fragile male ego," Mrs. Whitley's voice drops to a whisper on that last part.

"I'll do my best."

Then she laughs. "I doubt that, but still. I wonder if John will stop by for a visit today."

My heart breaks for her just a bit.

Years ago, when I asked what kept her fighting the cancer, she told me she was fighting for more time to try to make amends with her son. She wanted him to love her again. She told me how after Leo's death, she had a hard time being a mother. She loved her child, but he was a constant reminder of her husband. By the time she pulled herself back together, it was too late. His anger had taken root and grown.

But she fought, and still fights for him to come back around. A mother's love is the strongest bond in the world. My mother would've done anything for her kids.

"I hope he does."

"Me too, but if not, there's always tomorrow. And tomorrow is a day for miracles, Dr. Adams. I just know it."

Tomorrow is the big day. The chance to try a new way to fight cancer. So much could go wrong, but then again . . . it could go right. I try to focus on the possibilities rather than the failures.

This could be an answer to someone's prayers.

"Well, I have a surgery to get to, and you have an appointment with the phlebotomist," I tell her.

"Off you go then, no need to sit with me when you have

people to save."

"I'll see you tomorrow."

She smiles a wide grin that makes me feel like a child who pleased her mother. "Tomorrow, when you do great things."

I wink at her and leave, trying not to feel like I'm floating on air.

A few minutes later, I'm in the scrub room while my patient, Claudia, is prepped, and being wheeled into the operating room. I stand here, scouring my hands and arms, playing through the partial hysterectomy surgery in my mind. I've done this surgery over a thousand times, but I believe complacency is the mark of death. I won't allow myself to get comfortable when someone's on the table.

Once I'm fully scrubbed, I walk backwards through the doors and everyone goes into motion. My hands are covered, mask tied around my neck, and I walk over toward the patient.

"All right, Claudia." I give her a comforting smile, but the fear in her eyes is clear. "Do you have any last questions before we begin?"

"Just . . ." She shivers. ". . . want to make sure . . . I'll be okay."

Her teeth are chattering. "You're going to be fine," my voice is warm. "You're going to take a nap, and when you wake up, I'll have taken the tumor out. All of this is good, and you need to let me do my thing, okay?"

She nods, still with terror in her eyes. "Okay."

I can't let her be this afraid. I remember a few days ago, she told me she was a singer who toured for a long time before moving back to Chicago. I thought it was really cool that she knew so many of my favorite singers. "You know, before each surgery, we play music once the patient is asleep. I find that it really calms the room. How about this time, we start a little early, and you can listen to the music? Do you have a favorite song?"

She tells me the name and I nod to the nurse. The music fills the air and I watch her release a deep breath along with some of the anxiety. "This is helping."

"Good." I grin.

Claudia begins to sing, her soprano voice ringing out with each word. I let her go for a few more bars, and all the nurses sway and sing along. Her voice is beautiful, and I almost wish she wasn't going to pass out soon, but I watch the anesthesiologist push the drug into her IV and I know she's got just a few more seconds.

When her voice trails off as she falls asleep, I clear my throat and the surgical team moves into action. They know the drill. The nurse switches the iPod to my surgery playlist, and Bruno Mars fills the air, indicating that it's time to begin.

I go through my ritual. I stand on the left side of the patient, closest to her heart, lean my head back with my eyes closed, and count backwards from five. Five patients I've lost during surgery. I think of them, of what went wrong, and then I say their names.

Then I remember a few of the successes. I stand here, thinking of the cases no one thought I could win, and I smile. I replay the faces of the families when I told them I'd gotten all the cancer or that we were able to avoid the terrible outcomes they'd been preparing for.

The faith those families had in me was a gift. One I've never taken for granted. I say Claudia's name last and ask for a little help in ensuring she gets added to the column of successes.

I drop my head back down and open my eyes. I see Martina across from me, trust shining in her eyes.

I hold out my hand, and say the word that brings me back to reality. "Scalpel."

It's always a good day to save a life.

Martina places the blade in my hand and my heart swells with pride.

God, I hope I never have to count to six.

"**H**ello, gorgeous." Westin grabs me from behind, his strong arms wrap around me, and I grin.

"Hey."

"Just get out of surgery?"

I turn around, taking in the sight of him. He's seriously sexy and the kindest man I've ever met. It's what attracted me to him in the first place. Plus, he wants nothing serious, which is exactly what I want. We are perfectly happy in our non-relationship relationship.

I've learned the hard way that being a woman in a very male-driven job means sacrifices, and dating is one of them.

Plus, I already have a husband—the hospital. I don't have time for a boyfriend on top of it.

Still, Westin and I have a great routine that works for both of us. Neither gets upset or mad when the other works late or has to get up early for a surgery. We just go with it.

After my last relationship, I promised to never let my heart be tangled up like that.

"I did," I say as I give him a quick kiss. "All went well.

What about you?"

"I'm doing rounds today. I'd like to be doing something—or someone—else right now."

I laugh as his hand finds its way to my butt and he squeezes. Sex after surgery is really good. "Well . . ."

The door flies open and we split apart. Thankfully, we're behind the row of lockers so I have enough time to clean myself up.

"Hey, Dr. Adams," Tracy Allen, another doctor, smiles as she comes around. "Tomorrow is the big—"

"Nope!" I stop her there. "Tomorrow is abstract and all I'm willing to think about is today."

She nods. "Got it. Dr. Grant." She sees Westin and gives me a knowing smile. "I didn't mean to interrupt."

"You're not. Not at all. Thank you, Dr. Grant, we'll talk more later about the upcoming project." He shakes his head, but goes along with it.

"Sure thing."

No one in the hospital is buying what I'm selling, but I have to at least pretend we're not dating. Westin is the head of neurosurgery and the last thing I want is more people talking about either of us. We've had enough of that through the last year. There's a bid for chief of surgery coming up, and scandal—even a hint of it—could cost us both an opportunity. Not that I want it, but I know Westin does. Then there's the fact that both Westin and I know what a relationship in this industry looks like.

Too many friends have ended up divorced. It's hard to know that your marriage is second to your career—always.

I've lost a love once because of the choice to become a doctor. I won't lose another.

Tracy clears her throat. "Great, well, I have a consult I could really use your help on."

I look down at my watch, hating that it's so late. Claudia's surgery went off without a hitch and I was almost excited that I would get out of here early. Tonight is beer dip night at Rich's, the bar I go to. Usually it's Martina, my best friend Julie, and myself, but Julie mentioned really needing the night out, and while it's always the three of us, she may need it to be a duo tonight instead. I was hoping for a little girl time before Westin shows up.

Regardless, there's no way I'd walk away from Tracy or whatever patient she needs me to help with. Girl time can wait, patients shouldn't have to. "Of course," I say even though we all knew I'd never refuse her.

"See you later," Westin says with a smirk.

Ass. "Maybe."

We both know he'll be at my place later, like he always is.

Tracy and I head out and we talk about the mass she found in her patient. She's the head of OB-GYN and a trusted colleague. She shows me the patient's file, indicating the area causing her concern. We chat about what I see on the films and how I would proceed if the biopsy results come back as I expect. I operate on a lot more tumors than Tracy does and can usually get a good gauge on them before the pathology reports come in. Since my mom's death it's been my life's mission to eradicate cancer.

I don't care about anything but finding a cure for cancer and giving people whatever time is possible. Too many people die from this disease, and it blows my mind that we can find cures for the most random things, but for something that has touched everyone I know, we still can't find the perfect mix.

Come hell or high water, I want to be a part of destroying cancer's chances of taking one more person from this world. I've been a part of formulations, different approaches to radiation and chemo, but nothing has been fast enough or strong enough. It's frustrating, but it also fuels me.

"Here's the issue . . ." Tracy explains.

We spend twenty minutes really deconstructing Tracy's case. The tumor doesn't look cancerous to me, it seems more like a cyst than a tumor, but I can see where there's a reason to pause.

"So you think surgery is the best option?" she asks.

"It's really your only choice. I wouldn't leave the cyst in there. Plus, if it's not a cyst the last thing we want is for it to grow. The outer walls of the mass have me a little concerned, but I would be safe rather than sorry."

She nods. "Thank you. I know you were on your way home, but I appreciate you taking some time to look this over."

"I'm happy to help." I get to my feet. It's been a long day, and I'm beat. Tomorrow starts one of the biggest days of my life and I'd like to be alert. There's just one more thing I need to do before I can leave, and that's check on Mrs. Whitley. "We'll talk tomorrow?"

She nods. "See you then."

My phone pings with a text message.

Westin: I'm leaving now . . . are you tired or awake?

My teeth brush over my lip and I know exactly what that means.

I shoot off a quick text to Martina and Julie saying I can't make it and then I reply to Westin.

Me: Awake. Very awake. Give me a few. I have to check on a patient and I'll meet you there.

Who needs beer dip anyway? There's another thing I want much more right now.

I roll over and touch the cool sheets instead of the warm body I was expecting to find. Westin came back to my place after work, right? I swear he did. A whistling noise comes from the bathroom, and I grin.

Yup. He definitely did.

My imagination may be good, but it's not that vivid. I stretch my sore muscles and rub my eyes with a smile. Waking up with Westin Grant is the cherry on top of my sundae. He's the constant in my chaotic and unpredictable life.

The bathroom door opens and there stands my longtime— I don't even know what to call him—wearing nothing but a towel. Water drips from his hair and runs down his chest until it disappears into the towel at his waist.

"You're up," he smiles. "I thought I was going to get to wake you this morning."

"Not today. I don't think I slept more than an hour anyway."

"Do you ever?" he chuckles and moves toward me with that look. The look that says he was hoping to get his workout in this morning—with me.

"Wes," I warn as he crawls onto the bed.

"Ren," he grins.

"We can't," I shake my head at him and move toward the edge—away from him. "We both need to get to the hospital *on time* today. I cannot be late."

Today is when everything will really change. It's the day I've waited my entire professional life for. The day I'll finally be able to test whether my hopes for this new medication are right or epically wrong. I'm both excited and overwhelmed at the same time.

My clinical trial begins today. In the last five years, I've tried to find a mixture of drugs that will not only eradicate cancer, but also allow the women I treat to have hope for the futures they want. When an ovarian cancer diagnosis comes, we always treat first with surgery.

But what if we didn't have to?

What if I could save them from a hysterectomy and allow them to carry their own children? If my treatment works, I may be able to give them just that. With this combination of medications, I can shrink the tumor and save my patients from permanent infertility.

And if I can't, then . . . I'm not really sure what to think. I feel nervous, excited, and terrified all at the same time.

Will I screw up? What if I lose someone? What if I can't do this and it turns out I'm a fraud?

"I'll be quick," Westin jokes as his arms wrap around me. "Or I can hold you for a little."

I smile at him over my shoulder. "We don't cuddle."

"Only because you refuse to." His laughter vibrates against my neck and I shift away from him.

He's not wrong, it's definitely my fault, but I have my reasons. I'm good with how things are, and even though he gives me shit, it's all I'm capable of right now. Feelings lead to love.

Love leads to heartbreak. Heartbreak leads to me feeling weak, which I will never let myself be again. Besides, it's not like he has it all that bad. He gets sex without any expectations.

I roll over, pressing my hand to his cheek. "Don't pretend you don't like the way this works."

His warm green eyes roam my face. "I'm saying I wouldn't mind if this worked itself into something more."

I jerk back, surprised by this. Westin and I have an agreement, one that has worked well for us. "What are you even saying? What we have, it's . . . well, why make this complicated?"

"Complicated isn't always a bad thing, baby."

I tense at his term of endearment. Of course, he notices because there's not much he misses.

"We should get ready," I try to deflect, "I don't have time to debate what we are or anything else."

The last thing I want is to be a bitch, but today is a big day for me. He knows this, and if the roles were reversed, Westin would be the same. Part of the reason our convoluted quasi-relationship works is because we get this.

I don't have to explain my lack of emotional availability because we're both doctors. Damn good doctors.

"Serenity," Westin's deep voice washes over me as his lips brush mine. "There's always time for this."

"Not on clinical trial day. I need to be focused, steadfast, and you, my friend," I kiss him briefly, "know better."

His head drops to my neck, and he groans, and releases me. "I'm sure you'll text me to meet in the on-call room." He smirks as he stands and drops the towel, giving me a view of his perfect butt. "Where I'll gladly let you work off your anxiety—in many ways."

"Not today, Satan!" I yell while he re-enters the bathroom and closes the door.

As soon as he's out of view, my anxiety spikes thinking about how I was once where these patients' families are now. Fourteen years ago, I was driving my mother to her clinical trial for what we hoped would be the miracle we needed.

Fourteen years ago, it was me begging the doctors to save her.

Two months later, I was watching her casket be lowered into the ground.

There's not always a miracle, and I lost everything, including the person I thought I was. The girl who dreamed of a perfect life with a marriage, kids, and the affection my parents shared was laid to rest beside my mother.

I sit up, take a deep breath in for a count of four, hold it, and blow it out. I refuse to let anything ruin this moment—not fear, not someone else, and I'm definitely not going to allow *myself* to go down a rabbit hole I can't get out of.

Today is going to be a marathon and I won't allow the past to shadow the possibilities of what this could mean not only for me, but for the daughter who will be asking me to give her hope.

It's an hour before I need to be at the hospital. Thankfully, my condo isn't far and I can make it there in ten if I push it. Which I do often.

I head to the kitchen and brew a pot of coffee, check my phone, and attempt to decide what to eat. After a few minutes, I give up, not wanting anything and decide to get ready for today.

Westin stands in front of the mirror, brushing his teeth, wearing just the bottoms of his scrubs, which hang low enough to reveal the muscular cut above his hips. His light brown hair is cut short, and he has the most incredible green eyes. It's not hard to understand why every nurse, doctor, and intern fawns over him. He's every woman's version of the perfect man. Sexy, smart, rich . . . he's the total package.

"You've got that look, Ren," he grins at me in the mirror as he ruffles through his duffle bag.

Westin Grant is a very attractive man. I can't seem to help myself with him. I'm lonely in every part of my life, except when I'm with him. My feelings border on something more than friendship, but I can't afford to let myself go there. If I think about it, maybe his comment before isn't such a surprise. Every now and then, Westin will make a joke about finally calling this more than casual sex or moving in so we can stop with the back and forth. I never really thought much of it, but now I wonder if he has been hinting all along.

Does Westin really want more? Or does he like the idea of us together for real? Do I want more? The answers to these questions have to wait because I can't think about it today.

I can't think about anything right now. I have to stay light and playful and focused on the tasks of today.

"I like your butt," I say with a shrug. "Especially in scrubs."

He laughs, turns, and pulls me against him. "Yeah? Well, you're the sexiest thing I've ever seen when you're scrubbing in for surgery." Westin kisses my neck. "The way the soap moves up and down your arms, I can almost feel your soft skin." His voice is full of desire, and I'm trying to resist the pull. "I want to strip you down right there, touch your body, and finally tell everyone what we are."

"Is that so?"

"Yup," he runs his tongue along my ear and I shiver. "It's

too bad today isn't the day for a morning round."

I lean back, holding onto his neck. "Today is a day to save lives, and that's what this new dose of chemo is going to do. Then you can say you get to have mind-blowing sex with the ground-breaking, award-winning oncologist at Northwestern."

"So, I'm just your boy toy?" he leans in for a kiss, which I give freely.

"Pretty much."

He rolls his eyes and sighs. "Well, Dr. Badass, you better get in the shower before you're late for your own pre-trial."

"Do you think I'm crazy?" I ask.

His eyes narrow. "Crazy? Well, in what way?"

"For this . . . the whole trial. It could fail, and then what? Hell, what if the board doesn't allow it to proceed today and then I have to tell these people that I can't do it? I must be fucking insane for trying this!"

Westin deals with a different side of medicine, one that I'm a little jealous of. He saves more people than he loses. He can repair things, where I have to be methodical and sometimes it doesn't matter. Cancer will take their lives and I'll have no way to stop it. I'll watch a disease blacken everything around my patients, knowing I'm completely helpless. There are seldom times that Westin can't do *something* to help.

"You're not crazy, Serenity. You're brave, beautiful, and the best damn oncologist I've ever met. I think you'd be crazy for *not* doing this. You've already made it through phase one and two, this is the time to see where it can really go." Westin brushes my blonde hair off my face and smiles.

"And what the hell do I do if they cancel it?"

He pulls back a little. "Who? The board?"

"Yeah, there's no guarantee they'll push it through. I mean, they've approved it so far, but since Dr. Pascoe was out for the last two weeks, and the meeting got postponed, now I'm worried."

It's what has me feeling so uneasy. No one ever can predict the hospital's choices. One day they are on your side and the next the publicity is too much of a risk. We should've had this fully approved weeks ago, but Dr. Pascoe, the current president of the hospital, was dealing with an emergency and told me to push along as though we had the approval since delaying would change some of the patients' situations. Time is of the essence for us.

Westin releases a deep sigh. "There's a chance they won't, but it's all about how much you believe in it. Do you think doing this cocktail instead of surgery is worth the possible risk of a life?"

I look in his eyes, showing him the steel in my words. "One hundred percent. I know the data is inconclusive and can be argued, but I *know* it, Wes. If I could get this opportunity to prove it . . . I know this is the right dosage so that these women don't have to lose everything. We can shrink the tumor enough to remove it, treat the cancer, and leave the patients able to bear children. These women, some of them are in their twenties and thirties, and they have hopes and dreams. If it was me, and I had those dreams taken away, I can't imagine what I'd do. But what if I can give them more choices? What if they don't have to lose it all or die?"

He holds my gaze. "Remember this feeling, because if you suffer with a loss, you'll need this determination to push you through."

The memory of Westin a year ago comes back. I'll never forget how broken he was. We started our fling a year before he started his last trial. He was a cocky surgeon who wanted to be casual. Then his trial went downhill, and Westin retreated. No one could get him to talk, except for me, after he'd . . . worked off his pain. That was when our very casual fling became a friendship with sleepovers.

My chest tightens as I wonder if I'll be the same way if this doesn't work. "I can't go there," I say. If I admit defeat before the fight, it'll be a massacre. I need a victory.

"Good. You have to believe it'll work because it'll carry you through. And just know," he runs his thumb across my lip, "I'll be here every step of the way."

Sometimes, he does something and I don't know how to respond, and this would be one of those times. He says things that scare me, and I know he sees it. There are no steps for us. The next level doesn't exist. This is all I've got to give.

A long time ago, I learned that love doesn't guarantee happiness.

I will never love Westin.

I will never love anyone again. Not after finding out what losing love feels like.

"Westin," I say as a warning.

He takes a step back with his hands up. "I know, I know. I'm just saying as a doctor. If you need a consult, and of course, any kind of testing, to ensure it's working the way you hope."

That's not what he meant, but I'll give him the out because he gives me mine. "Right, sorry. I should've known that was it . . . I'm being stupid with all this. I'm sorry to think it was something else." I shake my head as though I'm embarrassed. Westin may be amazing, but he still needs to be a man. My father was the one who taught me about the need to preserve a man's delicate ego—or my mother did, actually.

My mother walked on water, but the real miracle was how she handled him. Mom was able to make him believe she needed him when we all know she could've done anything on her own, and probably better than he could.

She would tell me that men like having their feelings fluffed, and by doing so, they fluffed your own.

My mother was a smart woman. I miss her every day.

Westin needs me to fluff him a bit.

"Stop," he chuckles and wraps his arms around me. "You're overthinking things with the trial today. I wasn't clear. Speaking of the trial," he trails off and looks at his watch. "You better get moving."

If this combination doesn't work, then everything I've been working for is a waste. All the lonely nights, late hours, and faces of patients I've had to tell they can't have children have led to this moment. Right now, I can try to save women and give them time, but the cancer still robs them of something. It always does.

And my mind goes back to the one person from whom it took everything.

My mother.

I want to make her proud and prove that her trust in me wasn't for naught.

"Okay," I nod and rest my arms on his shoulders.

"Want breakfast?" he asks.

"I can't eat."

"Get ready and I'll go make something." He grips my cheeks and gives me a searing kiss. "You need to eat."

I stand here with my head resting on the wall as he leaves the bathroom. He's really perfect. There are times when I hate myself, and right now is one. I wish I were a bright-eyed girl who believed that love could save your soul. Rose-colored glasses may be stupid to own, but they make things beautiful.

I close my eyes as the steam floats around me, hating the hurt in my heart that I know won't ever heal.

"Ren," Westin knocks on the door, causing me to jump. "I got a call and need to head to the hospital now. I have a patient coming in for an emergency. I'll see you later?"

"Sure, see you at work."

"Dinner tonight and then stay the night at my place?" he asks.

"Maybe. I don't know."

I hear his chuckle at my response and then silence.

"What is *wrong* with me?" I ask myself. Maybe I should've gone for therapy, I could use some help here. "Focus. No time to debate your ridiculous issues today. This works for now. No need to muddle it."

I finish my shower and rummage through my closet. Dear Lord, I need a wardrobe makeover. Everything in here is drab and probably too big. It's not as if I have all that many reasons to dress up. My clothes consist of green scrubs and a white coat. On the rare occasion I'm not at the hospital, I'm usually in sweats or naked—either works for me.

Who needs pants anyway?

Grabbing the only semi-decent dress I own, I finish getting ready. Today, I take a little time to make myself look warm. *Whatever the hell that means.* I'm told constantly I look cold, put off, and damn near scary by the nurses. According to them, I don't smile enough.

However, my patients don't seem to mind. I produce results no matter what my temperature is.

My blonde hair is pulled back, and I line my brown eyes

with charcoal liner, happy I only stabbed myself in the eye twice this time. It's an improvement.

The phone blares Metallica and I smile, knowing who is on the other end of that call.

"Hi, Daddy."

"Serenity, my beautiful girl," Daddy's voice is beaming with pride.

"I'm not so beautiful right now," I chuckle. I have one eye with mascara on and one has a black blob of eyeliner under it.

I can precision cut a tumor without nicking anything, but putting on makeup? Forget it.

Daddy blows out a long breath. "You'll never see yourself the way I see you. So, today is the big day?"

"It is!" My voice rises with excitement.

I've bored my father with more details than the six-foot-three burly biker could ever care to know. I think he's now an expert on ovarian cancer and possible treatments. Although, he sort of was before. This victory is partially his.

My mother passed away two days after my twenty-fourth birthday with Everton, Daddy, and I beside her. Before that day, I can't remember ever seeing my father cry. But there he was, holding her hand, with tears streaming down his face. I held him as sobs wracked through his body, and he fell apart in my arms. He has only ever loved two things as much as he did Harmony Adams: his children, and the open road.

"I'm proud of you, Ren. I know I don't say it enough, but you're a remarkable woman. I wish your mother were here to see this." He clears his throat.

I wish she were too. "She's with me every day."

She's why I do this.

"Me too, honey. Me too."

If she hadn't died, I don't know that gynecological oncol-ogy would've been where I ended up. I don't even know that I would've finished school with a GPA high enough to get my residency at Northwestern.

Boys make you stupid and you lose focus on what matters.

My second alarm blares from the living room and I curse. "Damn it! I have to go, but I might be able to head up to the farm this week?"

Even as I say the words, I know it'll never happen. It's been a little over six months since I've been able to get up there. I've been so busy preparing for today.

"I'll believe that when I see it," he laughs. "Maybe you'll finally bring that boy to come meet me."

Not again. "Westin has to work."

"This is ridiculous, Serenity. It's been years that you've had these horrible excuses. Don't tell me that brain surgeons don't have a day off."

Sure they do, but the brain surgeon I frequently spend nights with doesn't need to meet my father. I can't even imag-ine the awkwardness of that meeting. My father wants to mar-ry me off and he's never going to see that happen.

"I'll check with him," I say, knowing I won't.

"Ren, love is . . ."

"Love is not something I'm going to talk about now," I cut him off. "I really have to go, Daddy."

"Kick cancer's ass, honey-pie."

"I will. Tell Everton I said hi!"

The phone disconnects, I grab a banana, and rush out the door. Time to make a difference in modern medicine.

3

On the walk to work, I go over the plan for my day in my mind. I want everything to go perfectly, however, I'm not stupid enough to believe that will happen. I've been a doctor long enough to know the only plan I should expect is chaos.

Today will be a little different since I'm going to be split between my trial and current patients. Twenty-five patients were admitted into this round of the trial, each with varying early stages of ovarian cancer. My research has shown that this medicinal cocktail that I put together should help significantly reduce the size of the tumor that is left if the patient wants to keep her ovaries and uterus. If I'm able to debulk enough of the tumor and leave the ovaries intact before the cancer is at stage II, I can treat the remaining cancer with this drug and the patient can keep everything without a hysterectomy. For any woman still wanting children, this will hopefully become an option. I can get them cancer free, and leave the possibility of having a baby open to them.

At least that's the goal.

I stand before the hospital, and look up thinking about how when I'm at the top of my game, I feel like I could touch God. Hell, I feel like I *am* a god some days, but I know I'm not. I'm mortal and so are the people here. It's my job to keep them alive as long as possible.

"Are you going to stand out here all day?" Martina asks, startling me.

"If I do, today hasn't officially begun yet," I smile, still looking up.

"If you don't start, you'll never know if it works."

"I'm almost ready," I tell her. "I'm just trying to get my bearings."

"All right then," she places her hand on my shoulder. "I'll let you freeze your ass off alone."

"Thank God for friends like you," I joke.

She bounces a little and rubs her hands up and down her arms. "I love you, Ren, but I love my fingers more."

My eyes squeeze closed and I exhale through my nose as she runs off.

"Wimp!"

Okay, Serenity, you can do this. You were made for this. You gave up everything to succeed, now do it.

Sounds easy enough.

I step through the glass doors and people move around. I love this place. I don't love many things, but this hospital is my safe place.

When my life fell apart years ago, it held me together. I took all the pain, disappointment, frustration, and channeled it into my job. No doctor worked harder than me and it paid off. I have rounds to get through, and then . . . I begin my destiny.

Okay, maybe destiny is a bit much, but I'm going to run

with it.

Deep in my heart, I have this overwhelming feeling that today will be the day in my life when something magical will happen.

I make my way to my locker, grab my coat, and head out to do rounds before my board meeting. Since Mrs. Whitley is the bright spot in my day, I head there first. She is in the rehabilitative wing since we know there's nothing that I can do, but I can't seem to let her off my caseload. Knowing that I could use a little brutal honesty and perspective before the trial begins, I make the trip there.

"Dr. Adams," she grins. "Today is a good day!"

"It sure is." I return her warm smile.

"I'm so lucky to have you as my doctor."

If she was lucky, she wouldn't be dying. I know that all the cards are stacked against us. Her cancer is advanced, she's not a young woman, and this isn't her first go-around either. I was fully aware, but it didn't stop my heart from becoming attached to her.

And when I lose her, it'll hurt more than I care to admit.

"Well, I don't know about luck, but I'm sure glad you found me."

She pats my hand, and then sighs. "Are you excited?" Her shoulder scrunches up as the excitement fills her voice.

"I am, but . . ."

"Nervous?" She fills in the blank.

I could admit it, but I won't. Nerves have no part in today. "Not really."

She looks me over with pursed lips. "Sure, honey. Doctors are not robots, although, maybe *you* are."

"How about we check your vitals and see how you're

doing?" I deflect. It's always a viable choice. "How did you sleep? Are you eating?"

She tells me about her pain levels and that her appetite is far gone. I wish I had something to help her, but there's nothing left to do but wait. Which is the absolute last thing I want to do.

My heart aches for her because no one sits with her, and she's lonely unless the nurses or I visit. I was by my mother's side every single day. I would go to school and spend the rest of my time beside her. The fact that Mrs. Whitley's son doesn't visit pisses me off.

There is such a thing as regret. He'll wish he'd come around when he still had time.

"Let's say you only have one day left to live, who would you have one last . . . night in the sack . . . with?" Mrs. Whitley asks this as I take her blood pressure. While it's not normally a part of my job, I'm happy to do whatever I can to justify hanging out with her.

"Anyone?" I ask. My first thought is of course Bryce. It doesn't matter how many years have passed—the memories haunt me. His smile, the way he brought every part of me alive just being near him. I miss him. More than that, I miss who I was when I was with him. I wasn't jaded, angry, or so sure that I would never find true love. He was my true love—until we fell apart.

Then I think about Westin and how, even now, he's not my first thought. I really hate myself for not being strong enough to forget Bryce.

I don't want to think of him. But he's a part of me. Bryce lives inside of my heart and no matter what I do to try to eradicate him—he doesn't leave.

"Anyone." Her fragile smile reminds me that time isn't on her side. Mrs. Whitley is fading. It's reality, and I can't make it stop. All day, she sits alone and stares out the window. It's hard to watch the life drain from her, so I come and spend my very scarce extra time with her. "Dr. Adams, I'm waiting."

Lord knows she doesn't do well with that.

"Hmmm," I ponder as I check her pulse. "Adam Levine?"

"Oh, he's quite a sexy man. My Leo would've been jealous of his hip moves." Her eyes light up since I know this is her choice too. She waffles between him and bringing back JFK from the dead.

"He is."

"You should find him. You're so pretty, I'm sure he'd like you. Most doctors don't look like you." She tells me each day how beautiful I am and that I need to marry Westin, since we're both doctors, and save the world. I wish it were that simple. I couldn't even save her.

"How so?"

"Well, most girls who are smart don't have a clue. Like my granddaughter, for example, Lord knows she could really benefit from a hairdresser and some makeup, but you're pretty. Lots of pretty girls aren't very smart."

I laugh at her commentary. "I'm not sure that's a compliment," I grip her hand with a smile.

"It is. And you should never argue with a dying old lady," she reprimands me. "I'm telling you that you've got it all. You should use what God gave you and get yourself hitched to Westin before he smartens up and finds a girl who sees what a catch he is."

That thought sobers me. I may not love Westin, but we've sort of been together for so long, I hadn't thought about him with another girl.

But today is not the day for these thoughts, damn it. I need to stay focused on the task. "You're not dying on me today, so we can argue this for a while longer."

Her cancer has spread so far there is nothing I can do. We fought a hard battle, round after round of chemo and radiation, but in the end, this horrific disease will take her.

"Oh, now, you don't know if that's true. We're all dying, we're just not dead yet. And stop trying to throw me off here, we were talking about you being a pretty lady that doesn't have a *real* boyfriend. That doctor of yours is going to get tired of you stringing him along. Now, back to Adam Levine and any other options we can think of."

"You're awfully feisty today," I laugh. "Besides, I don't need options because I have patients like you who keep me from being lonely."

It's partially true.

"Dr. Adams," she rests her frail hand on my arm. "How much longer do I have?"

If my heart could break, it would right now. I promised myself to always be honest with my patients about their diagnoses. It's a trust I don't intend to break, but it pains me.

"I can't answer that for you, I know that's not what you want to hear. All I know is, we'll do everything we can to make you comfortable," I assure her.

"Comfort for the body does nothing to soothe the soul," she says, and looks away.

This is the worst part of my job. It's the feeling of knowing I couldn't give her more time. The way my chest aches when I think of those I couldn't save. Each time I lose a patient I'm reminded how short our lives are. One cell turns dark and infects the rest.

"Did my son call?" she asks me as if on cue. Each day I watch the life drain from her blue eyes when I answer her.

I look at the clock, I have four more patients to check on, but I know right now she needs the comfort. "John called earlier, he asked for an update," I lie.

We talk a little more and she tells me a story about her husband. I've heard it at least ten times, but each version changes a tiny bit. I laugh at her jokes, smile appropriately when she tells me how magical their lives were, and I envy her a little. She's lived and loved with her whole being. She was able to hold onto her husband, Leo, until the day he died.

"I should get to my other patients before I'm accused of having favorites," I joke as I get up.

"You do great things today, Dr. Adams."

I smile and nod. "I will."

I wave goodbye and head to the lab. I need to make another check on all the trial documents, because I'm crazy and can't let this go. There's no such thing as being too thorough, right? I enter the lab, where Julie spends her days hiding behind her microscope.

We both went to medical school, but she'll never have to look at a patient and give them bad news because she chose lab work over patient practice. I definitely envy that on bad days.

"Ren! Tell me I look gorgeous today," Julie greets me as I walk in.

"Morning, Jules. You always do."

Julie, Martina, and I have been friends since college. They are the only people other than Westin I associate with outside of work.

Waiting for test results is never fun, but when the pathologist doesn't like you, it's torture. Thankfully, I have Julie on my side and she rushes my labs.

"For the love of God, you're not up here to check the packets again, are you?" She rolls her eyes.

I don't respond—she'll just give me hell. Instead, I make my way over to where the packets lie on the counter, counting each one, and reviewing the order in which the patients are listed.

My trial is being run as almost a lottery. Since phase I went off showing no major safety concerns, and phase II showed promising results, it's time to step it up and see how much we can accomplish. However, this time, two patients will receive a placebo that will not be aggressive enough to shrink the tumor the way I believe the new medication will.

As each patient arrives, they'll be given a number that corresponds with a packet. I have no clue which packets contain the medication until we open them. Of course, all the patients still receive chemotherapy, but not what I believe to be the right mixture to kill the tumors and those patients will most likely need a hysterectomy by the end of four weeks.

"You're going to make yourself crazy," Jules says as she leans on the table beside me.

"I'm already crazy."

"This is true," she agrees. "Talk to your brother today?"

I glance at her from the side and roll my eyes. She's in love with Everton, which is ridiculous since he's an idiot.

Jules is smart, beautiful, and comes from a very long line of doctors.

Everton is the quintessential bad boy. He drinks, smokes, rides a Harley like my dad, and we won't even talk about how he dresses. He's the complete opposite of her type.

"Don't look at me like that," she laughs and nudges me.

"Give up, Jules. You will never tame the beast that is my brother."

She sighs and rests her head on her hand. "One day he'll love me."

My friends are insane. That's all I can guess at this point because they all inevitably do this when it comes to my brother.

In high school, I lost my friend Gabby because she slept with him, and the next day watched another girl walk out of his bedroom. It was horrible and I hated him for that, but he will never change. Sure, he cares for Dad, but it's because he has free room and board and my father couldn't give a crap who he brings home.

After Mom died, my father stopped caring about a lot of things.

"Do us both a favor and forget that Everton exists. Please?" I tilt my head and jut out my lip.

"Whatever, let's talk about Doctor Sexyass." She grins as she fans herself with the file in her hand. "How is he?"

I roll my eyes, resting my arm on the table. "If he makes chief, are you going to call him Chief Sexyass?"

"Oh, no, he'll be Sir Sexyass. So much hotter, don't you think?"

She's ridiculous. "He would love this. Please don't ever let him hear that people call him this."

Julie continues on like I didn't speak. "I'd love to strip him down and do rude things to that man."

"You'd definitely enjoy it. I'll be sure to let him know you're interested. We didn't make plans for tonight if you'd like a go with Wes," I say jokingly.

"I don't get you." She drops the folder. "Are you stupid?

Seriously, what the hell is wrong with you, Serenity?"

Okay, that escalated quickly and in an odd way. I don't know what she's suddenly pissed off about. "What did I do now?"

Julie gets out of her chair and throws her hands up. "It's what you don't do."

"Which is?"

"Get jealous!" Jules yells. "You've been screwing his brains out for two years now and you never care when people talk about him. Hell, you actually pimped him out. It doesn't make sense. It's literally the stupidest thing ever. How could you be so uncaring, because that's not who you are. He's a great guy!"

I shrug. It's what it is. What does getting jealous do? Nothing. It's a pointless emotion that will only leave me feeling bad about myself. I'm not exclusive to Westin, so if he wants to date someone else, I have no right to stop him.

"We're both aware of what we are. I'm exactly that person. I care about Westin, but he's not mine."

Jules huffs in frustration. "So you wouldn't care if I walked up to him right now and stuck my tongue down his throat?"

I ponder it for a second. There's a tiny tug in my stomach thinking of him with someone else, but I don't trust that it's because of anything related to the grand idea of love. The whole idea that love makes you stronger is the biggest line of bullshit I've ever heard. There's nothing strong about love. My father loved my mother with his whole heart and when she died, he died with her. I loved Bryce, only to be left behind. I'd rather never feel those emotions again. I'd rather heal people, make things better and erase the damage life can cause instead of inviting it in.

But what if I did lose Wes? What if my life was no longer filled with those nights together? I've never thought about it because we just . . . are. Screw Julie for making me think this way.

Julie clears her throat, bringing me back. "Well?"

"I don't know. I wouldn't be jealous, exactly. I want to think if it made him happy, then I'd be okay with it."

"You're going to regret this one day, my friend. He's going to get tired of waiting for your frozen heart to thaw and find a warm body who wants it all. It'll be sad because you'll wake up, wondering why you didn't see how perfect he is for you."

Sometimes I wish for that. Not because I want to lose him. I do care about Westin. He's a wonderful man and he's been there for me in so many ways.

He's been the constant in my crazy life, and I don't want to watch him walk away, but I know he wants the happily ever after. I don't want to rob him of the life he desires and I'm not selfish enough to keep him if he can find love elsewhere.

One thing she said keeps reverberating inside my head, though.

"Jules?" I call her name with hesitation.

Her face shifts from irritation to concern at the tone of my voice.

Julie is the kindest person there is, which is why she wanted to avoid patients. To see someone hurting, sad, fearful, or experiencing any extreme emotion sends her spiraling. She could never tell family members bad news—she'd lose her mind. Despite that, when Julie saw me at the bottom of the barrel, she wrapped her arms around my waist and kept me upright.

I owe her everything. I don't know if I would still be functioning if it weren't for her.

"Ren?"

"Do you really think I have a frozen heart?"

The idea that people who actually know me see me that way hurts deep in my soul. I feel so much more than anyone might guess. I've learned to hide it well. Patients deserve my focus, not my worry about stupid things I can't change. Being part robot is par for the course, but Jules has also witnessed me on the floor, unable to get up.

I've only been there twice, but she was there both times.

Once when I lost Bryce.

The other when I lost my mother.

"No, Ren. I know you're not really an Ice Bitch, but it would be good to show others that. Westin especially. He loves you and you don't see it."

Again, she's wrong. "Westin may feel more than he allows other people to perceive, but he doesn't love me. We can't . . . he can't . . . it's not possible. We're comfortable, and what we have is all it'll be. In some part of my heart, I wish it was different. He is perfect and I know that," I tell her honestly. "I would fall for him in a heartbeat if I wasn't so damaged, disillusioned, or driven."

Julie laughs. "Stubborn, stupid, and masochistic were my descriptors, but those work too."

"Gee, thanks."

"You're not the only one who had a college boyfriend who hurt her. I thought David and I were going to last forever, but I date and *want* to find love again. You don't have to live your entire life based on one relationship. I'm sorry you guys didn't work out, but Jesus Christ, it's been fourteen years, let it go already."

Bryce wasn't just some relationship. He was more. He was

everything. It's different. "I know you don't understand it, but losing him and losing my mother, Julie, it was too much. I can't explain it, and I know you and Martina think I'm ridiculous, but what I felt for him, it's not like anything you could ever understand."

"I know what love is, Ren."

"This was love beyond measure."

She shakes her head. "But he let you go and you now have to let him go, so that someone else can find a way in."

"It's not the—" I start to say but the speaker on my hospital phone beeps.

"Dr. Adams, please call nurses' station seven."

I give Jules an apologetic look. "You're not going to listen anyway," she says, laughing sarcastically.

That's the one thing I love about her, she gives it straight and doesn't mince words. It's nice knowing what someone thinks without a filter—sometimes.

The phone picks up on the second ring. "Dr. Adams, one of your trial patients is here."

"Now?"

There's another three hours before the first grouping should be here. I've got the meeting with the board in twenty minutes, and we're not allowed to start before then.

"Yes, she flew in from out of state, and wasn't feeling great."

Damn it. "Okay, get her set up in one of the rooms. I'll be down soon, but let her know it'll be a bit."

"No problem," Martina assures me.

Julie walks over and gives me a hug. "I'm so proud of you, Ren."

"Thank you."

"Seriously, this is a pretty cool day considering we were two drunk morons in college, but do me one favor . . ."

Oh, for fuck's sake. Julie needs to stop watching chick flicks and come back to reality. "Julie."

"No," she puts her hand up. "Just think about what would happen if Westin really got tired of being an afterthought. Think what your life would be like. Think about how you'd feel. I promise it's not going to be good. You're not a callous person, there's no way that after this long your feelings aren't deeper than they'd be for a casual fuck."

He is more than that. He's a friend and puts up with all my shit. I've been guarded, and haven't allowed myself to want more.

Could I?

Am I ready to even consider it?

I don't know, but a part of me is pissed that Julie made me think about this now.

"I have to go," I say tersely. Today isn't the right time to think about this shit. I'm not ready and I have other things to focus on.

Damn her.

Julie smirks. "Love you too."

I head down the hallway, mentally preparing for the board meeting. We need to go over everything, ensure that I'm prepared and the hospital isn't at risk. Even though this isn't the first phase, they have to protect their asses.

As I make my way down the corridor, I smile and nod as I pass some of the heads of the departments. They will each grill me, going over each possible outcome and how I plan to handle them all.

When I get to the door, Dr. Pascoe, the president of the hospital, stands with a warm smile.

"Dr. Adams, it's nice to see you," he says.

"It's great seeing you, as well. How's Monica?" I ask. Dr. Pascoe and I are in a unique relationship. His wife, Monica, was my patient. She was diagnosed with cervical cancer three years ago and has been in remission for six months. To say that he likes me is an understatement.

"She's doing well, wants me to insist that you come by for the Fourth of July barbeque."

Well, that would be breaking rule number one, no friendships with patients.

It's better for them and much better for me.

"I wish I could . . ."

"But you won't," he finishes.

"You understand, don't you?" I ask.

Dr. Pascoe touches my shoulder. "I do, I'll let her down gently. Make her think it's a hospital rule or something." He gives me a wink.

He's a great administrator. I like him for personal reasons, but also because he puts the patients' needs first. The amount of red tape he sees in his job can be intimidating, but Dr. Pascoe ensures there are minimal hurdles when it comes to saving a life. He also treats each doctor who works for him as an equal. It's nice not feeling looked down upon.

"Thank you."

"Of course. You know that today is mainly a formality, right?"

"Nothing is ever that simple," I counter, because I know full well they can pull the plug if I say something they don't like.

"This is true," he chuckles. "What time do your patients arrive?"

"I actually have one here now. She wasn't feeling well, from what I'm told. As soon as we wrap up here, I'll head to her room."

He nods. "You didn't see her beforehand?"

My answer could make me look either responsible or uncaring. "I didn't. I didn't want to see her until I was fully green-lighted. If something were to happen in this meeting that pulled the trial, I didn't want to have given her misinformation."

I'd rather go with my best foot forward. Which I will, after I know I'm approved completely.

"Makes sense. Shall we?" He motions forward.

We enter the boardroom and my colleagues start to trickle in. I stand with my hands resting on the cool leather seat, trying to keep my heart rate steady. Public speaking isn't my thing, and it's definitely harder in front of a firing squad.

I've had to do this five times, whenever I've lost a patient in surgery, and each time was equally horrific. Not only was I broken over knowing I'd lost someone, but then to have to recount each moment, decision, and error in front of my peers, have my decisions picked apart . . . it's unimaginable.

A few of the doctors smile their encouragement, having been where I'm standing now, and I focus on breathing. All the chairs but one are filled, and Dr. Pascoe clears his voice. "I'd like to begin since Dr. Adams already has a patient waiting."

Everyone nods and I head over to close the door. But a hand presses against the wood, stopping me, and I gasp as I realize who it is.

"Sorry I'm late," Westin says with a smile.

"Late?"

Confusion spreads through me. He never mentioned he'd be here and I hadn't thought neurosurgery would be involved in my trial. All he'd said this morning was that he'd see me later. I wasn't aware he'd be part of the approval board. Westin may be the hot doctor, but he's also the asshole on these boards. He grills the doctors coming before the board, making them uncomfortable so they'll slip up.

Well, this should be great.

"Take a seat, Dr. Grant," Dr. Pascoe notions to Wes. "Hello everyone. As you know, Dr. Adams is now in the third phase of her trial with the new chemotherapy regimen for treating ovarian cancer. The first two phases proved, for the most part, positive, and delivered safe results. This phase will be run slightly differently, and we'll need a majority approval or denial."

Please don't pass out. Please don't throw up. Please approve this.

Westin clears his throat. "I'd like to say something before we begin. I am going to be waving my right to vote on whether the trial should proceed due to the personal relationship I have with Dr. Adams. However, I will participate in the inquiry in order to best serve the hospital and the patients involved if that's acceptable by the board. Chief?"

Dr. Pascoe's eyes move to mine and he nods. "I accept that. Does the board have any objections?"

A chorus of "no's" go around.

Great.

He looks to his secretary. "Please note the board does not object to Dr. Grant abstaining from the vote." Dr. Pascoe turns back to me. "Dr. Adams. You have the floor."

The table is in a "u" formation with a table, chair, and microphone in the middle. It's an intimidating seat, where all eyes are on you. I don't sit, I stand with my fingertips grazing the wood. Nerves fill my belly, making their way up my throat, but I swallow them down. I need to be a badass doctor right now.

"Hello, thank you for being here today. I can't tell you how exciting it is to be on the brink of a new medical discovery that could revolutionize the way we treat ovarian cancer." And I begin to launch into my presentation, my nerves growing less shaky as I get into the zone.

That is, until Westin raises his hand, interrupting my speech. "Dr. Adams, this is all well and good, and as doctors ourselves, we understand the desire to save everyone, but we also know that cancer isn't that clear-cut."

"No, it's not," I agree.

"So why detour from a known treatment path? Why should we risk this hospital's reputation?" He leans back with his brow raised.

Based on his aggression, no one in this room would believe that a few hours ago he was trying to shove his tongue in my mouth. I can't believe he's the first one to fire a shot at me, but I refuse to let him win.

I lean forward, looking directly in his eyes. "Throughout my entire career, I have studied different treatments and various drug cocktails to treat and shrink tumors in the ovaries. I have yet to find anything that has done exactly what this combination has done." My knuckles turn white from pushing down on the table with all my weight.

"That doesn't answer my question," Westin pushes further. "Why is your drug treatment worth allowing the possible loss of life?"

My legs start to tremble, however, my voice stays steady. I want these people to respect me and understand that this is exactly what we need to do. "Yes, it is possible we could lose a patient by delaying surgery if a tumor is resistant to the drug cocktail and doesn't shrink as we'd hoped. We may end up dealing with a number of other side effects, but the fact remains that these women are willing to take that risk. Your question is like me asking why a doctor would operate on a brain bleed when you could administer medication first."

Westin smirks, shifts closer, and shakes his head. "Let's not go there, Dr. Adams. This isn't remotely close to choosing to operate or choosing not to. You are asking us to let you give a mix of drugs that we don't have any proof will actually help reduce tumors. If it is not successful, not only will these patients need the hysterectomy you're trying to avoid, but their cancer may progress, requiring more aggressive chemotherapy later on."

In the bedroom, he's kind, loving, and takes care of me. Right now, he's acting like a prick who wants to dismember me. I don't know how to reconcile this, but I won't let him ruin today. He was the one who told me I was crazy if I didn't do this.

He held me in his arms, telling me he was proud and he'd be there each step. Now I'm wondering if he meant to push me down the steps. Then I remember this is Westin. He's not cruel and there must be a reason for him acting this way. I steel myself, keeping my demeanor professional and sure.

"Yes, they're different, but aren't they the same in some ways? Is the risk worth more than the reward? How do you determine the odds, Dr. Grant?"

"I'm not the one asking the hospital to stick its neck out for a trial that we aren't certain will yield any results at all. You are."

"I'm completely aware of that, but I've also proven in the last six months that I'm not throwing caution to the wind. I've shown positive results with the adjustments in the last three patients in phase two. A reduction that I've never been able to produce before with any other drugs in so short a time. I believe this round will show an even greater shrinkage in the tumors."

Westin leans over to the head of cardiology and whispers something before looking back at me. If looks could kill, Westin would need every doctor in this room to save his ass.

"Dr. Adams," the head of OB-GYN interrupts the staring contest I was having with my . . . partner.

"Yes?"

"As someone who refers a great deal of patients to you, I have a different opinion on this," Tracy's eyes are soft. She too has had to tell many patients the bad news. "I'd like to point out the repercussions of not pushing past the current protocols of medicine. If we are to keep with the status quo, are we not ruining our reputation that way? Are the advantages of taking the safer route greater than the advantages of doing something potentially groundbreaking?"

A few people move in their chairs writing things down, which I take as a positive sign.

"Exactly," I say. "We have to be better than our predecessors. As doctors, it's imperative to try to find not just the right treatment, but the best one for each patient. None of us have the answers or a crystal ball, but we have science and training, and I'm not taking a gamble I wouldn't take myself."

"You're telling me that if you had ovarian cancer right now, you'd attempt this trial? You'd risk the chemo, which we know doesn't always shrink the tumor, go through weeks of hell, and possibly still need a hysterectomy?" Westin asks.

"If I was in the position to save my eggs and possibly still bear children, yes."

"Even knowing there's no real proof? *Even if* you knew that you would be putting yourself at great risk?"

I lean against the table and look him dead in the eye. "Absolutely. I believe in this treatment. It's not always about life or death. To some women, it's about having a choice. Their disease is out of their control, but this is something they can choose. They aren't delusional about what the outcome might be, but it could be exactly what these patients need to keep fighting. They aren't too far gone that we can't at least try. If it fails, at least we will have done everything we can. So you asked me if I would do it? Yes. I would administer this to myself, my mother, and anyone I love, because it is working. The girl in the previous trial is alive with a tumor three-fourths the size of the one she came in with, and I will be able to operate this week to remove it. How much more proof do you need that this mixture of drugs is worth trying? We get to reduce the tumor, save the patient from a hysterectomy, and preserve the option for her to bear children later."

He nods and I look around the room at the others following his motion. "I appreciate the honesty, Dr. Adams. As you said, the risk of denying you would possibly hurt patients."

Everyone nods, looking to me.

Westin Grant may not be voting, but he just won the entire room for me.

He wasn't grilling me because he's an asshole trying to take me down. He was making me push past the nerves and bullshit to display my passion.

Once again, the question I asked myself earlier slams around in my head: *what the hell is wrong with me?*

Our eyes meet and I see the warmth there. Westin is on my side. A part of the heart inside me that vowed it couldn't love again cracks. Just a little.

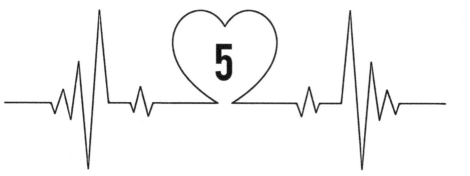

After my spirited debate with Westin, the vote goes through unanimously. The protocol was set as to how often I have to submit results, and the hospital has assigned two other doctors to consult. They'll act as my liaisons to the board, and also my tattletales. If there's anything that seems out of place, it's their job to report it.

The room clears out, leaving Tracy and Westin alone with me.

"Good luck, Ren," Tracy says gripping my arm. "I'm rooting for you."

"Thanks for backing me up."

"I'm always going to support anything like this. People's lives are too important to play political games with, right?"

I nod. That's where medicine gets its bad name, from the political bullshit that goes on behind the scenes. Denying people what they need, thanks to insurance or doctors whose egos hinder the decision to provide treatment that might actually work.

We've all seen it, and *good* doctors hate it.

Westin takes his time stuffing papers into a chart as Tracy walks out of the room. Once we're alone, I decide it's time Dr. Grant and I have a talk about what just happened.

"So . . ." I say, walking toward him.

His eyes lift and he grins. "Hey."

"Thank you."

Wes pushes his hair back and then rubs his chin. "For?"

"Being on my side."

He releases a heavy sigh. "I told you I was."

"You did, and then you seemed to turn for a minute there," I laugh softly, standing in front of him and leaning on the table. "I wasn't sure what you were doing trying to rake me over the coals. Especially since you never mentioned you'd be in the meeting."

"What would've been the fun in that? It was much better looking like you were caught off guard and then having your side piece tear you to shreds in front of your mentor. I mean, at least now people will believe we're nothing more than sex buddies."

"You're more than that, Wes." The words fall out effortlessly and I wish I could pull them back.

He jerks back slightly, runs his fingers through his light brown hair, and smiles. "How about that?"

Damn it.

"What?"

Westin gets to his feet with the folder in his hands and then taps me with it. "Growth."

I'm not even sure what I meant. Of all the days for me to decide to change something between us, why today? For two years I've been totally content with keeping things simple, then Julie says some stupid shit and I'm adjusting my thinking?

"Whatever," I blow off his comment as I push off of the table. "I was going to come looking for you anyway."

He chuckles. "I figured."

"Oh, did you?" I ask as we head out into the hallway.

"Well, that is kind of your thing. You often want to find me before a big surgery or something else where you need to work off some stress, don't you?" Westin jokes.

I'm not sure why that bothers me at all. He's right. But I realize it makes me sound like a crazy sex fiend. Which isn't the case . . . for the most part. We're friends, and I trust him in a way that I haven't allowed myself to trust anyone else.

"Yes, but that isn't why I was looking for you," I try not to look affronted.

"Really?"

"Yes, really. I'd like to think our time together at work is about more than me finding you for sex, Wes."

Westin jerks his head back slightly. "Okay, you're right, sometimes you come talk to me about a patient."

The small knot in my stomach constricts. He did something for me and I want to repay him. "Well, this time I was going to come find you to talk about us having dinner tonight."

"Tonight?" he asks.

"Unless you're taking back the offer . . ."

Westin shakes his head, leans against the wall, and smiles. "Nope."

"I was hoping that maybe we could have dinner tonight. You know, celebratory or whatnot?"

I suddenly feel very shy, unsure of exactly what I should be saying or doing. I know I'm not usually the one to initiate anything even remotely relationship-like, and I know I have to make a choice. Maybe we won't ever be madly in love with each other, vowing our lives to one another. However, I'm realizing we can be more than we are right now.

We can have dinner plans, movies, and friendship. I know that Westin gets my life. He understands the stresses of being a doctor. I don't need wild, heart-stopping, soul-shattering love. I need steady. I need a rock that will anchor me when I feel like I'm floating away. Westin could be that. Maybe Westin is the guy who is supposed to hold me up when I'm falling down.

I've never had that before.

Westin looks at me with his head tilted to one side and he touches my cheek with his thumb. "Are you asking me on a date?"

I shrug, smile a little, and look at my feet. "I guess I am," I look back up. "What would you say to that?"

Westin's brow raises, his hand drops, and he leans in to give me a tender kiss. "I guess I would have to say yes."

"Good."

He smiles and wraps his arm around me. "Good."

The two of us stand here, exhibiting a public display of affection at the hospital for the very first time. At work, we've always maintained a very professional relationship. I take a step back now, feeling a bit of unease about touching him in the open. I'm pretty sure every member of the hospital is aware of our relationship, but it doesn't mean I'm ready for it to be gossip fodder.

"Hi, Dr. Grant," a nurse waves with the tips of her fingers as she passes by the open door where we're standing and I roll my eyes. "You look very handsome today," she adds.

"Hi, Tammi," he smiles.

Stop looking at him, you stupid hussy.

Wait. Is that . . . jealousy?

No. It couldn't be. I'm not a jealous girl, especially when it comes to my non-relationship-relationship.

"I'll see you tonight?" Westin grips my elbow.

I nod, snapping back to reality. "Yes."

"I have two surgeries today. What time do you think you'll be done?"

"With the trial starting, I have no idea. I can't screw this up, you know?"

I say this carefully, aware of his own trial experiences and afraid to poke a wound. I don't know how he was able to pick himself up and continue on after losing six patients in his trial last year. I'm not sure I would survive that kind of blow.

"You'll do great, Ren. You always do. There's a reason you're the most sought out oncologist." He pushes my hair back and his voice is low. "People look at you and feel a sense of . . . serenity. You give them that because of what's inside your heart. You let them see how much you care, you give them that comfort because they need it as much as you need to give it."

My heart races and I realize Jules was right. Westin is a catch and I shouldn't forget the line of women waiting for their chance at more with him. But can I give more when I feel like I'm already at my threshold? Am I capable of putting myself out there to love again?

I've been holding onto my past for far too long, and it's time to move on. I haven't wanted to ever hurt like that again. I've learned how to be alone. It's been so many years since I've allowed anyone inside my heart.

It would be unfair to Wes if I were to offer more and then pull it back. Looking at him, though, I know that if anyone will be careful with me, it's him. Westin has been there, and I trust him.

I rest my hand on his arm and smile. "You're too good for me, but at least I know it. I'm . . . excited about our dinner. I'm excited about—"

My hospital phone goes off and I thank God for the interruption. I was about to say more, way more than I'm probably ready to say. We've taken things so slow, and I think that's why we work. He's patient with me, and I'm cautious about giving my heart away. Moving forward with him is exciting, but I want to make sure I don't hurt him either.

"Dr. Adams," I say into the phone.

"The trial patient that checked in early, she's really uncomfortable, and we need you to decide what she's allowed for pain management."

"I'll be right there."

Westin puts his hand up before I can say a word. "Go. I'll see you tonight."

I start down the hall and call out to him as I continue moving. "Thank you . . . for everything."

"Should we admit her as patient one?" Martina asks.

"Not yet," I fight back a smile. "Let's admit them the way we set it up. For now just put her as a trial patient without a number." This is really happening. "But let's get them set for their stay since tomorrow starts the next part."

"Got it!"

My trial is going to start today and my first patient with the dosage adjustment could be this one. I shouldn't be happy, but there's a hope inside me that I can't contain when I think of the lives that don't have to be destroyed because cancer seeps through every part of who these women are. Cancer is a growing thing, killing as it goes, and sometimes, it carries on after a person is gone, destroying the people they loved as they try to deal with the person's death.

I look over the chart. Allison Brown is thirty-eight years old, married with no children and has stage II ovarian cancer. However, this is her second time fighting cancer. She's the same age as me and the same age my mother was when she started her fight. Couldn't I have had a case a little less close to home as my first?

Releasing a deep breath, I straighten my back, and head into her room.

A beautiful woman with long brown hair and soft green eyes looks at me with a tired smile.

"Hi, I'm Dr. Adams." I move toward her bed and she shifts, trying to smother the pain in her face.

"I'm Ali."

I take her ice-cold hand in mine and cover it with my other one. "I'm going to get you something for the pain, but first I need to evaluate you and get you checked in for the trial. Okay?"

She nods. "It's really bad today. I had my last chemo treatment two weeks ago and it's lingering."

"I'm sorry. Let's get through your history quickly and then we'll go from there." Her chart states that she lives in North Carolina, which is where I went to college before I left to come to Chicago for med school. *Another thing that is a little too close for comfort.* "Your trial questionnaire says you were a very successful lawyer and being considered for a judgeship?"

"Until cancer kicked me in the face," Allison releases a sarcastic laugh. "My husband, Peyton, and I had a lot of plans until my diagnosis four years ago."

"I see this is your second occurrence?"

"Yes, I beat breast cancer once only to have ovarian cancer. Lucky me, right? I get through it all, with the hopes of still having kids, and then this . . ."

"I see. Were you able to harvest your eggs before that treatment?"

She nods. "Yes."

Good. That's at least one hurdle down.

I take her hand in mine. "We'll do everything we can to beat it again."

We continue through the questionnaire and I realize this woman could be me in so many ways. We're both very driven women who have flourishing careers. Allison married young, but they agreed to hold off on children until they were settled in their careers, and then cancer came back again, making that possibility even slimmer.

"Peyton drove me nuts, making me wait to have kids. I wanted a baby so bad." A tear falls down her face. "Now, though, I wish we hadn't waited. I could've had the baby and then . . . then I could just fight the cancer."

I've learned there are no words to rebuke that. She has her reality, and my job requires I understand her needs.

She brushes the tears away and clears her throat.

I give her a second to collect herself as I get to my feet.

"I'm sorry," she tries to smile. "Some days I'm really bad at keeping it together."

"Don't apologize," I reassure her. "You don't have to keep

it together with me. I'll handle that, okay?"

I like Allison and pray that this drug does what I want it to for her. I can't explain it, but I feel an instant bond with her.

"You're not what I pictured."

"Yeah? What did you expect?"

The more she talks, the less her discomfort shows. "I don't know, but your profile on the website doesn't have any photos or even much about you at all, just your accomplishments."

I smile at that. "It's by design. As a woman, I often find that it's difficult for those in the medical field to look at my resume instead of judging me by my photo."

"I get that."

"I thought you might," I reply. "Okay, everything looks good and I'll order something for the pain."

"Thanks, Dr. Adams."

"Don't mention it. I would like to go over the trial information if that's okay?"

She nods. "Please."

I give her the details, and then I get to the part I hate but can't leave out. "This trial is still in the early phases, and there is a great chance that you will still end up needing to have a hysterectomy. The chemotherapy mix may not shrink the tumor, and the other possible side effects may restrict your treatment options. You may also end up receiving the placebo, which then would guarantee that we would proceed with a hysterectomy. Do you understand?"

Allison squares her shoulders and then grimaces in a bit of pain. "I need to say this, and since you're my doctor, it cannot be repeated, right?"

"Of course, anything we say is between us."

"Not even to my husband?"

This gives me a slight pause. "Correct."

"Good. Then, I hand you this letter as my legal right to state what my wishes are."

I take the envelope she hands me and open it, expecting a DNR, only that's not what this is. It's a refusal of a hysterectomy signed and notarized.

"Allison . . ."

"No, I want to make this clear, Dr. Adams. I know what I want. I'm of sound mind, and understand that if I refuse the hysterectomy, I will die. I will not allow you to take it all from me. I would rather die of cancer than know I can never bear a child. While this may seem stupid to you or any other person, this is my wish."

I look at the paper, not understanding how she could choose this. "There are other options, surrogacy, adoption . . ." I trail off when her hand lifts to stop me.

"I was adopted, and while I had great parents, there was a part of me that wondered if . . . well . . . I know it is the only thing I want in this world, to carry a baby. I've dreamed of carrying a child, one that was really connected to me. I found a man who loves me and that dream was within reach. And then I found out cancer was going to take that from me. I harvested my eggs, hoping that once I got through the first hurdle, I could try then, only to go into the fertility clinic and learn there was a mass on my ovary."

I sit, feeling the pain in her voice. She doesn't cry, but it's clear that this is something she's not only thought about, but has planned for as well.

"I really have to advise you against this."

"I'm sure you do, and I appreciate it. But here's the thing, if I can't have my own baby, I don't have a life worth fighting for. I have tried, talked to counselors, my husband, parents, and everyone else, and I know in my heart that this is my last option. I would rather spend the rest of my life knowing I had the choice stolen from me not by surgery, but by cancer."

That's what this trial should give people, another option. The idea that women have to take all or nothing has plagued me. I wanted children once, but I got to choose not to have them. This trial is about giving people something instead of taking it away. While I may not necessarily agree with her decision, I have to respect it.

"And you understand that you're signing your death warrant by saying this? If the treatment doesn't work, or if you receive the placebo?"

"I do, and when I wrote that, I was in the office with a notary and my lawyer. Everything is clearly laid out. My only request is that my husband never knows of this. I don't want him to have to be in pain because of my choice. I can't listen to him plead and beg when I know that if I were to have the hysterectomy, it would kill me in another way."

I feel sick over this, but I can't deny her. As her doctor, I can't disclose this information to him and I will be the one to have to find another way to help him through it if the trial doesn't work.

"I hope that we find our way through this without either of these being the outcome. But if the medication does not work the way we want it to, there won't be another way to treat the cancer."

Allison wipes away a tear and attempts to smile. "I understand that. I hope and pray that this treatment works. When I saw this trial, I swear, it was like God answered my prayers. I believe in you and this trial. I really do."

I go to speak but the door opens. Both our heads turn and my heart stops as my eyes lock on the blue eyes I've tried to erase for the last fourteen years. Everything around me fades and all I can do is focus on one thing—him.

Bryce Peyton stands in front of me. His gaze is full of shock and confusion and I can't breathe. My chest is tight and I feel the blood drain from my face. Years have passed, but he's exactly as I remember. His dark brown hair is shorter, but his eyes are the same.

His lips part as he steps forward, but I take two steps back.

"Is that really you?" I ask as I shake my head in disbelief.

This can't be real. He doesn't live here and there is no reason he's in my hospital.

"Peyton?" the strained voice in the bed breaks the spell. Oh, God. Allison Brown called her husband Peyton, and it clicks.

Bryce is her husband.

His eyes glass over and I see the wall erect, shutting me out. He looks at his wife and smiles. "I couldn't find the doctor," he explains and walks over to her bedside.

"This is the doctor . . ."

"I figured as much," Bryce clips.

She smiles at me and then looks at him. "This is my husband Bryce, but I call him Peyton. He seems to have forgotten his manners. Peyton, this is Dr. Adams, she's running my trial."

It would be unprofessional of me not to shake his hand but if I touch him . . . if I let my hand touch his skin, I don't think I'll be able to keep it together. However, he takes care of that by glaring at me with disgust.

"If you could get my wife something for her pain, that

would be great. She's been waiting almost an hour for some help." Bryce grabs her hand, his rough fingers wrapping around hers as he holds it carefully. I remember the way his skin felt. How secure he could make you feel with just one touch. Each callous on his fingers would trail down my body leaving goose bumps in their wake.

Allison releases his hand then he kisses her lips. Tears well in my eyes but I push them down. I walked away from him. I gave him up, so I don't get to be upset.

"Dr. Adams, do I need to sign the papers since I'm one hundred percent in?" Allison asks.

All of this is too much, she made me promise to let her die if the trial fails her.

I look down at the papers in my hand and nod because I can't say a word now that he's here. "Yes, of course, then I can put the script through."

My feet drag as I make my way to the two of them, trying to stop staring at the gold band on his ring finger.

She signs the paper and Bryce watches me as my hand trembles, taking the form back. There's a crack in his armor as a look of sadness washes over him before he squeezes his eyes shut, and when they reopen, it's gone.

"Do you guys know each other?" she asks as we both study each other.

I clear my throat, trying to swallow the lump there and then shake my head. I'm not sure how to tell this woman that I spent half my life loving him, and that he broke my entire world. However, I'm not understanding how she hasn't put it together. If they're married, I'm sure they know about past relationships.

"Nope," he speaks before me.

Okay, I guess not.

"But she asked . . ." Allison tries to speak, but he continues before she can finish.

"I don't know. I've never met her before. Did you graduate med school from Duke? Maybe we went to the same school?"

Allison looks to me. I didn't graduate from Duke for med school and he knows that, but I did get my undergrad there. Still, something tells me not to mention it. "I graduated from Northwestern."

He shakes his head. "Then I have no idea where our paths could've crossed."

Really? Really? You have no idea? I have a million of them.

How can he act like I never existed at all? We loved each other once. We planned an entire life together. I'd be a surgeon and he'd be an architect, we'd have two kids, live in Georgia where the weather was warm and I could do great things in Atlanta. Everything about the life we planned was perfect. He was perfect, and together we were unstoppable. Or so I thought.

I try to control my shock, but I jerk my head back slightly. I never expected a grand reunion, but I hoped if we ever saw each other again, it wouldn't be like this. The tightness in my chest, the sinking feeling in the pit of my stomach, and the disbelief I feel is overwhelming.

For the first time in a very long time, I feel like I might break down and cry.

I need to get the fuck out of here.

"I'll get your prescription in," I say quickly. I can't be around him and keep my composure. "The nurse will be right back."

"Are you sure?" she asks curiously, glancing at the both of us before turning to Bryce. "You're acting weird and very rude."

Bryce brushes her hair back and presses his lips to her forehead. "No, sweetheart. I don't know her at all. She looks like someone I knew in college, but she died about fourteen years ago. Couldn't be the same person."

He had to have known. He had to have heard my name and known he was going to see me.

Allison touches his arm. "Oh, that's so sad."

Bryce looks at me. "Yeah, it is, but it was a long time ago and I had forgotten all about her."

And just like that, my heart shatters.

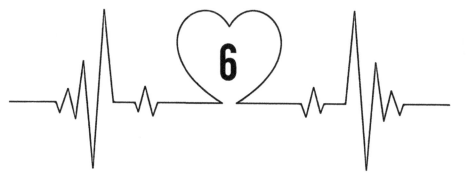

lean my head against the wall and my entire life comes to a halt. Bryce is here, and his wife was accepted into my trial and apparently she has a death wish if this doesn't work.

I don't know how I'm meant to endure seeing her and *him*—daily.

"You okay?" Martina asks. "You look like you saw a ghost."

"I think I did," I say quickly.

"What?"

I shake my head. "Please bring Ms. Brown her pain medication. I put a script through. I'll be back in a bit."

Without another word, I rush down the hall, past the break room, and head to the bathroom. I slide the lock, the loud click echoes through the small space, and I sink to the floor.

This can't be happening. It's just some horrible nightmare, because I couldn't have this kind of luck. Why is this happening to me? He's married and I'm his wife's doctor.

Oh my God, he's married and clearly moved on. Of course he did. A sob escapes my throat as the tears I've been fighting back fill my vision.

My head drops to my knees and I let it out. It could've been me, but I chose to leave and he moved on. The same should've been true for me. Instead, I've been stuck in a holding pattern. I wanted that life.

It's clear they love each other, and logically, I was stupid to believe he was like me—missing what we had. I never thought he would pretend that I never existed. That I died. That he didn't know me. We were *everything* at one time. God, I was so stupid.

I sit back up, look at the ceiling, and wipe my face. Damn me for having emotions. I'm supposed to be strong and here I am, crying like a stupid lovesick fool.

What do almost twenty-four-year-olds know about forever anyway?

Nothing.

Then I think about Allison and how she came to me for help that I don't know if I can give her now.

Ethically, I'm not sure that I can, or should, treat her. No. I won't treat her. There's no way I can work on my ex's wife. If she dies, will everyone think I did all I could? Can I actually help the woman who is holding the hand of the man I once loved? The man I still think about? The man who clearly doesn't think about me? The questions swirl around like a funnel cloud leaving nothing but destruction. How the hell can I do this?

I can't. That's the reality.

I can't be objective and I can't lie to Allison about the nature of my relationship with her husband, and that means treating her is a conflict. The rules are clear, and I won't risk screwing this trial up. I can't know any of the patients or their families. This is the biggest clusterfuck.

So much for my amazing day.

I need to finish checking the trial patients in, then I'll find a way to refer her to someone else. While I know that is the right thing to do, I feel sick knowing that means she won't go on with any treatment another doctor will suggest.

How can I turn her away when I *know*? I *know* what will happen to her.

"Serenity?" Martina's voice is soft as she knocks.

Shit. I get up and splash some water on my face, hoping to tone down the splotchy red spots.

"I'll be out in a minute," I call back to her.

"Ren, what's going on? Are you okay?" Martina continues, even with a thick steel door between us.

"I'm fine."

"Yeah right. Unlock the door."

I do as she says and her face tells me she's not buying it. Martina steps into the bathroom with me and crosses her arms over her chest. "Spill it, girl. I know you well enough to see there's something going on."

If I tell her, I could put everything in jeopardy, and there's no way I'm doing that. For now, I need to keep this to myself and figure out what I'm going to do. "I'm overwhelmed."

Her brows raise. "That's what has you locking yourself in the bathroom? Why not go to the on-call room, which is where you usually hide when you need it?"

"I don't want to see Westin," I say honestly. He's the last person I want to see right now.

How is that for timing? I finally start to give my heart a small chance at healing, and the cause of its destruction shows back up. Okay universe . . . I hear you. No love for me.

Martina watches me closely, but seems to buy it. "What made you say you saw a ghost?"

Shit.

"That patient reminded me of my mother."

It could be true.

"Oh, Ren." Martina's arms wrap around me. She pulls me close and disappointment floods my system. I have two real friends in this town and I just lied to one.

I hate myself for this. I loved him and the lies I told myself when we ended were that it was for the best. Bryce wanted things from me I couldn't give him. We were so hot and heavy in college, the world couldn't touch us. Until I got into med school.

Then what I thought was unbreakable broke within weeks.

Seeing him brought it all back.

He was the only bright spot in my life and then the world went dark, and I retreated, vowing never to let myself be hurt again.

Now he's here and all that I buried is right back at the surface. Once I remove Allison from the trial and find a way to convince her to do the right thing, he'll be gone and I can go back to my life.

I pull back, not wanting Martina's comfort when I don't deserve it. "I need to take care of something, okay?"

"Of course. Let me know if you need my help. Just so you know, two more trial patients checked in."

I'll deal with the Bryce and Allison thing later. It's my job to be a doctor and treat the others who came to me. My issues aren't important in comparison, so I'll do what I'm pretty damn good at—putting them aside.

"I'll be right there."

She heads out and I stare at myself in the mirror. I take a deep breath, reminding myself of the person I am now. "You are not the same girl you were. You're a doctor, a friend, and a strong woman. No man can make you feel unloved and unworthy. You can do this."

It's been many years since I've had to utter those words aloud, but I need them today.

I head to the room of the second trial participant and pray I can avoid seeing Bryce. Luck has never been my friend, though. As I place my hand on the door of my next patient's room, he exits Allison's room. Our eyes meet and I see the conflict in his blue eyes.

My pulse races at the sight of him, but I remember he's not mine and he doesn't know me anymore. I guess he was right, that girl died fourteen years ago when he let her go so easily.

I turn my head, and enter the room to do what I was put on this earth to do.

After the remaining patients are registered and have the instructions for tomorrow, I sit in the on-call room charting notes. There is one patient I have to release, due to her scans coming back outside of the trial range.

I enter her room and she looks over with hope in her eyes. "Dr. Adams? Hi, I'm so excited about this trial and . . ."

"Lindsay, I got your scans back and I have a few concerns," I say as delicately as possible.

"What's wrong?"

I step closer, hoping to ease her tension, but there's nothing that will comfort her. Telling her that the tumor has grown again and that this chemotherapy won't help is a devastating blow.

My emotions are on shut-down mode. I'm not Serenity Adams, daughter, sister, friend, and kind-of-sort-of-girlfriend. I'm Dr. Adams, world-class surgeon and kicker of cancer's ass. I don't have feelings, just facts.

"The scans show that there's no way I can save the ovaries, even with this treatment. The tumor has grown and I'm afraid I need to schedule you for surgery immediately. If I find what I believe I will, you won't be eligible for the trial anymore. I'll have to perform a full hysterectomy. I'm very sorry."

Some doctors follow up with more, but there's no point. Most people only hear the first sentence, so I try to give the bad all at once.

The hope that was in Lindsay's eyes is gone and is replaced with tears. They fall as the words I spoke start to sink in. "That's it? There's no chance? My uterus too? This is the end for me, isn't it?"

"It's not the end. I'm still going to do everything I can to fight the cancer, but most likely the scan isn't showing the whole picture, so I have to go in surgically to determine and deliver the best course of action."

I will fight to the end with her.

"I can't afford . . ."

"Hey," I stop her. "You're my patient and there are a lot of things we can look into. I don't want you to worry about that. My nurse Martina is very good at getting financial help for patients."

"I don't know how to do this," she admits with tears in her eyes. "How do I tell my fiancé that . . . that I won't be a complete woman anymore? That I can't carry our kids?"

I make a mental note to help her find a support group and counseling as well as financial help, if it comes to that. Lindsay is twenty-six years old and it's possible she'll have a complete hysterectomy if I find what I believe I will. I can't imagine having to make this choice at her age.

"Believe me, this isn't what I want to do, so if I get in there and it's not what I think it might be from looking at the scan, I'll take what I have to. We will have our reproductive team there in case there are any eggs they can freeze, and then you could at least have a surrogate, but I want you to be prepared for whatever the possibilities are."

Most of my patients have already had eggs harvested, but Lindsay wasn't one of them. She couldn't afford it, but since I'm going in, it won't be considered an elective procedure. If I can get anything for her, I will.

"The possibilities have ended," she says looking out the window. "I don't care. Take it all."

I take another step closer, place my hand on her shoulder, and watch her lip quiver. "I'm going to do what I can, okay?"

She nods.

"Why don't you call your fiancé and family? I'll schedule you for tomorrow morning and give you some time to talk to everyone."

A tear falls down her cheek and my heart breaks for her. "I really hoped . . ."

"I know. I did, too."

Of all the patients I met today, Lindsay was one I most wished I could help. She's young, and I thought her case would show the most promise. Most of my patients are in their late thirties to early forties, married, and some already have kids, but Lindsay doesn't. This could've possibly given her the life she envisioned.

Lindsay doesn't look back at me. She stares out the window with tears streaming down her face. I pat her arm once, and quietly leave.

Feeling helpless sucks.

I walk to the nurses' station and fight back my own wave of emotions. Today has drained me in so many ways, but seeing the pain and devastation in Lindsay's eyes was the icing on the cake. How can this job be so rewarding and utterly heartbreaking at the same time? When it's good, it's great, but when you have to deal with the ugly parts . . . it's too much.

"Schedule Lindsay Dunphy for exploratory and possible hysterectomy surgery tomorrow morning at eight, please," I tell the surgical nurse on the desk. "Ensure the reproductive team is available as well. Also, she is to be removed from the trial."

My phone dings with a text.

Westin: Are we still doing dinner?

Shit. I look at the time and hunger hits me in the face. I didn't even realize it was past eight and I haven't eaten a thing all day. The last thing I want to do is see Westin tonight. I haven't even considered what it will be like seeing him. I've never lied to him, and it's not something I'm looking forward to doing now if he asks about my patients. I'm not ready to talk to him about what all of this means.

Coming face to face with Bryce has brought up everything from my past and I worry that I can't do this. On the other hand, how the hell do I cancel on Westin after dinner . . . and whatever more came with it . . . was my idea?

My life is a shit show.

Westin put his neck on the line for me and I owe him this much. I'll have to find a way to put my crap aside.

Me: I'm leaving in a few. Your place?

Westin: I have a pizza waiting.

Me: Great. I'm starving and today has been stressful.

I'm hoping he reads the warning and will understand if I'm not myself.

In so many ways, today has been awful. But it's not over yet. I have one more blow of bad news to deliver. Putting Allison off is wrong, and I need to deal with it now. My chest tightens because this isn't medically necessary, but it's mentally and—at least in my head—ethically required. Treating her, lying to her, and knowing that I might not be able to be objective, is never going to work.

There's no easy way to do this. I'm going to have to look her in the eye and tell her that I can't treat her, and let her *husband* explain why.

I put Lindsay's file down and start to walk toward Allison's room with heavy feet. Dread fills me with each step I take and I wonder if I can really take her out of the trial. Can I walk in there and admit that I'm too weak to do the right thing and tell her the truth about my relationship with her husband? Will she understand that what she asked of me is impossible now? I know in the pit of my soul that this is the right thing, but then why does it feel wrong? I stop walking, press my back against the wall, and breathe.

Damn it. Pull it together, Serenity. You have to do this. You don't have a choice, because you know this will ruin everything you've built. It's a conflict that will keep you weak and unable to give her the care she needs.

I'm weak when it comes to him, though.

I always have been.

I always will be.

There is a line and I can't cross it. I made the choice years ago to let him go, and I have to do it again.

Pushing myself off the wall with the determination to get this over with, I gather all my strength to say the words. When I turn the corner, I come face to face with Bryce, and all my plans disappear.

I gasp with my hand over my pounding heart. The years and distance have done nothing to stop the ache that seeing him causes. Having him here right now has brought that to the forefront. Looking into his blue eyes stirs things inside me I never thought I'd feel again.

My life has been steady since I left Duke University. I had to make a choice that day, and I chose to come home to my mother and attend med school close to home. When I did that, it was the end of my love story with Bryce.

Sure, we tried for a few months, but absence didn't make our hearts grow fonder. I closed the book on us and when I needed him most, he wasn't around.

Now here we stand, with the pages flipped back, and I'm reliving it all over again.

"Bryce," I breathe his name and try to get control of my pulse.

"Chick," his deep voice practically croons my name.

That name. No one has called me Chick since him. No one

even knows about the stupid name. Hearing his voice caress over the nickname, my chest is tight and I want to scream.

Instead, I go to what matters . . . getting answers. "What are you doing here?"

"Allison . . ." he pauses.

"I don't mean the hospital, I mean standing here, now," I clarify. "I figured you'd be with your wife."

I'm trembling inside, but using every ounce of control to keep my outward appearance together. How can I look at this man after fourteen years and still want to cry? How can he bring me to my knees with a single look? It shouldn't be this way. I'm a goddamn doctor who has faced incredible odds with grace and poise, but Bryce Peyton is the lynchpin that could destroy everything.

He rubs the back of his neck. "I came looking for you."

"Why?"

He rubs the back of his head and looks away. "Why do you think, Serenity? It's been damn near fifteen years, and now I see you again out of nowhere? I thought maybe we should talk before all of this goes sideways."

No, I've been here since the day I left, it's him who showed up out of nowhere. Which makes no sense. Why would he ever think this was a good idea?

"Sideways, you mean like lying that we don't know each other?"

Bryce looks up and releases a heavy sigh. "I didn't know what to say."

I huff. "So your first instinct was to lie?"

"It's not like I thought I would ever see *you* as her doctor. So, yeah, I lied."

Well, that's a great way to function in a marriage. Not that what Allison is doing is any better. Still, it doesn't even make sense, this web of lies. Why not just tell her and then we could all make sense of it? She'd never want me to treat her and I wouldn't have to.

"How could you not know it would be me as her doctor? You're at my hospital, in my trial, you had to put two and two together. I don't know any other Serenity Adams, do you?"

He rocks on his heels. "I never knew the doctor's name when she mentioned this trial. Allison has seen countless doctors and tells me about every trial under the sun. There are so many details involved in these things, and the doctors' names usually aren't pertinent. I learned to let her lead with this and don't ask questions. When she told me she was accepted into this one, I came with her without hesitation."

I close my eyes while shaking my head. "How does *she* not know? I don't understand any of this."

He waits and I finally bring myself to look at him again. "She doesn't know you ever existed."

Pain once again lances through me. I wanted to believe I had meant more to him. He proposed to me, loved me, was willing to risk everything to make things work, and then I left him.

"Well, then."

My mind reels, knowing this won't work. It's not good for anyone involved, and if she doesn't even know that he and I were engaged at one point, there's no way I can pretend. It's not fair to her. She deserves a doctor who will be one hundred percent committed to her care, and keeping secrets could derail her. It's a conflict even if in the eyes of an ethics board there is no transgression. In my eyes—it is.

His eyes meet mine and I see the anger burning. "Don't

judge me. I did what I had to in order to survive you leaving me."

"It wasn't like that . . ."

"It was exactly like that, Chick. I asked you not to go, and you did. Then you moved on."

He acts as though I wanted to go. As though leaving the man I was engaged to was a goal. It wasn't. My mother was sick, and I had to be here for my family. He chose to go to grad school.

"You can't really believe you were the only one broken. You have no idea how hard it was for me."

He puts his hand up. "I can't do this with you now. I needed to talk to you before you see Ali again. She's been asking a lot of questions and we need to be clear."

Bryce takes a step closer to me and I smell his cologne, instantly transporting me back in time. He's the same in so many ways, but things are different too. His voice still sounds the same, I've replayed it a hundred times in my head, but his hair has a few grays that definitely weren't there when we were kids. I wish I could say it makes him look less attractive, but it doesn't.

All the more reason why I can't do this. I can't even look at him without my stomach dropping and my heart feeling as if it's going to fly out of my chest.

"I plan to be very clear because I'm not going to do this . . . I mean . . ." I stammer and then take a moment to compose myself. "I can't treat Allison. I'm sorry, but I need to release her from the trial today. There's another doctor that she can see, but my treating her is not a good idea."

"Why?" he practically yells.

"Because it's a conflict of interest. The rules are very clear that in a trial I can't treat anyone I know, Bryce."

"You don't know her."

Okay, sure, but that's semantics.

"I can't be her doctor and pretend like I don't even know you. This trial is too important to me, and I can't be objective, which makes this dangerous for her as well."

"She didn't do anything wrong."

"No, she didn't, but I'm not comfortable. I can't administer her medication in a clinical trial when I was romantically involved with her husband."

I start to walk away, but he grips my arm. Every muscle in my body locks at the feel of his skin on mine. The memories assault me all at once, the love, the hate, the making up, and then the letting go. My breathing comes in short bursts as I use all my strength to stop myself from falling to the ground.

"Serenity, don't do this." The gritty sound of his voice calls to my heart. "Please, don't, I'm asking you to think about this for a second."

"Please let go of me." I keep my eyes shut with my back to him.

His hand drops and I turn, and he starts to pace. "It was a shock to see you. That's all. We were a million years ago and this isn't about us, it's about her. She doesn't deserve to be thrown out of this trial when it's the only thing she's talked about for weeks. It doesn't matter that we knew each other, we don't know each other now."

"I can't lie to her. I can't tell her I've never met you when that's the furthest thing from the truth. And it doesn't matter what we know or knew, it's not allowed."

His eyes turn pleading. "You're her only chance. Do you understand that? She gave up everything and denied the hysterectomy she probably should've gotten because of this. You're going to penalize her because once upon a time we thought we loved each other?"

I pull in a deep breath and shake my head. I didn't think I loved him, I did love him. The fact that he admitted he didn't love me stings. And knowing Allison's intentions, knowing more than he does, it's just too much. There are some burdens I'm not strong enough to carry. Still, I can't break her trust and tell him that. I have to stick with the fact that it's about us. I can be the bad guy. "It's not a good idea. I'm sorry that you're upset, but there are rules for a reason."

"You're a doctor. It's your job." Bryce's fingers wrap around my wrist, stopping me from walking away, and I can't breathe. "And you owe me."

I rip my hand back, breaking the connection. "Owe you? What do I owe you?" He makes me angry, sad, happy, and destroyed all at once.

Bryce moves closer, forcing me to take a step back, but I hit the wall. He looks away and then rubs his hand over his face. "Owe is the wrong word. I guess I mean that this is incredibly hard. Seeing you, and having Ali in the room, it's got me confused, and I'm sorry. Look, all I'm asking is for you to think about what this will do to her."

That's the thing, it's bad for her as well. What if she finds out about us? Not that there's been anything recent, but we weren't just some thing once upon a time. "How could she not know anything about us?"

He releases a deep sigh. "When you left, I lost my mind. I was a mess, I wouldn't talk to anyone, and I went to Houston where no one knew about us. My family followed my lead and . . . I don't know, it never came up. I didn't want it to come up. I loved you with my entire heart and you broke it."

"I'm sorry, Bryce. I wish I could help you, but I can't lose my trial. There are other people in this trial to think about. It wouldn't be fair."

I see the defeat in his eyes. "You're right. I thought you, of all people, would understand what it's like to watch someone you love need help. I'm asking you," his eyes fill with unshed tears. "I'm asking you not to punish her. I'm begging you to at least think about it. We don't have to tell her because it's in the past. We're in the past and we've both moved on. Please, Ren, please don't do this."

Our love was the kind people write songs about. We were the love story that writers pen. Two people meeting in the most innocent way, falling in love, and then ripped apart by tragedy.

We had the beginning, the climax, and then the fall, but unlike in fiction, we never were redeemed.

I left as promised and Bryce never followed.

He moves back farther and everything inside of me is con-flicted. "I can't . . ."

"Please, just think about it tonight," Bryce says as he dis-appears around the corner, leaving me stunned.

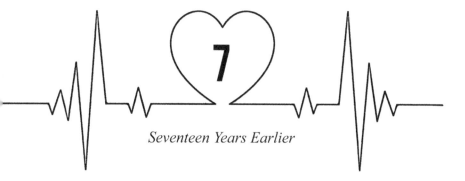

Seventeen Years Earlier

"Hi," a deep voice rumbles behind me. I put up my hand to dismiss the idiot who will only ruin my buzz. "I just thought we should meet."

I shake my head, uninterested in whatever he's selling. "No thanks."

"Well, considering you're going to be my wife. It would probably be best that we get the pleasantries out of the way."

I turn with my mouth agape. "Excuse me?"

"You heard me," the stranger says.

"I'm sorry, who the hell are you?" I ask looking him over. The first thing that captures my attention is his eyes. They're light blue with green swirls, but more than that he looks at me like he knows all my secrets.

We stare at each other for a beat, taking each other in.

My best friend, Laura, starts to laugh.

Neither of us speaks, yet I've never felt so in tune with someone. "I said I'm going to marry you one day." He shrugs as though it's something you say daily. "Just thought we should meet before the wedding."

I smirk, and take a sip of my beer. "You're pretty sure of this, huh?"

"Well, I'm sure that I've never seen anyone as beautiful as you before," his smile grows, and mine does as well.

"Oh, God," Laura begins to laugh. She grabs her drink, downs it, and then gets up. "You should sit. I have a feeling you're only getting started." She pats him on the back, and heads to the dance floor.

"Well, since we're apparently getting married, maybe you'd like to tell me your name?" I ask.

"Bryce Peyton. It's a pleasure to meet you . . ." he trails off. For the first time, I catch a little glimpse of a twang, but it's not prominent unless you're listening closely.

"Serenity Adams."

"That's a beautiful name."

I shrug. Truth is, I hate my name. My parents said the minute my mother held me, she had an overwhelming sense of serenity. She also could've been smoking pot through her whole pregnancy, but I never understood what she meant until right now. The minute Bryce sat down I felt a sense of calm wash over me. It was like my life suddenly clicked into place. Two halves forming into a whole. He completes me and I don't even know him.

"So, Bryce Peyton, future husband of mine . . . what are you doing here?" I try to play indifferent, but I can't stop looking at him. His brown hair hangs slightly into his eyes, and without permission my fingers lift and brush it to the side. I draw my hand back, embarrassed, but Bryce takes my hand in his. "Sorry," I say, feeling awkward.

"Don't be." He squeezes my hand. "Honestly."

"Is there any valid reason to start our predestined marriage off on a lie?" I reply playfully.

"My roommate needed to study or more like sleep with his girlfriend, so I decided to take a walk. As I passed this bar, I felt the need to come in and see it. Then, I saw you. And I know it makes no sense, but I needed to talk to you."

"And here you are . . ."

"Here we are."

My heart sputters as he says 'we.'

"Yes, we," I smile. "Let me ask you some questions," I play along.

"Shoot."

"Are we going to be happy in our marriage?"

Bryce takes my beer, drinks some, and puts it back in front of me. "I believe we will. You share well and I'm a giving man."

"Hmm," I muse. "Do you randomly propose to girls in bars?"

"Never."

Good to know, I think to myself. "And what's your major?"

"Architecture."

"Interesting," I tap my chin. "I assume you built a lot of Legos?"

He chuckles and I wish I didn't enjoy the sound of it so much. "Guilty. What about you, future wife, what are your career goals, other than making me deliriously happy?"

He's smooth. I'll give him that. I lean back in my chair, taking my beer with me and watching the way he studies me. Bryce's gaze is intense, but there's a warmth to it. I don't know that I've ever had this kind of a reaction to a man before.

I've been hit on plenty of times at the bar, but never wanted more than a free drink. Just the idea of him getting up and walking away makes me want to ask him to stay. However, I promised myself no boyfriends or anything like that before I graduate. There's no way I'm screwing up my chances at med school.

Yet, here I am, wondering what it would be like to see him again. I'm clearly nuts if his game is working.

"I'm finishing my undergrad, but then I'll be going to med school."

"Wow, a doctor. What year are you in now?"

"Junior," I yell over the music. "I should be a Senior, but I took a year off."

"Well, another thing we have in common."

I raise my brow. Not many kids I know with ambitions like mine take a year off, but my mother was fighting cancer and I wanted to be there to help. Once she was out of treatment, I dove headfirst into school.

"You took a gap year?" I ask.

Bryce grins. "Yeah. Felt I needed another year to figure my goals out. Plus, it's a lot of schooling, huh?"

I take a sip of my drink. "It sure is, but after is much worse. You know, that means you'll have to accept that my job is demanding. Do you think you can handle that and still love me eternally?"

I'm having way too much fun with this. It's a little crazy, but I'm sure I can scare him off with this one.

Bryce leans forward, his fingers tangle with mine, and his deep voice is filled with promise. "I guess we're going to have to marry each other and find out."

If it's possible, I just fell in love with him. I should lay off the alcohol, but instead, we spend the next hour talking and by the end of the night I know without a doubt, this is the man I'm meant to marry.

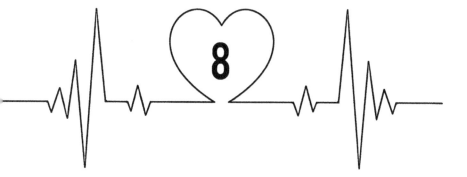

8

I stand outside the door of Westin's apartment wondering how many more bad decisions I'm going to make today. Instead of going to Allison's room and telling her the truth, I ended up here.

After Bryce left me standing there, I couldn't think straight, so I grabbed my coat and rushed out.

I drop my head back and release a deep sigh. I'm a fool. This is the last place I should be.

The door opens. "Ren?" Westin's voice is full of concern.

"Hey," I give my best attempt at a smile.

"Why are you standing out here?" He laughs while leaning against the doorjamb.

Good question. *Because I was debating how to go home without looking like an idiot.* "Just got here," I lie. I've been standing here for more than ten minutes.

"Okay, you coming inside or do you need to go get some sleep?" Wes asks.

He knows me well enough to give me the out. How sad is that? I'm so fucked up in the head that I require loopholes in every part of my relationships. I need some serious therapy.

"No, I'm coming in." I release a nervous laugh. "I'm so beat, I can't think straight."

Westin extends his arm as I enter the apartment. His high-rise building has a completely different feel than mine. Mine is an older building, where Westin's is new and very industrial. The ductwork hangs from the ceiling, the floors are concrete and the counter is stainless steel.

Like Westin's exposed brick walls, I'm raw and jaded, and the mortar that holds me together is chipping.

His arms wrap around me from behind, and I sigh. Being held right now is what I need. I close my eyes and lean my head back on his shoulder. When we're alone, I can let my walls down just a little. It's when we step outside the cocoon that they go back up.

"I like when you're this way," Westin's deep voice is low against my ear.

"What way?"

His lips touch my neck and I shiver. "Unguarded."

It's easy when you're in a bubble to pretend the world outside is a farce. I don't have to be anything but me when we're alone. Westin doesn't care because our expectations are just this. When we're together, we can give what we want to each other, and when we're apart, we don't have to do anything.

"I had a long day. I need us tonight."

I turn, looking into his beautiful green eyes, and touch his cheek.

"First we eat," Westin demands. "Then you can have all the *us* you want."

Westin kisses my lips before releasing me. He heads into the kitchen that never gets used, except to heat up pizza or some other kind of takeout, and smiles.

"Are you going to keep me in suspense?" he asks.

Oh, God, did he hear about my breakdown in the bathroom? Does it say on my forehead: Hot mess. Ex-fiancé is back in town.

"About?"

He shakes his head and then places the plate in front of me. "Your day . . ."

"Oh." I shrug. "It was . . . hard."

That's the understatement of the year.

Westin grabs his pizza and watches me. I've never held back on this stuff with him. We both share our days freely, but I don't know that I should. If he finds out about Bryce's wife, I don't know what he'll say. Or maybe I do, and that's why I haven't said a word.

"Ren, what's going on?" he pushes.

Fuck. I'm doing a really bad job at keeping my feelings off my face. I need to tell him something.

"I had to remove a patient from the trial," I explain. Lindsay was a difficult part, so I start there.

Oh, by the way, the guy that has had me a complete mess for the last seventeen years is back, his wife is my patient, and basically told me that she'll refuse all the normal treatment if the trial doesn't work. Plus, I'm dying inside.

"For?"

I tell him about her cancer and the scans. The whole point of the trial is to see if this can avoid a hysterectomy. If I have to remove her uterus and ovaries, there's nothing to test.

He leans against the counter in front of me. His green eyes vary from inquisitive to concerned. "You know you have to report this to the board, right?"

"Yeah," I reply hesitantly.

"Losing her from the trial adjusts your ratio. I'm saying that you have to keep your information correct. If you lose another patient, they could shut it all down until you have the numbers back."

My head falls along with my heart. I didn't even think about that. If I remove Allison from the trial as well, I could be forced to postpone the entire thing. All those other patients would be affected by that. It could mean they lose their chance and I don't know when I would be able to start it again.

Is everyone else's life more important than just finding a way to deal with Allison?

Can I really not handle this, or am I being stupid?

I rest my elbow on the island with my head in my hand. "I can't lose this trial," I admit.

He rubs my back. "I know, and maybe it won't be a big deal, but in order to prove the results, you have to have the numbers. You barely qualified for this stage of the trial because of the woman who dropped out."

God, I didn't even think about that. The first stage of the trial was a success and showed enough promise to push to the next, but there are minimums for patient numbers and I'm right at that number for phase three. If I lose Allison too, I don't know what it'll mean for the whole thing.

I look up at him, hoping he has the answers I need. "What if I lose another patient? One of the patients, Allison, is possibly dropping out. I'm waiting on her scans to determine if she qualifies. So *if* I lose her, then what?"

Westin runs his hands through his hair. "I don't know, it would really depend. I'm just giving you a heads-up. I would do whatever I could to keep the rest in the trial."

This could change everything. It's bigger than me, Bryce, and Allison. It's about the families of patients who are hoping this could save a future they envisioned. My former love life shouldn't destroy their chances.

I'm not really in love with Bryce. He's married and I have a life now. It's been years. I'm strong enough to put my emotions aside to help Allison. Not to mention, this trial is life or death for her. I don't want her to die. I don't want any of my patients to die, but I really don't want her to die.

And Bryce was right, I don't know her. I'm not treating a friend or a family member, she's the wife of a guy I was once in love with. I don't know if that's really an ethical violation, but if anyone finds out, it could be viewed as one. It's a risk—a big one. I feel a pit in my stomach that's growing with each second. Letting her out is what I should do, but then I think of the other patients.

They need me to be stronger than some woman who can't put aside her bullshit.

And Allison needs me. She came to me for treatment and that's what I'm going to give her. I'll give her the best medical attention I can and ignore the man who used to look at me with loving eyes.

This trial is everything that matters.

My entire life has led to this one point, and I won't allow the man who I haven't been able to get out of my heart derail me.

Westin's hand brushes against my cheek. "You there?"

"It's been a long day," I say while taking his hand in mine.

He nods. "Do you need to forget, Serenity?"

The deep timbre of his voice sends shivers down my spine. Westin may not be the man I loved and have been trying to forget, but he's the one in front of me. He's real, he cares, and he's here.

I do want to forget it all. I want to go back twenty-four hours to when Westin and I were in my apartment, tearing each other's clothes off to exorcise our demons together. No judgment or expectations, just us.

"No talking, Wes." I rise and stare into his emerald eyes. "No emotions. Not tonight. I know earlier . . ."

He places his fingers over my mouth. "No talking. No explanations."

The hunger swirls in his gaze. He knows exactly what I'm asking for and he's going to give me everything I need.

I walk through the doors of the hospital with purpose. I'll get through Lindsay's surgery, and explain to Bryce that he's to stay away from me if he wants me to treat his wife at all.

It's the only option I have if I want to keep my trial. My heart doesn't matter in this, only medicine does.

"Ren?" Bryce's throaty voice calls me.

I can't avoid him even when I'm trying.

He extends a cup of coffee and his lips tilt up in a tentative smile. I don't want a peace offering. I want him gone so I can go back to pretending I don't have a heart. It was easier that way. My life was clear and concise, not muddled with feelings that make me vulnerable.

"I'm fine," I say, rejecting his offer of coffee.

"Right. I'm not trying to bribe you," he explains.

I shake my head with a grin. "If that was your idea of a

bribe, you've got a lot to learn."

He chuckles once. "Yeah, I just . . ."

"Thank you," I say and extend my hand. If he's going to be nice, there's no reason for me to be rude. I'm sure it took a lot for him to come to me like this. It's not easy when one person holds the keys to your happiness. I know this all too well.

I remember when my mother's doctor was abrupt and unwilling to offer us even a little hope.

"I'm not sure how you take your coffee anymore, but I went with memory."

"I appreciate it." I take a sip and hold my reaction.

Bryce remembered exactly how I take my coffee. Time may have passed, but this one moment shows that I wasn't a blip on his screen. Although it changes nothing for either of us.

"So did you think about what I said?"

It's all I've thought about. There are so many variables and I don't know what the right thing is anymore.

I release a low sigh, feeling the anxiety boiling inside me. "I have a patient who was removed from the trial and I need to operate. I really wanted to think through this before I made my decision, because you and I know this is messy."

He scratches the stubble on his face. "It doesn't have to be. We're not the same people anymore, Ren. It isn't like we're having an affair. I'm asking you to be her doctor. To save someone who hasn't done a damn thing wrong in this situation." He steps closer and I move back. "I'm not . . ."

Being this close to him stirs the pain I've tried so hard to bury. "Please step back," I request. "If you want me to pretend we don't know each other, you have to do the same. Your wife being my patient is a complication, and we both—"

"Dr. Adams," Westin's voice stops me from speaking.

Jesus Christ.

My stomach drops as he approaches. "Pretend you don't know me other than as Allison's doctor," I whisper to Bryce.

Westin comes to the side of me and extends his hand. "I'm Dr. Grant, nice to meet you."

Bryce looks at me and then back at Wes. "Bryce Peyton," he says as he shakes Westin's hand.

"Bryce's wife is one of my trial patients," I explain. "We were discussing the process."

"Well, you're in great hands, Dr. Adams is the best." Westin gives me a grin. "There's no one like her."

Bryce clears his throat. "Good to know."

The contrast between the two men is striking.

Westin is tall, lean, with green eyes that you can get lost in. He's got lighter hair and keeps a constant short scruff that I love. There is no doubt about his confidence. Each smile is effortless and real.

Whereas Bryce is more muscular and darker. He carries the weight of the world on his shoulders and I can see how tired he is. The energy around him is different, harsher. But when those blue eyes are on me, I can't breathe.

"I need to check on my patients," I say with a nervous laugh. "I'll check on your wife, Mr. Peyton, and we can go over the information later on."

Bryce's eyes narrow slightly and then he nods. "Okay."

He walks away, and Westin wraps his arms around my middle. "Sorry I had to run out this morning. I got a call in the middle of the night and didn't want to wake you."

I don't know when he left, but I didn't really think much of it. It happens often for the two of us. It's part of being a doctor, and my mind was elsewhere. "It's fine."

I try not to feel uncomfortable with him once again initiating a public display of affection, but I set this tone. Me going to his house last night was what I needed, and I still want to move forward, give more of myself to him.

The feeling that we're being watched overcomes me. My chest grows tight and I turn my gaze to see what is causing my unease. As I scan the room I realize Bryce is still here, and find his eyes trained on the two of us. His fists are clenched at his side as he sees me in Westin's embrace. It would appear to anyone watching that we're a couple.

Maybe this is exactly what I need him to see. I don't want him to know I've spent the last fourteen years thinking about what we could've been. He needs to believe I moved on.

I move my fingers up Westin's arms and hold onto the back of his neck.

"Are you going to take a day off this week?" Westin asks. "We could try to get away for the weekend . . ."

I don't like myself for playing any sort of game, but I need to protect my own heart right now.

"I don't know, I think I'm going to visit my dad and brother."

Westin's face falls slightly. I glance back over to see Bryce walking away. I watch as he disappears around the corner and then I step back.

What the hell am I doing?

I'm out of my fucking mind. I need to get out of here and fix myself.

"Just let me know if you change your mind."

There's no way I can stick around Chicago. Besides, my family is why I'm in this mess to begin with.

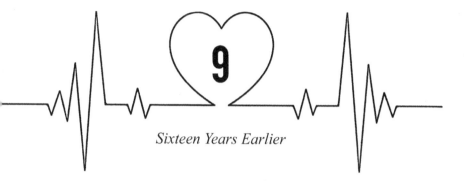

"**M**y father wants me to go to Rice University, which is where he went," Bryce informs me as we lie on the couch, curled up after watching a movie.

"Where is that?"

"Houston."

I sit up. "Houston? But that's so far."

He gives me a reassuring smile. "It is, but I'm not going there. We're both going to Penn State."

I release the breath I was holding and nod. "Well, if I get in."

"You will."

I applied at the same time he did, and he already got his acceptance. There's no reason to think I won't get in, but still . . . I'm worried. If I don't get accepted, I'll have to go to either Johns Hopkins or Northwestern. Both are excellent schools and offer what I want, but Penn State is where Bryce will be.

"We should discuss the options."

He pulls me back down so I'm lying on his chest. "We

don't need to, because we'll work it out. If you go to Johns Hopkins, we'll be close, Northwestern is the only one that would be hard."

"But we'd make it work?"

"I'd make anything work if it means I have you."

I rub my fingers across his lips. "You say the sweetest things."

"I say only what I mean."

I love him. I love him more than I've ever known was possible. He makes me so damn happy, and I now understand why my mother does what she does for my father. I used to think they were crazy in their devotion to each other, but here I am.

Maybe it's because he's my first love, but I don't think that's the case.

I think it's because Bryce is the other half of my soul.

"What would you do to keep me?" I ask playfully.

He looks away as he makes a humming sound. "Well, first, I'd have to kill any man who tried to take you away."

"How could I ever love anyone else now that I've known what loving you is like?"

"Good answer, Chick."

I groan at the stupid nickname. "Stop with that."

"What? It's cute. You're like a little chick."

Did I say I love him? Because right now I'd like to choke him. "I'm going to find something you hate and torture you with it."

He laughs and then brings his lips to mine. "You could try."

"I swear, you make me crazy."

"In the best way."

I wish I could deny it, but that would be a lie. We've been

together for nearly two years now and each day just gets better. I never thought that a chance meeting my junior year would lead to me finding the only man I want to be with.

In my heart, I know there is no one else who will ever love me like Bryce does. There's not another soul that could make me feel like the world is full of color and life. He will forever be the only person for me, and I know this.

It's why I will do everything I can to hold onto him.

A love like this is worth fighting for.

"You know I love you," I tell him as my fingers rub his chest.

"I do and I love you . . . until my last breath."

I smile and then kiss him. "I don't want to lose you."

"Hey," his voice is soft and comforting, "I won't let you lose me."

"Don't you think we're being naïve?"

"There is not another human on this planet who will ever love you the way that I do, Serenity. You're all I want and all I need. If that makes us naïve, then I don't want clarity. We love each other and one day, you'll be my wife. You will be the mother of my children, and we're going to make this work, no matter what it takes."

"The idea of not having you . . ."

"It's not a possibility." And then his lips touch mine once more, sealing his promise with a kiss.

10

"What the hell, Everton?" I ask as I look around the house I grew up in.

It's absolutely disgusting. There are plates piled up, cigarette butts lying around in soda cans, and the floor has a layer of filth on it. In all the years we've had this home, it's never looked like this. My mother would be rolling in her grave if she saw this.

"You don't get to judge."

"Judge what? This is nasty! You're supposed to be taking care of Dad and the house. How is this okay? Seriously, Ev, I know you're a lazy asshole, but this is insane."

Everton huffs and walks into the other room. My brother has always been a slob, but I didn't think I'd walk into this. I march into the living room where he sits on the couch about to light up a cigarette. I rip it from his mouth before he lights it and break it in half.

"What the fuck?" he yells.

"You're out of your damn mind. Mom died of cancer and you're smoking? In the house with Dad?" I tack on. "Dad, who had a cancer scare a few years ago? Not to mention what I do for a living. This is reckless and inconsiderate, even for you. What are you doing with the money I send every month?"

He rolls his eyes and grabs another cigarette from the pack, which enrages me. "Go to hell, Serenity."

When he lifts a hand to light his cigarette, I lose it. I grab the whole pack from his hand and run to the kitchen. I hear him behind me so I quickly throw it in the sink and run the water.

"Bitch!" he bellows. "You come here after six months of being in your fancy life and think you can boss us around?"

"My life isn't fancy, I have what I have because I work! I work every single day, unlike you. Damn it, I thought you had things under control!" I run my hand down my face. "Where's Daddy?"

He rolls his eyes and grabs a beer from the fridge. "Find him yourself. You're good at working."

My brother storms out of the room, slamming the front door, which causes me to jump. I can't believe the selfishness that comes from him. I bust my ass to send them money each month. I know my father's medical condition has made it difficult to keep the business afloat. It's hard to work on bikes when your fingers cramp all the time. I'm so sick of trying to save people who aren't willing to help themselves.

Regardless of my brother's issues, I can't allow the house to stay this way. My father isn't a young man, and his lungs can't handle breathing this in daily.

I spend some time doing the best I can to make it livable. I throw in a load of laundry, strip my father's bed, open the windows and try to air out the smoke smell, and then order groceries online. This is probably what I should've done from the start instead of thinking my jackass of a brother would use the money I sent correctly.

Once I've done what I can, I head down the long dirt road to the shop.

My parents inherited the land, and being the hippies they were, they lived off it. We have a garden with vegetables, everything runs off solar panels that backs up to a generator for the non-sunny times, and Daddy converted the old barn into a garage.

He built it this way in case the government ever wanted to destroy us, so we could hunker down here and never leave. My parents were very weird.

"Baby girl?" My dad comes down the dirt path, wiping his permanently black-stained hands on a rag.

"Daddy," I sigh with a smile. His brown eyes sparkle in the sun and happiness paints his face.

I don't see him nearly enough, since he's a little over an hour's drive from Chicago. I wish I could come more often, but it's hard to get away from the hospital. He's changed a bit since the last time I saw him—there's a slight limp in his gait and more salt than pepper in his hair. It makes me realize how long it's really been.

"Well, isn't this a surprise?" His smirk says more than his words.

"I needed a break."

"I'm sure. It's tough saving the world all the time. Sometimes you need to save yourself."

I nod, and his arm tightens around me as he pulls me to his side. "I missed you, Daddy. I'm sorry I haven't come more. I just needed to hug you."

"Sure you did," he laughs. "So, what's got you all torn

up?"

Damn intuitive man.

I grunt while I squeeze him harder. "Can't a girl just miss her daddy? You persuaded me to visit on our last call."

There are times in life when you need the loving arms of a man who never fails you—and this is one. My father is my rock, and while that rock may be a little misshapen, he's always honest.

"Sure, she can, but I know bullshit when I hear it. I've been around a long time and you're not very good at lying anyway."

Nothing gets by Mick Adams.

"You're so pushy."

We start to head back to the barn a few feet away. Dad has this way of making you feel like he's telling you everything you need to hear in the silence. While no words are exchanged, there's much being said. He waits with his hand on the door.

"Well?"

I internally groan. "Why do you think there's anything? Why can't it be what I said?"

"Because I know you, baby girl. I also know you don't come visit your old man unless something is making your head all jumbled and you need to flee. And it's usually a boy. You've also always been an easy read."

I huff, "Gee, thanks."

Easy read, my ass. I fled because people suck and I'm in a no-win situation. I don't flee because of boys. Well, okay, just the once—and then maybe a little this time. *Whatever.*

He guides me to the couch that's sat there since as long as I can remember. It's dingy and smells like fuel, but it's home.

My father crouches down, lifts my chin, and tells me more with his eyes than I want to hear. "Out with it."

It's time to tell him, and pray he doesn't fly off the handle.

"Fine. If you really want to know, I'll tell you. It's Bryce," I say the name, bracing for impact.

"What about Bryce?" My father's tone is razor sharp. He's never hidden his feelings about Bryce.

"He's back."

Daddy doesn't say a word. He sits like a statue as I wait for him to speak. "Ren, you can't . . ." He looks away. "You can't even think about going near him."

"His wife is dying," I tell him and watch the pain lance through his eyes. "He didn't know I'd be her doctor. I didn't know she was his wife when I accepted her in the trial. But, it's not like there's an option of avoiding him if I'm treating her."

"He'll drag you back down. You'll be worse than last time. You can't treat her, it'll kill you."

"Not this time."

Daddy doesn't say a word. He sits like a statue as I wait for him to speak. "Ren, I've never liked the man."

"I know."

"He broke your heart. He made you cry for weeks. I thought you were going to kill yourself at one point." My father stands and grips the back of his neck. "I'm telling you, being around that man is going to destroy you."

"I won't let it." I shake my head. "I won't let it get that far again, and things are different because he's married. That's a line I would never cross."

"That's what you think now. But do you really think you can stop your heart from feeling? Do you think you're strong enough to battle this? Because I promise you, darling, you and Bryce are unfinished business," Daddy pauses, giving that a minute to sink in. "Can you tell me that seeing him didn't mess your head up enough to take a drive out here?"

Lying to him is futile. He knows it's not something I can do. Not because he is so vehement about being dishonest, but because I respect him more than anything. "It's more complicated than that."

"No. It's not, Serenity. All a man has is his word. If he breaks it once, he'll do it again. He told you he loved you and would marry you, and then, when things got tough . . . he disappeared."

Tears threaten behind my eyes. "I'm so confused."

Dad inches closer and gives me the answer I came for. "Walk away."

Only, I don't want to be the woman who destroys someone else's life. Allison needs help as much as the other patients in the trial. Sure, there's a part of me I buried long ago that is being resurrected right now, but I can handle it, right?

I'm not that girl anymore. The one who was idealistic about love and happiness. I didn't know true loss like I do now.

God, I'm so conflicted about what to do.

"Would you let Mom go without treatment that could change her life?"

"Ren . . ." his voice is full of warning. "You can't compare that."

"I can, because if I don't treat her, she loses. He married her and loves her. I know the stakes, Dad. I'm not that same girl who lost it years ago. I'm stronger than I've ever been. He can't hurt me. I know the rules."

"Emotions don't play by the rules."

"Neither do you." I smirk, hoping he'll let this drop now.

He laughs and nods. He knows I'm right. I don't think the man has ever played fair. He fights hard, loves harder, and is the most honorable person I know. "Rules were never my thing. It seems you're more like your old man than I hoped. If you were like your mother, you'd do the right thing."

"Mom wouldn't want me to let someone innocent suffer. She'd push me to be stronger than I think I am. If this woman was anyone else, I'd have no issue with treating her. But because seventeen years ago I fell in love with her husband, now she can't have a chance? It's not right."

Daddy places his hand on my leg. "Your mother was too sweet for her own good. I just hope it's not your life that's ruined. You are strong, I know that, but you have a bleeding heart, exactly like her, and that gets you in trouble. I think it's telling, based on how you live your life."

"What does that mean?"

"It means you're a fantastic doctor. You let people come and go without an attachment. You live alone and your boyfriend of the last two years has never met a single person in your life other than people you work with. You've closed yourself off from any chance of loving and losing. We both know that when you love, you don't hold back."

I don't want to hear any more. He, of all people, should understand why I've lived this way. He lives up in this run-down house in the middle of nowhere with my brother. His friends who once swarmed this garage aren't around anymore. When Mom died, so did he.

"Are we done for now?" I ask. I came here for clarity but that's the last thing I feel right now. I need to stop with this conversation before I say something I'll regret.

Dad looks at me for a minute and lets out a deep breath. "Why don't you come help me with this alternator since your brother is no help these days?" My father's arm wraps around my shoulder as we head into the bay.

Which reminds me, we need to talk about their living conditions. "Daddy, the house . . ."

"You were up there?"

The shame in my father's eyes brings me to my knees. The last thing I ever want to see is his pain. At the same time, this is completely unacceptable. My brother is clearly too inept to handle running the house, but being a doctor and living just over an hour away doesn't put me in the best position to pitch in.

"Yes," I pause and he looks away. "Where's the service I set up to clean the house?"

"I fired them."

"Dad! Why?"

He shakes his head with his lips pursed, the anger growing in his features. "I don't need strangers coming in here to clean your mother's house."

"Mom is gone, Daddy. She's gone and you can't live like that."

My father is a proud man, I understand that, but he can't do this all on his own. The farm was paid off when I was a kid, then my mother got sick. He mortgaged the house, shop, land, and anything else we had to pay for her treatments. Of course, he was so desperate to get cash to help his dying wife, he was completely taken advantage of.

Deep in debt, my father has to keep the garage running overtime or there's nothing to pay the bills, plus he has to run the farm single-handedly without my mom. I send what I can, but Chicago isn't exactly a cheap city to live in.

"I appreciate your help, but I'm doing fine."

"Fine?" I lean back with my arms crossed. "You think that

was fine?"

"You're not living here, what do you care?"

I blow out a loud breath. Why are men so damn hardhead-ed? "Because I love you, Daddy."

"I love you too, baby girl. Are we done now?"

We're not anywhere close to done. All he's done with is fighting back without offering a solution. I'll be the one who gets things in motion—as always. The two of them will screw up and it'll be my burden to fix it all again.

"For now." I pat his back.

"Help me with that car, would you?" Dad extends an olive branch.

"Sure." I smile and walk over to my tool chest.

My father and I used to spend hours in this shop. So much that he had to get me my own set of tools because I was work-ing so much. In here I let myself just be, no thoughts of ex-boyfriends, no pain and suffering, only my dad and me.

We dive headfirst into the alternator that's busted, arguing about what we believe the problem is. Fixing cars is much dif-ferent from being a doctor. It's mechanics so there's no guess-ing. I can take apart an engine and know that it'll go back the same way. It's mind-numbing, but it feels good to just zone out that way.

Once the car is running again, I clean up a little, feeling much more at peace.

I lean my hip against the front end, pull my phone out, and sigh. Three missed calls from the hospital. I listen to the voicemails, thankful it's nothing life-threatening. However, I need to get back to the city.

"You leaving?" Dad asks as I put my phone in my back pocket.

"Yeah, I need to get back." I look down at my ruined clothes. "And shower. However, I'm calling a housekeeper tonight and you're going to let them clean the house."

He opens his mouth but I lift my hand to stop him.

"And, you're going to tell Everton if he smokes in the house again, I'm going to beat the shit out of him. No more, Dad. I'm serious. You can't breathe that in." I point at his chest. "Years of dirt, exhaust, and all the other crap has done a number on your lungs. If Ev wants to kill himself, that's on him. There's also food coming, and you need to eat it, which means no junk food! Open some windows too, you need fresh air. Oh, and you need to take your pills. There's a reason the doctor is prescribing them."

"Okay, fine," he acquiesces.

The changing roles of adulthood are impossible to grasp. This would've been a lecture I heard as a teenager. Don't smoke, don't let others influence your life, clean up, eat right . . . and now I'm the one telling him.

"You're not just agreeing so I'll let it drop?"

"Go back to the city and save people," he chuckles as he guides me toward my car.

"I worry about you," I say as I get to the door.

Now, even more than I did before. I'm going to have to find a way to be around more. I need to be there for my dad. My brother also needs a kick in the ass.

"You don't need to worry, Ren. I'm fine."

The house was not fine, none of this is, but I also see the finality in his eyes. He's done talking, so now I need to make my plans and hope he follows them.

As I open my door, I can feel the turmoil coming from him. He may be done with listening to me, but Daddy isn't done talking.

"I gotta say this to you," he coughs. I knew he couldn't keep it in. "I loved you the moment I saw you. I wanted a boy so much, but the second you came out, I felt it. Your mother felt it."

"Felt what?"

"Peace."

He's never hidden the fact that when I entered his world, I changed it. He used to say that having children is when you realize nothing you knew in life was true. My brother and I altered him to his core, we made him more.

I always wanted to know what that was like, until I didn't have someone I wanted to share it with anymore.

"You have this power inside you that you don't see. You save people. You repair them. You helped me. My point is this." He lets out a heavy breath. "Don't ever allow someone else the power to break you. The man you love, the one you share your heart with, should always treat it with care. He shouldn't forsake it."

"Daddy," I start, but his hand raises, stopping me.

"No, listen to this if you hear nothing else I've said." He releases a deep breath. "There are different kinds of love. The kind that saves you and the kind that breaks you. Bryce wasn't the saving kind. He stole a part of you and you've never gotten it back."

My father made his mind up about Bryce a long time ago. No matter how many times I told him he was wrong, it didn't matter. I was his baby, and someone hurt me. Fathers are supposed to protect their little girls, and he couldn't mend my broken heart, no matter how he tried.

I never told him the full story about why I left, partially

because I knew he'd tell me I was a fool.

We all were.

I came home for him and my mother, even though they told me not to.

I also lied about not getting into Penn State . . .

I nod, unsure what to say because I'm still not ready to share my truths. "Thank you, Dad. For everything."

"Anytime. You know I'm here."

"I do."

"Good, drive safe. I'll be expecting you before another six months go by." He gives a pointed look. "And be careful, Ren."

I grip the wheel a little tighter, knowing he's not talking about the drive home.

11

I park my car in the underground garage and lean my head against the seat rest. The things I thought were working in my life are now riddled with flaws.

My brother is clearly not taking care of my father.

There's still a piece of me that loves Bryce even though I've deluded myself into believing there wasn't. Just the thought of him makes my heart race, my palms sweat, and I wonder what it all could've been like if I had gone to Penn State. Everything would've been different. We could've been happy, but our lives went in opposite directions and now I'm treating his wife because I have no choice unless I want to lose my trial or another candidate applies, is accepted, and gets up to Chicago by today. After talking to my father, I know I'm in over my head.

And then there's Wes, none of this is fair to him. I care about him, I want to want a future with him, but Bryce being back . . . complicates things.

It's not simply raining on my parade, it's an entire ecosystem failure.

Julie: Want to go out tonight? I'm off and I need vodka.

Vodka sounds like a great idea.

Me: Yes. Where?

Julie: How about we go to Rich's pub? Low-key and you know we can get a sucker to buy us drinks.

Me: Perfect.

I have two missed calls from Westin, but I don't feel like talking to him. Right now, I want some space from my life. Westin, Bryce, Allison, the trial, my worthless brother, and everything else can disappear for a night. Monday starts the actual distribution of the chemo, and I decide I deserve a weekend for just me.

The next few hours pass with a text from Westin that goes unanswered, and I don't even have the energy to give a shit right now. The last thing I need is to say something stupid and really screw up things. Usually on our weekends off, we spend them together, but there's nothing left inside of me to pretend today.

I walk down to Rich's, needing the atmosphere that always grounds me. It's a hole in the wall place, but the bartender is generous with the alcohol, and it's cheap. When you're a broke med student, cheap is your favorite word. But it's become so much more than a dive bar. It's my favorite place for advice I don't ask for, and it has the best burgers in Chicago.

"Hey!" Julie smiles and pulls me in for a hug. "You look

like you need a drink."

"I do."

She smirks. "Good. Let's get drunk and you can tell me all your problems."

There's not a chance of that, but the drunk part sounds good.

We hook arms and enter.

"Trouble one and two are here," Rich, the owner, yells as he slaps the bar top.

"What a welcome," Julie laughs. "I knew you missed us."

Rich comes around, hugs us both and then wipes two barstools. "Sit, it's been a while since I've seen you."

Rich is a character. He's probably pushing seventy now, but you'd never know it from the way he moves around. He and his wife bought this place when they were in their twenties and have survived through it all. Each patron that walks in becomes family, and he loves his family.

It's what keeps those who come through the doors returning over and over again.

"So, what's new with my girls?" Rich asks.

"Ren started her clinical trial," Jules says.

"You did?" The pride in his eyes is humbling. He's almost like a second father to me.

I nod. "Yeah, Monday it really starts, but all the preliminary stuff is done," I explain.

"Well," he grins. "I'll be damned. I knew you two were going to change the world the first time I saw you both."

He's so full of shit. We were two doe-eyed med students the first time we stumbled in here. I had moved back here to help with my mother, lost Bryce, and was trying desperately to pretend I was okay. I was drinking more than I should have, and sleeping with as many guys as I could to feel anything but my longing for Bryce.

"He lies." Julie rolls her eyes.

"I do not." Rich puts his hands on his hips. "I knew you two were going to do great things. Just took you both a little while to realize it."

"I'm glad someone knew we were special," I giggle.

"You're special, all right," Rich says with sarcasm. "What are you troublemakers drinking tonight?"

Julie and I look at each other and answer. "Vodka."

After a few martinis, I'm pretty damn numb. I don't care so much about all the shit in my life. Julie rests her head on the bar and spins her glass.

"Rem-member when we drank lots of these?" she stammers.

I laugh as my head drops back, causing hair to sway. It feels funny. "I 'member."

My phone dings with a text.

"Ugh," I groan. "Westin again."

Westin: I don't know where you are, but you said you'd be home by five. It's late and I'm worried that you're not okay.

Me: I'm fine. Just hanging with Jules.

Westin: Okay then.

"What does he want?" Julie asks.

"More."

"More is less," she giggles. "More is never happening with

you."

"More sucks," I respond. "You know why you don't give more? Because you give more and then they want more of more," I ramble. "I'm tired of it. I won't give nothing anymore."

Julie lifts her head, slaps the wood, and straightens her back. "Yes. Give nothing because men don't give us enough."

"Yes!" I agree.

"I think you're an idiot, though," she shrugs.

Why am I an idiot? I'm the one who started this revolution of how stupid giving more is.

"What the hell?" I ask feeling miffed.

Julie raises her glass toward Rich, indicating we need more. "Because Westin is more than any of us will ever get."

"Westin is not perfect."

He has flaws and people need to understand that. I'm so tired of hearing how great he is because sometimes, he's not. When he loses a patient, he's a dick. When he can't figure out a way to fix something, he's awful. When he doesn't get his way, he's a big-ass baby.

He's a man.

I know he's great in so many ways, but he's also a showman. The good impression he makes is carefully orchestrated. Westin wants to be the Chief of Surgery. He's playing a game and we're all the pawns. Anyone that doesn't see that is blind.

"I never said he was," she clarifies.

Didn't she? "Why do you keep bringing this up? It's the second time in a few days."

Julie shifts to face me. "Don't tell me you don't hear the rumors about the women wanting to take your place, Ren. He may not be perfect, but he's pretty damn close."

"You don't know everything. He's got ambitions and if you think he won't step on all of us to get there, you're crazy."

She sways in her seat a little and puts her head back down. "Like either of us wouldn't if we had the chance?"

"I'd like to think I wouldn't step on my friends to get to the top," I say, because I want to earn the title of chief, not politic my way to that seat. Which will probably be why I never get it.

Julie laughs once. "You would and neither would Wes. He may have aspirations and goals, but he's not an asshole. He wants to get it the same way that we do."

Wes isn't that way. He's kind and she's right. He wouldn't purposely destroy anyone to reach his goals. "True. So that leaves you. And we all know that you couldn't hurt anyone," I reply. "You're too damn nice."

"This is true," she sighs. "I'm happy in my lab, and you're happy with people."

She's right again. I want to be the person on the front lines of medicine. Being chief is a lot of paperwork, politics, and pissing people off. I'll stick to the patients, where I can make a real difference.

"I have to pee," Julie giggles as she hops off her barstool. "Don't do anything stupid!"

"Okay," I say as my head lolls to the side. "I'll be right here."

I never drink like this, but it feels good to relax for once. I feel like the last fifteen years of my life, I've had a great big stick up my ass. It was college, mom being sick, med school, internship, residency, and now it's just constant death. Not to mention my father isn't going to be around forever and my wayward brother can't do shit.

I'm tired. I'm tired of always doing the right thing.

I'm tired of always being a damn adult.

When do I get to have fun? Never, that's when. My friends enjoyed the first four years of college, but I wasn't at bars or frat parties, I was studying or with Bryce. It was my choice, I know this, but I thought I had more time.

When Mom got sick, everything changed. My entire life became about cancer. I need a little fun once in a while.

"This seat taken?" A deep voice I'd know even in a crowd of screaming people asks from beside me.

Our eyes meet and there's an ache in my heart as I take him in. He looks tired and desperate, and yet on the outside, you only see perfection. Bryce Peyton was trained to never show emotion, but I can see it. There were always fissures in his stone-cold façade that I was able to pick up on. There's pain and fear in those gorgeous eyes, things he thinks he's hiding, but I see his wife's sickness is weighing him down.

Wife.

Remember that, Serenity. It's not because of me or being around me. It's because his wife is sick.

"I'm waiting for my friend," I explain and turn back to my drink.

"Not what I asked," Bryce says as he sits without my answer.

"Well, the seat is taken, but I'm sure you'll sit anyway. Not like you care about what makes me happy." I mumble the last part and then drain the rest of my martini.

It's clear that he's not going to respect my request for him to stay away from me.

"I'll move when your boyfriend gets back," he tosses out and then orders his drink.

A whiskey neat.

Some things never change.

"I never said Westin was here."

"He has a name." Bryce smiles and I glare at him.

"Yes, he has a name. Why do you care?"

Bryce shifts so we're close enough that I can smell the mint on his breath. "I don't. I'm married. Remember?"

I roll my eyes and lean back. "Yes, you are. I remember."

The two of us continue to stare at each other and I work hard to read him. I'm not sure why he's here or why he felt the need to talk to me, but Bryce is fighting his own demons.

"So, we meet again—in a bar." Bryce clears his throat, breaking the eye contact, and I fight back the desire to trudge down memory lane. We're not those people anymore.

I lift my glass, letting Rich know I need another. At this rate, he could bring me the bottle of Tito's and I'd be happy. Who needs olives after the fourth—or was it fifth?

"Shouldn't you be with your wife?"

"She's sleeping and I needed to work," he explains.

"Work? In the bar?" I question.

Bryce rolls the drink around his glass before bringing it to his lips. I'm just drunk enough to allow myself a momentary lapse in judgment as I think about what he once tasted like. The memory of a mix of whiskey, mint, and just . . . him, sends my pulse into overdrive. I remember how he'd kiss me with his entire body. It wasn't just his mouth. I could feel all the energy he carried flow through the two of us, causing an overwhelming surge of emotions.

He kissed me with tenderness and power that battled for dominance.

I remember feeling drunk afterwards even though I hadn't had a drink.

"Does it matter? I needed a drink, and here I am."

Lucky me. "Yeah, here you are."

Where the fuck is Julie? I really need her to get back here.

"So, you and the doctor?"

My eyes narrow and I try to piece together why he's asking. This is the second comment now about Westin and I can't help but wonder if it's bothering him. It shouldn't, considering he's the one that actually moved on. Of course, he doesn't know anything about my life and I'm not about to admit how pathetic I am.

"Westin and I have been together for a few years," I admit.

"I don't see a ring," Bryce notes.

"Unlike you, who found someone and got married. Although I'll admit Allison seems great."

He takes another long sip before finally speaking. "She is. She's been good to me, and," his eyes meet mine, "she saved me after I went down a dark road."

My breath hitches as the passion in his gaze tells me so much more. We were always in tune with each other when we were together. Bryce could look at me and I'd know what he was saying. It was like we were two halves of a whole that came together without any gaps.

"Because I left?"

"Yeah, Ren. You left and shit went downhill for me."

"Don't think it was so easy for me either," I counter. I'm still recovering from it, and him being here has reversed what little progress I've made.

He looks up at the television, sighs, and then his eyes close. "I didn't sit down next to you to fight."

I don't want to fight either. All I want is for things to go back to the way they were. I liked my life a few days ago. It wasn't perfect, but I was . . . content. Westin and I were going to turn a corner and now I feel as though I ran into the wall—a wall named Bryce.

I play with the stem of the martini glass. "Then why did you sit?"

"I don't know. I saw you and started to walk toward you. I swear it was like I couldn't stop myself."

His admission stuns me. There's a hint of defeat in his voice. Bryce is struggling just as much as I am.

"Why were things so dark?" I ask.

He pinches the bridge of his nose and then takes a long, slow slip of his whiskey. "You think I wanted you to leave? I was a wreck after you decided to go to Northwestern. We were stronger than that, Chick. We were supposed to go to school together, start our life, and you came back home and then it was like I didn't matter anymore."

He mattered. He always mattered. Hell, at one point, he was all that mattered.

Maybe we should talk about all of this that lingers between us? Closure is what we're both lacking. If we could get it out there, we could finally put this thing to bed.

"Oh my God. I met this guy right by the bath—" Julie's voice breaks the intense moment. "Well, hello there." She looks at Bryce.

He drains the remnants of his whiskey and stands. "It was great to see you, Dr. Adams. I appreciate you lending me your seat, miss."

Looks like closure has to wait.

"I'll see you tomorrow, Mr. Peyton." The formality sounds foreign coming from my lips. He's Bryce. My Bryce. The one who I met in a run-down bar like this one what feels like a million years ago, but he's not mine anymore.

12

Knock, knock, knock.

I really need an IV to cure this hangover. Vodka is not my friend today. No, today I hate vodka and all the promises it made about how much better I'd feel if I drank it. I do not feel better. Instead, I have a splitting headache and I've spent a few hours in front of the toilet.

"Ren?"

My head falls back. I groan when I realize who it is, and I rest my hand on the door. I don't have the energy for today. I wanted to spend today in bed, hating my life and enjoying a little pity party I was going to attend.

"Ren, I saw your car," Westin's voice says from the other side of the door.

I twist the lock and unhook the chain, knowing I need to deal with this now. Westin deserves better from me.

"Hey," I croak, clear my throat, and try to smile.

"Are you sick?" he asks with concern lacing his voice.

I shake my head. "No, Julie and I went to Rich's bar."

He smirks. "You blew me off for that?"

"I didn't blow you off, Wes. Or, I didn't mean to. Either way, please know I'm being thoroughly punished for my sins."

"Since last night was a bust, I'm stealing you for the day," he informs me. "Go get dressed, we're going out."

I look at him with my brows raised. "I'm sorry, what?"

He takes my hand, pulling me toward the bedroom. "Get ready, Ren. Don't fight me, just listen for once."

I stop walking, cross my arms over my chest, and fight back a smile. "What are you up to, Westin Grant?"

Our eyes are locked, and he moves close, his strong arm hooking around my back, and pulling me in so we're flush against each other. "I'm doing what I should've done a long time ago," he says, watching my reaction. "I'm not going to let you drive the car anymore, Serenity. I want more and I'm tired of waiting for you to be ready."

I gasp as the fire burns in his gaze. "What if I'm not ready now?"

His lips turn into a sinful smile. "Then I guess I'll have to make you ready."

If this were a week ago, I would've been thrilled at this take-charge kind of change in him. I might not have been on board right away, but I wouldn't feel as though I was being pulled apart. Now, though, I'm at war with the girl I was and the woman I want to be. I think about what it was like to let a man run my world, and how that ended. My heart is irrational and it's torn. I remember the way it was for me a long time ago with Bryce, and even though I can't have it, I crave the closeness and love I felt.

Westin must see the hesitation, because he doesn't allow me the time to let it grow. Within a second, his lips fuse to mine. The force of the kiss knocks me off my feet and he slams my back into the wall. His body molds to mine and I'm completely lost to him.

My tongue slides against his, feeling the dominance radiating from him. I moan into his mouth as his hands roam my body. Westin knows how to please me. He moves his fingers down to my core, pressing in exactly the right spot.

I would much rather get undressed right now than go wherever he's planning to take me.

"Westin," I groan. "Bed. Now."

He moves his lips to my neck, kissing his way back to my lips. "Not until we go on our date."

That's not fair. I want Westin to do what Westin and I do best and then we can think about the date. I want to forget and he is the one thing that makes the chaos that riots inside of me calm.

I pout and he chuckles. "Not fair."

"Neither are the games you've been playing."

"I'm not playing games. I've been honest from day one that I'm not a relationship girl. I like what we have. I started to think I wanted more, but now I don't know anymore . . . what if we don't work out? We would have to work together, see each other daily. I'm scared, Wes. I'm scared of letting you in and then messing up what we have."

I make myself stop talking, because *I* am a mess. I'm frustrating, unsure, insecure, and all of that has become clear in the last few days. I have spent the last fourteen years hardening myself to being vulnerable to a man. My work, my family, and my focus have allowed me to survive that way. The fear of opening myself to being hurt again leaves me restless.

He pushes back a little, and his nose flares but his voice stays even. "I know, but I'm asking for one date. One chance to see what it could be like if you let your guard down and open your eyes to what we have. Not this half in and half out shit you've been doing. We're both mature adults. We can handle working together if it fails. We can be friends if this ends, but God, Ren, can you handle walking away?"

Doubt plagues me and I wonder if I'll regret this moment for the rest of my life. If I say yes, am I giving him hope that doesn't exist? If I say no, am I willing to lose what I do have with him?

Julie would punch me in the face if she was here.

"No, I can't, but don't . . ."

"Don't say another word, just get dressed and meet me in the living room," he kisses my lips and walks away.

Damn it. I guess we're going on our first real date.

Westin takes me to the movies, which I haven't done in— forever. I seriously think college was the last time I've gone to see a movie.

"What are we seeing?" I ask as we get to the cashier.

"You'll have to wait." Westin's arm wraps around my shoulders and my hand rests on his chest. To anyone who walked by, we'd look like a couple, and for right now, we are. It feels . . . nice. There's no baggage or pretending when I'm with him. I can laugh, be weird, and I don't have to impress Westin. He's been around long enough to know my quirks.

He gets two tickets to a horror film and I'm slightly giddy.

Westin buys popcorn, a huge soda, Reese's Pieces, Starburst, and Whoppers.

"Who is eating all of that?" I ask as he hands me the popcorn.

"We are. We're going to eat shit food, watch a movie, and pretend for a few hours that our lives aren't serious all the time."

I nod once. "Okay then. I can get with this."

We get to our seats and I sink in, ready for the movie. I'm suddenly overcome with gratitude and regret for being so stupid these last few years. Westin is real, he's here, and he cares about me.

Comparing what we have to what I had with anyone else isn't fair. In all honesty, I'm dumb for wanting what I had before. Bryce broke me just as much as he claims I broke him when we lost each other. I don't want to endure that again.

My hand covers Westin's, wanting to have some kind of physical connection. His eyes meet mine and my heart begins to race a little. "Thank you for this, Wes."

"You're welcome. Today has been long overdue."

If I gave myself permission to move on, it could happen. Even as crazy as our lives are, we could be happy . . . if I wanted to be. If there's anyone who's going to be the one to get through, it's him.

Thankfully, the lights dim, stopping the conversation before it gets intense. The movie is terrible. I mean, absolutely ridiculous and not scary at all. Throughout the entire thing, we both make comments, laugh, and throw popcorn at each other.

It's the most fun I've had in far too long.

"How could anyone think that movie was even halfway decent?" I ask as we walk out of the theater.

His fingers link with mine and he pulls me against his side. "I have no idea, but I'm glad you had to suffer along with me."

I grin while looking in his eyes. "Whatever. I only suffered because it was so bad."

He laughs. "I liked how you squeaked when you got scared and grabbed my arm."

"I didn't get scared! Also, I don't squeak."

"I'm pretty sure I heard you."

I giggle and nudge him. "I think you need your hearing checked."

"Know any good doctors?" Westin smirks as I stare up at him.

"Funny."

He leans down and kisses the top of my head. "Cute." Suddenly, he stops, grabs an empty box of popcorn, and tosses it in the trash. "I hate when people don't clean up after themselves."

I feel my lips turn up into a warm smile. Here's a guy who lives in a very expensive loft, has money for days, but still stops to pick up someone's trash.

"Sweet," I mutter aloud. I release his hand and hold onto his arm as we head toward Millennium Park.

As we walk, Westin tells me about his meeting with the chief and his hopes to get the position. Then we switch topics and he brings up a case he has that has him a little stumped. I love listening to his passion as he talks about his hopes to find a way to help his patient.

"I have faith you'll find a way," I tell him.

"You do, huh?"

"I do. If there's anyone who won't give up, it's you," I laugh.

Westin wraps his arms around me and starts to tickle me. I squirm in his grasp, but I can't stop myself from giggling. I'm ridiculously ticklish. He stops, but doesn't let go.

We stand here, in front of the park entrance, and he looks down at me with adoration in his green eyes. "I'm only relentless on things that matter."

"I'm glad you are."

"Are you?"

I nod.

"Well," he taps my nose. "I'm gl—" He's cut off when a bike zooms past us and he grabs me closer, tight against his body. My pulse spikes, as it was a close call. Wes looks down at me. "You okay?"

"I'm fine," I smile. "Thanks to you."

When I'm around Westin I feel a sense of safety in a sea of uncertainty. He holds the rudder, keeping us on course. He doesn't control me, but he comforts me. I can relax. I can breathe.

We continue walking, with me clutching his arm as we reach the famous Chicago bean, where tons of people are milling around, snapping selfies and smiling. Westin and I love coming here during our days off. It's a fun area where we can be normal people.

His arm wraps around my shoulder and I burrow into him. It's freaking cold out.

"I like this, Ren."

I look up with curiosity. "Freezing our asses off?"

He laughs. "No, being like this."

My heart starts to race as he moves back to this topic. I knew it was coming, but I don't know what I'll say if he pushes. There's a part of me that's ready to move on with my life and another part that's definitely not.

I'm terrified to love anyone else. In my experience, the people I love leave or die. They let me go, and I don't want to think about it right now. I want to enjoy this little slice of heaven that Westin has given me.

"Let's not talk about it tonight. Please." I close my eyes.

"I've had the best day with you and I don't want to ruin it."

"I'm not saying I want us to get married or any of that shit, but I want—" I place my fingertips on his lips to stop him.

"Tomorrow we can talk about it. But I want to enjoy tonight with no heavy stuff."

He pulls his jacket around us both with his chin on top of my head. "One day you're going to have to give in and move on."

I inhale his clean scent, rubbing my ice-cold nose against his chest. "Why do we have to change things?"

Westin pulls back, takes my face in his hands, and sighs. "Because I watch people die every day. I see regret in their eyes and I don't want that with us. It's been two years, and I've been a patient man. You've got issues with love, and I get that, but I'm not *him*, Serenity. I'm not the guy that fucked your head up. I've been the guy who held you when you cried, supported you, and if you don't see that we're more than fuck buddies . . . I don't know what else to say."

My stomach sinks as the truth in his words sink in. I open my mouth to speak, but Westin silences me before I can say a word. His lips press against mine and he kisses me with so much passion my head spins.

I hold his wrists as his tongue enters my mouth, sliding against my tongue and stealing my breath.

He pulls back and I pant. "Westin, I want . . ."

"What do you want?"

You. Us. This. I think. But fear holds me back and I hate myself for it. "I want us to try, but I'm afraid."

He pulls me back to his chest, forcing me to look up at him with so much warmth in his eyes I could cry. "I'm a desirable doctor that many women would like to date."

There is no doubt about that. "I know."

"I can't waste time if you're never going to come around."

"I'm not saying never. I'm not even saying I haven't now."

Westin's phone dings and he grins looking down at the text.

"What?" I ask.

"Nothing."

"Everything okay?"

He shrugs. "Yeah, it was one of the nurses letting me know something."

Something Julie asked me floats around in my head, sending a jolt of jealousy through me. What if Westin is seeing someone else? As of right now, I don't have a right to care. I was deluding myself before to think I really wouldn't be upset.

A violin starts to play "Radioactive" and we both start to dance a little. Here wrapped up in each other's arms, in the middle of the park, the two of us sway to the music.

This song is fitting—most days I feel radioactive. As if I'm a dangerous chemical that's ready to blow at any point, poisoning those around me.

The song shifts after about thirty seconds, where suddenly drums, a guitar, and a keyboard start playing the next song, which is a much more upbeat melody.

Our arms fall, as we both look around to see a hoard of dancers moving in, and they're all synchronized.

"Holy shit!" I look around as the batches of flash mob dancers head into the center joining in. "It's a flash mob! I've never seen one and I've always wanted to."

"I knew you were upset that you missed the one in the hospital." He leans down, kisses my cheek, and heads into the mob, leaving me stunned.

The music is loud, phones are in the air, and Westin is out there, dancing in perfect time with them. The song changes again, but he doesn't miss a beat. I can't believe this. How did I not know Westin dances in a flash mob? My smile is so wide, it's hurting my face, but I can't take my eyes off him. He continues through two more songs before it ends. The crowd around me starts to clap and everyone starts to disperse.

I rush over to him, grab his hand, and pull him away.

"That was . . ." I shake my head with wide eyes. "I mean, you do flash mobs! How? When? You were amazing!"

He chuckles as we move out of the way.

"How long have you been doing these?"

"Only when I can. Remember the eight-year-old with the brain tumor last year?"

My smile falls as the child's sweet face fills my memory. He was adorable, with the biggest smile I'd ever seen. Westin was absolutely devastated when he lost him. I'd never seen him so broken after a surgery.

"I do." I take his hand.

"Well, he loved flash mobs, he'd watch them for hours on YouTube, so I found a group that does them, and started learning. We had the one in the hospital for him, and then I kept finding ways to practice."

My heart grows to ten times its size. I can't believe he has the time to do this, but the reason he learned is what touches me so deeply.

"I'm speechless, Wes."

He grins. "It's a lot of fun, and something that reminds me of him. I'll never forget that kid, but when I dance, it's all smiles and good memories."

The feel of Westin's skin against mine warms me to my

core. "I never knew about this."

Westin's hand touches my cheek. "There's a lot you don't know, Ren. Things I want to share with you. All you have to do is say yes."

"I literally don't know what to say. You blow me away."

"In a good way?" Westin grins.

"Yes," I laugh at the silly look on his face. "In a very good way."

"How so?"

I pull myself closer to his chest, loving the way I fit with him in this moment. We've had the best night, and I want many more like this, and like the ones we've always had. The nights with my feet tucked into his lap as we chart. The times when we're so exhausted we just collapse into bed without needing to explain.

"You make me want more. I can't promise I won't pull back, but I can't imagine my life without you, either. Next weekend, I need to go back up to my father's house and make sure things are okay. Would you like to come?"

His head tilts to one side as if I'm a conundrum he's trying to solve. It's as if he's seeing me for the first time. My stomach tightens as he watches me.

"Is that a yes?" I ask after the intensity starts to worry me.

"I'm not known for chasing a woman. You make me want to run . . ." I open my mouth, but he stops me. "Not away though, Serenity, but to you. So, yes, I'd love to finally meet your father."

My eyes fill with tears that don't fall. I don't cry. I shove down the feelings he's stirring within me. "I've been running from love for so long I don't know if I can stop even if I want to," I say, looking away. "I'll try, but be patient with me."

Westin pulls me flush against him, causing my eyes to flash to his. "I'm faster than you are. I'm ready to show you."

"You might not catch me," I warn.

He may run faster in the physical sense, but I've been running from love for years. I'm good at it, and I don't know that I can ever be caught.

His lips press against my forehead and he releases me. "I might not, but it won't be because of speed. It'll be because of you."

That's what I'm worried about.

Westin takes a few steps back, and the cold air is like a punch to my chest. With each step, I feel his loss. This is what it will be like. Him over there and me standing here, waiting to make a move.

I think about my father's words about a different love. The one where I wouldn't be left in the pits of hell. The kind of love that Westin offers wouldn't take anything from me. I watch him retreat, and think about the tightness in my chest increasing as he moves farther back.

Can I let him go and stand here, watching him leave me?

My feet are becoming one with the cement, and I'm making the choice to stay.

As he takes another step backward, I know what I have to do. I have to break the chains of fear and go to him.

He's right for me.

He's good for me.

Westin is who I want to build a future with.

It's as if the moment I made the choice, the ground became a cloud, helping me get to him. I close the distance, wrap my arms around him, and hold on tight. Life goes on around us, but time stands still. It's as if what's been broken inside of me for so long just healed a little. The hole may never be filled, but Westin can patch it. Every part of me knows what I want. There's no hesitation in my heart. He's the right man for me, and I have to get closure so I can fully move on.

Fifteen Years Earlier

"I got in!" I yell as I rush into Bryce's arms. "I got in!"

"I knew you would."

God, this is such a relief. I got into Penn State and now we can solidify our plans. It'll all work out. I feel like I can breathe.

"I'm glad you were confident."

Bryce shakes his head. "You're insanely smart, got into Yale, Northwestern, and UCLA, so . . . yeah . . . I was confident."

"None of those are where I wanted to go though, that's what you're missing."

UCLA was never a real option, but my professor urged me to apply. Yale was an option if he was going to Cornell, but we both wanted Penn State. Now, we have it.

"We have dinner tonight," Bryce reminds me.

"Shit. I have to study."

"Chick, not tonight."

I really can't blow this biology final off. There's a reason I got into every school I applied to—because I work my ass off.

He is the only thing I do outside of school.

"Can we please do it another day?"

"No."

I groan and cross my arms. "Why are you being so rigid?"

"Because today is important."

Worry starts to creep in. Is it his birthday? No, that's in three months. Our anniversary? No, that just passed. What the hell is important about today?

"Why?"

He rolls his eyes and then kisses me. "It is, go get ready."

We are clearly not going to come to an understanding here, and today is a day for celebrating, I guess. I'll study once he goes to sleep.

I rush out of the room and do as he says. I shower quickly, shave my legs, and look for something cute to wear. Once I'm all dressed and ready, I come out to see him in a suit.

Bryce looks really freaking good in a suit.

"Who . . ."

He grins and his eyes roam my body. "Whoa yourself." Slowly, he rises to his feet and stands before me. His hands cup my face as though I'm a delicate flower and then his lips touch mine.

The kiss is slow, sweet, and has my heart pounding.

When he kisses me like this, it feels like everything disappears and all that exists in the world is Bryce and me.

He does that to me. When we're together, I'm not afraid of anything. I know that he'll be here to hold me up. My hands grip his shoulders as our lips move together.

Has anyone ever felt this breathless and cared for?

With my eyes closed, I take everything in. The way his cologne fills my nose, the musky notes giving a slight burn. How the fabric of his jacket is rough against my fingertips, and how his soft, warm skin causes my nerves to ache from his touch.

I commit it all to memory, so I can recall it anytime I need to feel like nothing in this world can harm me.

After another few seconds, he releases me. His forehead rests on mine. "I would die for you, Ren. Do you know that?"

His statement makes my breath hitch. "What?"

"If anything were to happen to us, I wouldn't survive it."

"What is going on?"

He releases a heavy sigh and steps back. "I just keep thinking about how much I love you and how it feels so intense. All I want is to hold onto us. It's crazy, right? Do you feel it?"

I do. It's sometimes scary because it's overwhelming. It's as though nothing in this world matters as much as him, and that's not normal. We're only twenty-three and yet I know that he's the one.

"I feel it," I say. "I love you so much sometimes that it physically hurts."

"Yes."

"And then I worried we wouldn't be together and we'd fall apart."

He takes my face in his hands again. "Never."

I smile at that. "Good."

"Marry me."

My eyes lift to his, surely I misheard him.

"What?"

"Marry me, Serenity." Then, Bryce drops to his knees. He holds my hand and pulls a box from his pants pocket. "I planned to do this at dinner, where I would tell you everything in my heart. You see, there is no one else for me. I found you that night and I knew that what we had was special. I told you that one day you'd be my wife, and I meant it then and I mean it now. Marry me. Be my wife. Let's have a hundred kids. Marry me, Chick. Be my everything—until my last breath."

I can't see his face as the tears are streaming down. I drop to my knees and wrap my arms around him. "Yes. Yes! Yes!"

And then, neither of us really care about dinner.

14

Okay, *I can do this. I'm going to go in there, and do my job.* Today starts the actual administration of the drugs. All of the patients have been tested, folders numbered, and there's no going back now. Allison will remain a part of the trial or need to be replaced within twenty-four hours in order for the trial to proceed. Since I don't have another patient that meets the age and stage requirements and still actually has a uterus, she's going to remain a part of the program. Also, she deserves the treatment. I'm her doctor, I took an oath, and I'm going to try to save her, no matter who she's married to.

I push open the door to Allison Brown's room and find her and her husband holding hands and smiling, and he stares at her the way he once looked at me. I draw in a deep breath and force a smile.

"Good morning, Allison." I enter the room, keeping my eyes on her. I'm with Westin now, this shouldn't matter. "How are you feeling?"

She looks at Bryce and then back to me. "Hopeful. I feel like maybe this is going to work and that maybe we can . . ."

Maybe they can have a baby.

Bryce's eyes meet mine and I look away, hating myself for even going down that line of thinking.

This is what is wrong with me and why I'll never be happy. It always comes back to him.

I follow the words on the paper, needing to do what I came in here to do without letting my ridiculous thoughts run away with me. "Well, everything looks great. Your labs are good, scans came back as we hoped, so now we'll start to administer the medication and monitor you." I force my gaze to hers. "Do you have any questions?"

She nods. "I know the waiver said that there would be patients who do not receive the trial dosage. Will those patients be made aware of that?"

This is the part that is pure torture for everyone involved, but mostly for me. Knowing that two of my twenty-four patients won't get the drugs they're hoping for is absolutely horrible. I'll still be treating their cancer, but if they get the placebo, they'll most likely need a hysterectomy by month two.

"No, as the trial paperwork stated, this is a placebo trial, meaning no one will know who has the drug and who has the placebo." If a patient knew they were on the placebo, they'd drop out, which means it has to be a blind trial. "However, we will still be treating the cancer with traditional chemotherapy to show the difference," I explain.

"So she could still need a hysterectomy?" Bryce asks.

"Yes," I say while I nod, doing my best not to look at Allison and answer as though I don't already know about the letter she gave me with her demands. "That's correct, but I will be following the size of your tumor very closely. The rules state that I can't do anything until the end of the trial, which is when

I won't hesitate to do the surgery." I look into Allison's tear-filled eyes.

I stare at her, begging her with all that's in me to understand the consequences of her actions. "I know it's scary, but I've treated this type of cancer for a long time, and as much as this trial is important, you're more important. I won't hesitate to alert you if the tumor grows to the point that the trial is no longer relevant. We can decide then."

I can pretend to empathize with what she must be feeling, but I can't, really. There's a science behind medicine that takes out the human emotion. I work hard not to lose sight of that in dealing with my patients.

All I can do is pray that if it really does become a life or death situation, she'll choose life.

"I don't like this," Bryce says. "I don't understand how it's fair. So you get to decide who gets the combo and who doesn't?" There's an edge to his voice I don't appreciate.

This is exactly what I worried about.

If each patient received the same dosage, we'd never have a clear picture of how this combination works. I need to see comparisons of the same women receiving different drugs to make an accurate conclusion. Especially if we want this to be a viable option for other women across the world.

"Peyton," Allison tries to calm him.

"No, this is completely ridiculous. We can go back to North Carolina and get the same treatment that we know will work."

"Allison," I pipe in, but get cut off again.

"You only care about your trial, *Doctor*," he sneers. "I care about my wife."

"I care about your wife as well, Mr. Peyton," I say quickly. This could go off the rails very quickly if I don't get control of this situation. "I don't get to pick who gets what medication. It was done by a lottery that assigned each patient. It's the only way to keep things fair and balanced," I keep my tone even.

Until I open the sealed envelope, I won't know which patients get the placebo. The worst part is that I'll have to keep my reactions hidden so I don't tip off a patient.

"This is bullshit, baby." Bryce pushes Allison's hair back and presses his lips to her temple. "We can get the surgery and adopt, or have a surrogate. I don't want to play these games with your life. We can go home. We can have everything we wanted, Ali. It doesn't have to be like this. I love you."

My heart aches at the mention of their future. I want to be able to look at him without the wonder of what could've been.

More than that, why the hell do he and Allison make a difference in my life? They don't. I made my choice years ago when I let us go. I didn't go after him, beg him to take me back, and he didn't come after me either. We drifted apart, both caught up in our new lives and new priorities.

Yes, I would've married him if we'd stayed together, but we didn't, and he married someone else.

Westin is a good man who cares about me more than I deserve. This is the closure I need. Right here, Bryce has moved on and so have I.

"You can definitely do that," I break up their moment. "However, there's a chance that you could avoid the surgery that will strip you of the option to have children, which is what I believe brought you here." I hate to be underhanded, but if Allison walks, then all the other patients will suffer as well. "If you want to do that, my suggestion would be for me to do your surgery today so that you have the best options for fighting the cancer. I can get you in . . ." I look down at the clipboard as though I have a schedule there. ". . . in the next hour?"

"Good," Bryce responds.

Allison turns her head to Bryce and I see a tear roll down her cheek. "That's not what I want, Peyton! Even if I don't get the medication, I won't go down that road. I want the chance. I want to carry our baby inside of me, and if I weren't here right now, there would be no options. Please don't take that away from me."

He shakes his head, lifts his gaze to me for a moment, and then back to his wife. "I just want you."

I just want to leave this fucking room.

"I want you too, but this is important," her fingers glide against the skin on his cheek. "It matters to me. We're here for a reason and Dr. Adams is our best chance."

"I love you," he tells her again.

I close myself down, not wanting to hear another word. I've been trying to deal with all of this like a mature, professional woman, but this is too much. Hearing this is over the line.

"I love you more."

"Until my last breath," Bryce says, and I can't stop myself.

I gasp as pain lances my already raw heart and I'm taken back to a memory I've long since tried to forget, thrusting me back into the past.

"I can't go to Penn State with you."

His eyes fill with confusion. "What do you mean?"

"I can't do it. My mother is sick and my family needs me."

"I need you!"

I release a heavy breath and touch his face. "And I need you, but her cancer isn't going to get better and I can't imagine what this is doing to my dad."

He steps back, disbelief etched in every part of his face. I know this isn't ideal. It's the last thing I wanted to do, but in my heart, I know it's right. My mother gave everything to me. This is the least I can do.

"And what about our plans?"

"Plans change, Bryce. We're not talking about forever. I'll go to Northwestern, you can go to Penn State, and we'll make it work—like you promised."

That seems to deflate him a bit. "I just . . . I got us an apartment and I was ready for this."

"I know, baby. I wanted all that too, but you understand, don't you?"

"How far is it to Chicago from there?"

I close my eyes and breathe the word. "Eight."

"Eight hours?"

"I don't like this any more than you, but I'm asking you to not make this worse than it already is for me. I want us to work this out."

We don't fight. We never have. We talk and then we figure it out. This is not the Bryce I know and love. He's always understanding, but right now, he's making me feel guilty about something that's out of my control.

"I just want you!" he yells.

"I'm not leaving you, I'm just going where I'm needed."

He shakes his head and I can hear his rebuttal in my own. It took me two weeks to work up the courage to talk to him about this. The mere idea of leaving him tore me to shreds. After talking to my brother, I knew I had to do it. Everton said that Dad is close to tears each day and that Mom is barely holding on.

She's sick from the chemo and the only hope they have is this trial she was accepted into.

My family needs help, and I'm able to give it.

"I'm not trying to be a selfish asshole, Chick. We just were building our life. We're engaged and everything was laid out." He runs his fingers through his dark hair and then sighs. "I'm sorry. I know this isn't what you hoped for from me, and yes . . . we'll figure it out. We'll have to make whatever time we can see each other work."

A tear falls down my face, and I rush to him. My lips touch his cheeks, nose, and then finally his mouth. "I love you, Bryce Peyton."

He shakes his head, worry filled in his blue eyes. "Until my last breath."

"Until mine."

"Hello? Dr. Adams?" Allison asks, forcing the memory out of my head.

"Sorry, we're ready to start, are you ready?" I ask.

Allison studies me warily, and I use every muscle in my body to keep from looking at Bryce. I never want him to see how much those words affected me. Allison needs me to be her doctor right now.

She closes her eyes and then when she looks at me, I see the answer. "I want to be in this trial. I want my damn life back. So yes, the only hope I have is you."

I nod once, pulling myself together and refusing to look at Bryce. "I'll have your medication started. You'll be inpatient for three days while we deliver the chemo, then you'll come in for testing and other things before the next round," I explain very matter-of-factly.

"I re-remember."

I hear the fear in her voice, and even though this woman has everything I wanted, it's also my job to give her comfort. I take a step toward her, still refusing to even glance at Bryce, and touch her arm. "I know it's scary and a lot to think about, but know that I'm going to do whatever I can to fight this with you. You have a team of doctors that believe in this trial." I smile and she returns my smile with her own.

"Thank you." She pauses. "For everything."

The meaning is clear. It's not just about the trial, but for fighting for her because we both know what happens if she didn't get to try.

"I'll be back in a few minutes to get you set up," I promise.

With strength I didn't know I had, I exit the room without looking at him. My father was right, I'm powerless to him and that's going to be my downfall.

As I stand in the hallway, I clench my fists, inhale, and will myself not to lose my mind. He can't make me weak here. When I'm in this hospital, I refuse to be anything but at the top of my game. People need me to be the one who controls things, and being messed up won't benefit them. Above everything that matters in my life, being a doctor is what I cling to. I won't allow Bryce to set me back.

After a few seconds, I regain my sense of self, and head to the lab where I'll finally find out who the two doctors assigned to track the trial are. They'll ensure all my documentation is in order and be able to discuss anything that might arise. As much as I always thought it was stupid, after serving as one of the advisors for a colleague, I realized it's actually a great policy. Well, providing I don't get some asshole.

I open the door excited, but my excitement evaporates when I see Westin standing there, holding an envelope, talking to another doctor.

"Yes, the patients are given a number," he explains to Dr. Wells. "Dr. Adams will then correlate the number. We need to make sure there are no discrepancies before we sign off at the end."

Dr. Wells looks over the file. "This all looks great."

No. He can't be an advisor and auditor on this. He can't, because that would just be the biggest cosmic joke ever. He'll have to come and meet patients, oversee everything I do, and I'll have to check in with him. This can't be happening to me.

"Wes?"

"Hey," he smiles. "I was just looking over your paper-work."

"For?"

He scratches the back of his head, which is his nervous tell. "I'm one of the advisors on the team."

And yet, it seems this is very much happening.

I'm not sure why the hospital would sign off on this. He and I are romantically involved and even though we keep it quiet, people know. It's sure to be viewed as a conflict by someone. Not only that, why the hell would he want to do this? After everything last night, this is a huge mistake. Maybe I can get him to hand it over to another doctor, one who doesn't know me quite so . . . intimately.

"Can we talk for a minute?" I ask and jerk my head to the side.

My nerves can't take much more of this. I feel as though I'm coming apart at the seams. Nothing has gone right since Bryce Peyton showed up in town.

I release a deep breath from my nose when we reach the hallway. "How?" I ask quickly.

"I didn't—"

"You didn't think this was important to tell me? You didn't think I should have even been given the slightest heads-up? Or do you not think this is a very, very bad idea, Westin?" I rub my forehead. "All night you had to mention it and not a word!"

There are rules about what can be shared and I've already mentioned cutting Allison from the trial. I won't be able to hide that there's a history between myself and one of the clients, not after how I felt in that room a few moments ago. He needs to recuse himself from this.

"I'm professional enough to handle this, Dr. Adams," he bristles.

Oh, Dr. Adams, is it? Got it.

"I'm not implying you're not, *Dr. Grant*. I'm simply stating that you and I are more than colleagues and I would like to avoid any possible signs of favoritism and impropriety," I return with an equal amount of terseness in my tone.

Westin crosses his arms. "I'm more than capable of it."

My throat gets tight as Westin stares me down. If he's somehow figured out that my patient's husband and I share a past, the entire thing could get shut down. I didn't report it, which is clearly a violation, but maybe I can save this. No medication has been dispensed, there's really nothing that's been done questionably at this point.

"Why are you doing this? Why would you take this, knowing what we are and where we're going?"

"We aren't breaking any violations or rules. Dr. Pascoe is well aware of what we are. I submitted documentation of our relationship this morning before I officially signed on."

I jerk back a little, my chest tight as though I've been punched. "I know it was important to you, but I didn't think you'd go this far. I didn't think you'd do this behind my back. I wasn't ready to put paperwork in."

Westin looks up and sighs, and then his eyes meet mine. "I see. I guess I misread the signs on what we were—nothing new there."

That stings.

"That's not what I was saying. I want this. I want us, but you and I both know that appearances, especially in a clinical trial, are important. We have to do everything above board. There can't be the slightest hint of any ethical boundaries being crossed."

"I know that, which is why I submitted the paperwork. I went to Dr. Pascoe and offered to step aside, but he wouldn't hear it. I am one of the only doctors in this hospital that has extensive knowledge in clinical trials as well as the necessary protocols. There are four other doctors overseeing it, I'm not here to make things harder for you, Ren. I'm here to help."

I shake my head, not sure what the hell to think. "You still went behind my back."

"And I'm sorry for that. I really am. I didn't want to, but I couldn't tell you either. I did what I thought was going to protect us both and give your patients the best opportunity at success."

Westin gives me a few seconds to work this out in my head. A part of me knows he's right, he did the right thing, what we probably should've done months ago, when we were still pretending we weren't a thing.

"So, this means what?" I ask. "You're overseeing the trial?"

"No, I'm just here to advise and make sure that all the paperwork is in order."

I rub my forehead and release a heavy sigh. "Right."

"Serenity, if I thought, for one second, that me being on this trial would harm you or your patients, I would walk."

"What if it harms us?"

His shoulders fall and he sighs. "If I lose you now, then we were never meant to be. I've been chasing you for two years, Ren. Two years that I've waited for you to want more. You've given me these little slivers of you and then you pull them back each time you get too close to feeling anything. I want you. I want us. But I know that both of us put our patients and this hospital first, and that's what I'm doing. I'm good at my job. I wasn't trying to hurt you by going to the chief. I did that because it protected us both." Westin touches my cheek, his green eyes full of conflict. "I'm sorry if that upsets you, but it was the right thing. I care about you more than you know," his hand drops. "I will never ask you to do something that would harm your career by keeping secrets, Ren. Don't ask me to do it either."

My hand falls and Westin walks away, leaving me completely screwed. My new boyfriend and my ex, working on the same trial . . . what could possibly go wrong?

15

"**D**o you want to wait for your husband?" I ask Allison as we stand in her room, ready to dispense the medication.

"If we can," she says nervously. "I don't want to be alone when this starts."

"It's no problem. We can wait a few minutes," I smile.

"Sorry, he had to handle something."

There are four patients still waiting to start the chemotherapy, and one of them will be the final placebo. I have been able to keep my face completely stoic with each patient so far. Hopefully this will be the same, but this one feels different.

"Please don't worry about it, we're not going anywhere," I reassure her again.

Dr. Grant, please come to the nurses' station, the loudspeaker blares.

I look over to Westin who gives one nod. "Go, we'll be fine," I tell him.

"I'll be right back." He touches my arm and then leaves.

Allison clears her throat, watching me with a smile that

indicates she wants to say something. "Boyfriend?"

Oh, God. I can't girl talk with her, but I can't be rude either. Why is my life suddenly so difficult? I really liked when it was simple. Not sure what exactly the right thing to do is, I give her a little, hoping she'll drop it. "I guess you could call it that."

"Sorry if I'm overstepping." She chews on her lip.

"You're fine."

That's a lie. None of this is fine. I send a prayer out for my name to be called so I can get out of here without saying something dumb.

"It's the way he looked at you, it was clear that there's something going on between you guys."

Dropping it is not happening.

I look back at the door wondering what she picked up on. We were fighting not even two hours ago.

"It's not like that . . ."

Allison laughs. "Nothing ever starts like that, does it? But he's really good looking . . . and a doctor."

I move over to the side of her bed, and check the lines of her IV. "Yeah, he's a good guy."

Please drop this or let the ground swallow me up, either would work.

"How long have you been together?" she asks.

As much as I may hate this, Allison is sweet and I don't really have an out right now. I can be aloof or choose to be the person I am. I love my patients and I believe healing isn't only about medicine. People have to want to fight and be willing to put up with an immense amount of struggle in order to feel better.

Going through hell is an understatement.

I've prided myself on being their friend through it all, and Allison deserves the same thing.

"It's been a few years, but nothing serious until recently," I admit.

"Ahh . . ." She pushes her hair back. ". . . I see."

"See?"

"I'm assuming he finally decided to shit instead of getting off the pot. Men are so stupid when it comes to women. Peyton was that way." Allison rolls her eyes. "I swear, it was like pulling teeth to get him to finally pop the question."

Now I'm suddenly interested in this conversation.

"Oh? Why is that? You guys seem so happy," I say in spite of myself.

I should never have asked, but I don't know when I'll ever have this opportunity again.

She leans in, playing with the edge of the blanket. "I was never supposed to really marry Peyton. We were childhood friends, and our parents basically arranged our marriage at infancy. Both of us come from traditional families, but we never seemed to get the timing right. I always loved him. I was that stupid girl with big eyes for the hot guy, but Peyton never saw me that way. I was just the annoying family friend."

My pulse pounds in my ears as she tells me the story I've wondered about. Did he fall in love with her right after me? Were they kept apart because he met me? Then I wonder, why had I never heard about her when we were together? I sit on the edge of her bed, waiting for anything she's willing to share.

"We both ended up going to Penn State, which is where I bumped into him after years."

Penn State.

I feel the walls closing in, but I mentally hold my hands

out to stop it. "Grad school?"

She nods. "Yeah, I was supposed to go to Yale, but my father graduated from Penn so that's where I went. Anyway, I saw Bryce and he looked so . . . sad, so . . . different than I remembered. We talked a lot. It was nice knowing someone there and not feeling so alone. He was in a bad state and we happened to be there for each other. He never talked about what was wrong, but I assumed it was someone else."

Me. It was me.

The way she described him is nothing like he was before that. We were happy, ready to tackle the world, but when I got up here and saw the state of my family, Bryce and I couldn't hold on.

We drifted like ships out at sea with no steering. We were on opposite currents, without a way to chart the course back to each other.

I never really thought of him as sad at the end. He was so angry and disappointed. My heart aches for the man she describes.

"I'm glad you found each other, then." The words hurt but I mean them.

"Me too. He asked me out, even though he clearly didn't want to, and then we grew to be more. It was a long time before he finally said he loved me, though. We'd fight so much and I threatened to end things, and a light switched on."

So he didn't just run to her arms. He didn't love her right away. It shouldn't make me feel better, but it does. I've spent so much time getting over him, it's nice to know it wasn't easy for him either.

"I guess he needed the push," I say, not able to look at her.

"Most men do," she laughs lightly. "So, what was your

sexy doctor's push?"

If only it was Westin who needed the urging. "It was actually me," I tell her the truth. "I was broken by a man a very long time ago, and I didn't want to ever endure it again. I've wasted a lot of time trying to shut myself off and Westin never gave up on me."

She touches my hand. "I'm sorry."

"It's fine. Wes is a great guy and I'm lucky to have him."

"I don't know how you work with him, though. I'd kill my husband if I was around him all day."

I shake my head. Sometimes I do want to kill him, like when I learned he was advising me. "Well, it helps that we usually only see each other when we need a break . . ."

"Yes!" She giggles. "I've always imagined that's how it really is."

"What?"

"You know, sneaking off to have sex in random places, the no rules in your relationships, like a mix of a soap opera and television drama. Tell me details, you know I basically have been celibate for a year now thanks to this fucking cancer. Please, let me live vicariously through you."

That's a visual I could've done without.

"We *really* don't have to go there," I say, because nope. I can't do it. I can't talk about my sex life, no matter how sweet she is.

"Fine," she grumbles. "Do you love him?"

"Do you love who?" Bryce's voice fills the room.

I rise, wondering how long he's been standing there. Did he hear the conversation and cut it off because he didn't want to know?

"Babe!" Allison waves him over. "There you are! Dr. Adams had to keep me company while we waited for you. We're starting the first dose and," she squeals. "It's finally happening."

"Let me go grab Dr. Grant and I'll be right back," I say moving out of the way.

I head out of the room, but Westin is gone. "Martina," I call out. She pops her head over the stack of papers. "Where's Dr. Grant?"

"He had to check on a patient, he said he'll be back soon, but to go on and get started without him."

This is just great. My advisor is now missing and I have other patients waiting, plus a surgery this afternoon. I sigh and recalibrate my emotions.

"Okay," I say as I enter the room. "I'm going to administer the medication. You'll be here for two more days, and then you'll be able to leave until your next appointment."

I go over the speech I've given all day about what to eat, and when to call me or head straight to the hospital. There's a lot of scary possibilities and I like my patients to be informed. Allison and Bryce hold hands as I open the envelope.

I remove the bottle, write down the code on the bottom, and my heart sinks.

She's on the placebo.

There's nothing I can do now but watch the cancer spread and know that she will die. The medication alone will not be enough. I know it in my heart and for the first time in my fifteen-year career I feel the bad news on a personal level.

I keep my back to them, not wanting to give anything away, and place the vial in the machine. Each second, I feel the nerves in my stomach clenching. This is wrong. This is so very wrong.

How do I face her?

The decision was hers, but would she truly let herself die because she couldn't carry a baby? She can still have a child— her and Bryce's child.

But then I remember the letter. She won't. She had to know and be advised at that time. I explained that to her as well, and she's made her choice. When she first gave me the letter, while I disagreed, my code of ethics required me to accept the patient's decision about her treatment. But that was when she had a high probability of the trial working for her. But now that she has the placebo, this is just all too real.

And I'm lying to everyone and have no one to talk to.

I close my eyes and pull myself together. I can't give anything away. The rules are there and there was a chance this is how it would play out. Allison knew her risks and I need to keep that in the forefront of my mind.

Once I have a good handle on my emotions, I turn to face her. "All set," I smile and touch her shoulder. "A nurse will come check on you soon. If you need anything else, just call."

She takes my hand in hers. "Thank you, Dr. Adams. Thank you for this. I-I can't," Allison starts to get choked up. "I can't tell you what this means to us. It's like since we came here, everything is working out. This is all going exactly how it was meant to go."

Funny, I feel the complete opposite way about her showing up.

"I'm glad. Now rest and I'll be back soon," I squeeze her hand, look at Bryce, and walk out of the room.

I can't believe she has the placebo. This is exactly what I worried about. Damn it.

A hand wraps around my arm as I'm walking down the

hall, causing me to stop.

I turn, but gasp when I see Bryce's face. "She doesn't have the medicine, does she?"

"I don't know what you're talking about," I say quietly, pulling my arm back. I smile at the nurse who passes me in the hall.

Once she's out of view, Bryce begins again. "I saw it on your face."

I don't know that I would believe it from anyone else, but he knows me. And he's seen every emotion dance across my face before. Bryce once knew me better than I knew myself. "I can't talk to you about any specifics regarding the trial, Mr. Peyton."

He scoffs. "Don't give me that shit, Chick. I know you. I know when you're lying. Allison doesn't have the drug."

I have to hide any emotion and be the lead doctor right now. He's exactly like any other patient's husband who wants answers. I understand it, but I won't jeopardize this trial. "I'm very sorry you think you saw something, however, I can't tell you anything other than that she is receiving a dose of chemotherapy."

"Serenity," he nearly chokes on my name. "Please don't lie to me. Just tell me the truth. She has the placebo and she's going to be fucking crushed."

That makes two of us.

"I'm sorry I can't say more about this, but know that I'm doing everything I can to treat Allison within the bounds of the study while also respecting her choices."

Bryce takes a step closer, defeat radiates off of him. Somehow he figured it out, and I won't confirm it either way, but I'm breaking watching him like this. No matter what I feel for him, seeing someone you love in pain hurts worse than being in pain yourself.

Tears fill his eyes and he shakes his head. "Please, Ren."

"Bryce," I sigh. "I don't know what you think you saw, but you have to trust me to do my job."

He wipes his eyes before the drop falls. "I know you. I know what I saw and the fact that you haven't said she has it confirms what I thought."

"I can't say anything about the trial, don't you get that? Stop asking me for things that I can't do. I agreed to treat Allison and now you need to go back to your wife, hold her hand, and be supportive. I can't discuss this with anyone, especially you."

This isn't about just him and his wife. I'm sure that's not easy for him, but if I say something, I'm risking everyone.

"I'm not just anyone."

He's right. He was once more than that, but he's not anymore. "No, you're Allison's husband, and she needs you."

Bryce takes two strides and pulls me into his arms. He holds me, tucking his head in my neck. My arms are down at my sides, and I can't move. For years I've wondered how this would feel and it's exactly like I dreamed. I close my eyes, breathing in the musky cologne that is all him, committing it to memory. His soft hair touches my cheek, and I fight the urge to rub my face against him. My heart races and the world around me disappears as the man I loved more than anything is touching me.

This is wrong, but I can't make him stop.

I don't know how long we stand like this, like two lost people searching for something to hold onto, but the sound of his sob breaks me. I wrap my arms around him, holding him close as he cries.

After a few seconds, he releases me. "I'm sorry."

"It's okay . . ."

"No, it's not. Fuck." Bryce rubs his temples. "I hate this. I hate that I'm falling apart. I hate watching her suffer. I hate that I have to lie about all of this."

I step back, needing air and some space. "Lie about what?"

I'm the one who is going through hell lying to Westin, Julie, him, Allison, my patients, and most of all myself.

"This. Us. That we know each other."

"It was your idea not to tell her," I remind him. "You didn't want her to know what we were."

He leans against the wall across from me, both of us keeping our distance.

"Not that, I can't do this. I can't feel like this and I can't ask you what I want to. I have to go back to her . . ." He looks down the hall.

Back to her.

Back to the woman he belongs to.

"Yeah, you should." I look down at the ground.

Bryce doesn't say another word, he pushes off the wall and walks away, leaving me a complete mess. Just like the night I left him.

"So we'll talk every day?" I ask again as I stand in the driver's side door.

"Every day."

"And you won't forget about me?"

Bryce rolls his eyes and then takes my hand. "Do you see this?" He lifts my hand with the diamond sitting there. "This is not something I'd forget. It's my grandmother's ring, it's a family heirloom and only family wear it. You're mine. You're my family, Chick."

I do my best not to swoon right here, but sometimes, the man says just what I need to hear. "You're mine too, Bryce Peyton." My hand rests on his chest and I hold back the tears. "Don't you forget it."

He smiles at me as though I'm crazy, and maybe I am. I have loved this man for the last two years in a way that has left me stunned. I'm still unsure that I'm making the right choice going to Chicago, but I'm hopeful we'll stay strong.

"I'll see you in a few weeks."

I nod. "And then we'll see each other a few weeks after that."

"We have to keep making plans because you and I don't let the other down."

"No," I say with a sigh, "we don't."

He leans in, kissing me softly. "I hate that you're not coming with me, but I understand why you're not."

It's the first time he's acknowledged that he gets it. My heart is filled with gratitude. "Thank you."

"For what?"

"For letting me do what I feel in my heart."

He moves to the side, taking my hands in his. "I know you love your family and I'd be the worst kind of prick if I told you not to go. I was just scared. Fuck, I'm scared now. I don't want us to drift apart, so you can't let that happen."

"I won't."

And I mean that vow. I will not let us falter.

"You better get going, baby. It's going to be late and you have a long drive."

I lift my hands to his face, and kiss him hard. The tears I fought to hold back fall without permission. The salty beads touch our lips, mixing in with our goodbye.

"Don't cry," he says as his thumb brushes the moisture away.

"I'm going to miss you."

"I don't blame you," he jokes.

My laughter is short and comes out almost like a snort. "You're stupid."

"I've never claimed to be anything but."

I just keep trying to drag this out. Not ready to go weeks without seeing him. It's going to kill me to drive away.

"I should go . . ."

"Yeah, you should."

I fight the strength to get in the car, feeling like I'm leaving half of my heart behind, and maybe I am, because it will belong to no one else.

"I love you."

"I love you, Serenity. Until . . ."

"My last breath," I finish for him.

And then he closes the door to my car, and our hands are on the glass, not able to touch, but needing a connection. I put the car in drive, tears falling freely and then his palm falls and I drive away, leaving the man I love behind.

"John," I say with a smile as I see Mrs. Whitley's son.

"Dr. Adams."

"How are you?"

He looks over at the door where his mother is. "I'm okay. I

was able to get a few hours off and came down here."

"She misses you."

I see the shame pass in his eyes. "I wish I could make it more, but with work and the kids. It's just . . . hard."

I have to push aside my own feelings about this wonderful woman and remember that everyone deals with things differently. It's not my job to judge this man, but I can't help but think of my own mother and how I would've gone back in time for just one more minute with her. One second where I could hold her hand, feel her love, or hear her voice.

"I understand, but she doesn't have a lot of time left and she loves you so very much. I don't want to see you regret anything."

John's hand goes to the back of his head and he squeezes. "I have regrets that a few days can't solve."

The fixer in me is screaming to tell him that what he's doing now won't help things, but I stay silent. "Well, I'm sure you made her day being here today."

"Hopefully I can come again in a few days with the girls."

I give him a soft smile. "I really hope so too. I know she'd love to see them."

He nods once and then starts to walk away. When I'm right at the door he calls my name.

"I know you think I'm a shitty son for not being here, and I'm sure I am. She talks about you all the time and how much time you spend in her room. Whether or not we're here, I'm glad she's had you."

I think about my brother and how he's handled losing my mother. I want to tell John all of it, but I'm not sure if I should. How many times did we tell him to go more and he didn't? Countless times. Fuck propriety. If I can stop anyone from spiraling like Everton, I'm going to do it. "I lost my mother to cancer," I say. "I know the pain of watching someone you love die, but she's going to die, John, and I promise, you'll wish for the time you're squandering now. You'll want to reach for the phone or just sit beside her and you won't be able to. Come back with the girls because I promise if you don't, you'll regret it and never be able to fix it."

He doesn't say anything as he walks away.

I turn, take a few deep breaths and plaster a smile on my face. "How's my favorite patient?" I ask as I walk into Mrs. Whitley's room.

"Tired," she croaks. "Lots of pain today."

I look at the chart, noticing that her vitals aren't strong either. A nurse walks in and I write some notes. "Up her fluids and let's give her another dose of morphine for the pain."

Mrs. Whitley is starting to fade. I'm not ready to say good-bye to her. I need her in my life more than ever. Part of me hates myself for getting attached to her. It was never a surprise she had cancer, I'm the one that diagnosed her. But each day I find myself more drawn to her.

"John came today," she tells me as I sit beside her.

"He did?" I smile, wanting to let her have this moment so I pretend I don't know.

"He . . . he sat here and told me about the girls." She coughs.

"When did the cough start?"

She ignores me. "I saw pictures."

That's great, but I'm worried about her lungs. I stand, put my stethoscope on and listen to her lungs. Her breathing is shallow, but she sounds clear. "Tell me about the cough."

Mrs. Whitley takes my hand. "Let me tell you about John."

I sit on the edge of her bed and realize she doesn't want Dr.

Adams right now, she needs a friend. Her days are filled with a lot of nothing, unless we visit with her. Today, she wants to tell the story, and I want to listen.

"Okay." I smile and place my hand over hers. "Did John show you pictures?"

Immediately, her face brightens. "He did—they're getting so big. I hoped he'd bring them, but they were on a video on the phone. He said they'd come again soon."

She speaks and I listen, offering my happiness when she pauses. You can see the weight lift off her shoulders as she relays the information about her grandchildren and son. John stayed for just under an hour, but it made her entire day.

Even with her health deteriorating, her spirit has definitely taken a turn for the better. We talk about the trial, but mostly I just enjoy listening to her.

I imagine if my mother were still alive, this is what she would've been like. Whenever we visited her, she was happy, feeling like she could beat the odds. I hear the hope in Mrs. Whitley's voice, and I pray that she'll get more days like this and I hope John returns tomorrow.

"It's nearing, isn't it?" she asks me after about twenty minutes into my visit.

"What is?"

She looks at me with knowing eyes. "You know what I'm talking about."

"No, you're having a small setback, but we're all going to do what we can."

Her hand touches mine. "Tell me about your doctor."

"I think he's upset with me."

"What did you do?"

I scoff. "Me? Why couldn't it be him?"

"Because I know you and he's dreamy."

"You're smitten with him," I say as I push back her white hair. "I don't blame you, he's a catch."

Mrs. Whitley's eyes close but she has a soft smile there. "Be sure to make it better because time isn't a luxury we can afford to spend."

"No, it's not, but he's hurt and so am I."

She pats my hand, looking as though she's drifting off. "Time heals all wounds."

Time heals all wounds, but when you're fighting a broken clock, each second counts.

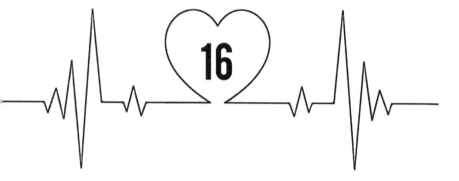

16

"**S**o, how did it go today?" Rich asks as he places the cheeseburger platter in front of me.

"Great," I say before shoving a fry in my mouth.

If great means embracing a married man in the hallway of the hospital like a moron. Because that's what happened. I stood where anyone could see us, which wouldn't be a big deal if I didn't melt into him. I hug family members all the time in comfort, but it doesn't ever look like that, though.

I spent an hour in Mrs. Whitley's room. When I left, she was resting, but her vitals improved and I felt comfortable with where she was at. The fluids seemed to give her a boost and I'm glad we caught it when we did. Westin had to rush into an emergency surgery, and was still operating last I checked.

Here I am, asking him to go with me to see my dad in a few days and I'm in reverse down memory lane with a man who doesn't love me. The truth is, I don't love him like that, but I can't stop my heart from feeling this ache and letting my memories take hold of my mind.

I tell myself to put it behind me, and I believe I have, until

I see them or hear something. Then I'm thrown back in time to where I felt safe, my mother was alive, and I had hope for a family and a marriage. Bryce made it so easy to trust him with my heart, and as soon as things got difficult, it was as though we meant nothing.

I just want it to stop hurting, but my mother always said you had to go through the pain to get over it. So maybe that's what this is? I have to feel all the shit I shoved down for years, pretending it didn't exist, so that I can really move forward.

"I knew you'd do good, but I also think you're a liar." Rich's brows rise. "I've known you long enough to see when you're putting on a brave face."

Of all the days I have to be readable, why this one? "Can you pretend today that I'm telling the truth?"

"All right, but you and I both know what happens when you keep it bottled up. The pressure builds until it all explodes."

Oh, it's exploding and I'm going to be the one who gets hit from it. I won't survive this blow.

"I know, but today I can't," I admit.

Rich gives me a small smile and touches my hand. "Maybe tomorrow then."

Hopefully tomorrow my skin doesn't tingle where Bryce touched me and I don't smell his cologne on my scrubs. I'd really like to not replay the way he held onto me for dear life every ten seconds. If all of that could go away, I could think straight and realize how wrong I am and snap myself out of it.

"I don't know what I'm doing anymore . . ." I say to Rich without meaning to say it aloud.

Rich stops wiping down the counter and looks at me. "Doing with what?"

I look into his wise eyes, hoping for some guidance because I'm drifting. "I loved someone a long time ago. I loved him in a way that was almost unnatural. It was fast, reckless, but it was like breathing for the first time after being held underwater. It was beautiful, painful, strong, and yet so weak because it fell apart like we were nothing."

Rich nods. "I know that kind of love."

"Is that what you shared with Ester?"

"Kind of. We were crazy kids who were on a warpath of destruction. It was this bar that grounded us."

Ester was an amazing woman. She was always kind to us, made sure we were working hard, studying, and eating. I swear, it was her mission to feed us. I'm pretty sure that was all part of their game plan, keep people fed and they kept coming back.

"Do you miss her?"

He looks at the photo of her that sits behind the bar. "Every single day. Much like your father feels, I'm sure. Her death rocked my world, but we had a good life."

"Yeah, he misses my mother. So much that he fired the cleaning crew, scared off the home health aide, and is leaving it up to Everton to handle the house. Which means the place is a mess."

Rich chuckles and grabs the rag. "Sounds about right."

"Men," I roll my eyes with a smile.

"You know, when a man truly loves a woman, he'll never move on. We all have that one person. Sometimes we marry them, spending an eternity trying to prove we're good enough for her. Other times, we lose them and spend our lives wondering how we were so stupid to let that woman go. Sounds to me like you're one of those 'other times.'"

I dip my fry in the ketchup, swirling it around, thinking

about what he said. "I'm in between. My sometimes and other times have collided. For the first time, I *want* things to work with Westin and me. He's good for me and we're good for each other."

Since the night we went on our date, I find myself thinking of what a future would look like with him more.

His smile is full of pride. "I hoped you'd say that. I've known that man a long time, Serenity Adams, and he's a good one. He's got a lot of love in his heart."

"But my heart is at war and I don't know what to do."

Rich touches my hand. "You know what to do, you just don't want to do it. War is just a fancy word for conflict, there's a right and a wrong and you're battling with which side to choose. Is this love you had once right for you?"

"No."

"Is Westin?" Rich asks.

"Yes," I look up, pleading with my eyes to tell me what to do.

"Then you're not at war. You just need to choose your side and do what's right to avoid bloodshed."

My eyes close as the truth of his words washes over me. I should've sent Allison and Bryce away the day they showed up. I knew it in my gut that this was a bad decision, but I didn't want to screw up the trial, or at least that's what I told myself. The truth is that I was afraid I'd never see Bryce again.

Which is exactly why I knew he should go.

"Why do you have to be so smart?" This conversation needs to stop here for my own sanity.

Rich grins. "I'm old. With age comes wisdom, which is why you should listen to your dad when he says something."

My father would love Rich for saying that.

Someone down the bar calls Rich's name for a drink, and he winks at me and heads to help his other patrons.

Dad was right when he said this was a bad idea, but I thought I had it under control. I was so wrong.

"Ren."

I jump. "You have got to be kidding me," I groan as Bryce sits down next to me. Speak of the Devil and he shall appear. "What are you doing here?"

"I need to talk," he says.

"No, I don't want to talk. I need to forget you. I need to eat food, get some sleep, and kick cancer's ass tomorrow. What I don't need is to be followed by my patient's husband."

Today isn't the day for us to talk. I'm too broken down and I have no fight left.

"You have to help me," he starts.

"Why is that, Bryce? Why do I have to help you?"

"Please, I know you don't want to hear this, but don't you see we can both get what we want?"

I'm suddenly not very hungry. Instead, I feel like I could be sick. I push the plate away and release a sad sigh. I want to be angry, I should be furious, but I'm just sad. I feel as though someone has beaten me down and I don't like it.

"I'm not getting anything I want. In fact, I feel like this is some cosmic joke."

"I know," Bryce sighs and he sits on the stool in defeat. "Believe me, of all the doctors in the world, you were the last person I anticipated would walk through that door. I never thought we'd be standing here today. It sure feels like the laugh is on us, huh?" His hand rests on the bar, close to mine, but not quite touching.

Seeing a little fleck of sadness in him softens me just a bit.

"I guess it is."

Bryce releases a half laugh. "You know, I wondered about you for so long." He stops talking, looking at me with shame in his eyes. "I dreamed for years about seeing you again and how I'd be so angry and that I wouldn't care how you'd been. My visions of how it would go were nothing like this. But I gave you up when I started to fall in love with Ali."

"Please don't do this," I plead.

I'm trying to not care about him. I want to move forward, put Bryce behind me and look toward the future, but he's making it unbearable.

His hand touches mine, and my stomach drops.

Bryce continues on. "I don't want to feel like this. I don't want to think about you. I don't want to remember what it felt like when it was you I woke up next to." My heart races as he continues to talk, and I pull my hand away. "When I saw you again, it was like I was thrown back in time."

This is wrong, but here he is, saying all the things I wanted to hear years ago. "You need to stop," I say while clutching my chest. The ache is so great I worry I'll crumble. "Bryce," I sigh. "I can't help you. I can't do this anymore. You need to go back to North Carolina and find a new doctor. This is too hard for me." A tear falls down my cheek as I admit my defeat for the first time aloud. "I have someone I'm trying really hard to move on with, and you being back . . . it's destroying that chance."

He has to go. I'll lose the trial or find another way to help the other patients. But if he stays, I don't know who I'll be at the end of everything.

Bryce's eyes blaze as he pushes himself back. "Do you think this is easy for me? My head is messed up. I have a *wife*,

Chick. A wife who's sick and needs my full attention and support."

"So go," I point to the door. "Go back to her. Go back where you belong, Bryce. Live the life you had and let me move on. Just go," my voice cracks.

He leans forward on the stool. "I want to, but I can't. I just want to get this *thing* between us resolved so we can put it behind us."

"Well consider it hereby resolved. You're married and your wife needs you. There's nothing more I can offer you." I place a twenty on the bar and walk out.

"I should be used to your back walking away by now," he yells as I take a step down to the busy street. I stop, my heart racing and tears filling my vision. "I watched you do it all those years ago. I thought you'd come back to me, but you never did."

The world just stopped and I can't think. "That's not how it happened," I breathe, my voice shaking on every word.

"I loved you, Serenity. I've loved you from the first moment I laid eyes on you and I never thought I'd recover from losing you."

I turn, feeling breathless and unsteady. His eyes are filled with years of regret and disappointment. "I called you . . ."

He shakes his head. "You called after months! Months of me trying to find ways for us to work it out."

"You stopped calling me as well. You were angry because I had school and my family to attend to."

Bryce takes a step closer. "I had commitments too, but you were my number one."

All this time, the two of us held onto this. Despite the fact he's married and I've been with Westin, there's been this . . . thing . . . festering inside of us.

"That day . . ." I start, but choke on the words.

"You broke my fucking heart."

"So you broke mine to get back at me? You ended things on the worst possible day." He ended them on the day my mother died.

"You left!" The anger in his voice breaks me out of the sadness that was threatening to overwhelm me. "What does it matter what day it was? Every day was the worst day. Every time I called or begged you to come, you were too busy."

Yes, I left, but it was fourteen years ago and I had to.

"I never wanted to leave, Bryce. I didn't have a choice! I did what was right for my family, and fuck you for not understanding that. You wanted my world to revolve around you, but I wanted more. When we met, I told you I was going to be a doctor and that meant sacrifice."

His chest heaves as he glares at me. "And I guess I'm the one who has to sacrifice now . . . again, for you."

"How the hell are you sacrificing now? I'm the one who's in the impossible position of treating your wife. Do you think this isn't hard on me? Do you not understand that I've spent the better part of fifteen years wondering about you, replaying things with us? I loved you more than you could even fathom. When I lost you," I choke on the sob that rises up. "I lost a part of me."

His head jerks back and the heat from his breath causes steam to flow around us. "My love for you has dictated everything in my life. I love Allison, more than I ever thought I could, but it is nothing like what we had. Imagine what seeing you now is like. Imagine knowing, as you hold your spouse's hand, that there's still a part of you that's looking at the girl you once swore would be in her place."

I feel weightless and my head is spinning. "Please don't say these things."

"I don't want to feel them, Chick. You have no idea how disgusted I am with myself for feeling this way. I'd never, *ever* hurt Allison when she's sick—I wouldn't leave her or betray her or do anything to make her life worse. But I do want to exorcise these demons that you're resurrecting so we can all move on and I can protect her. I don't want her to suffer another devastating blow and I could've done something to stop it."

I close my eyes and fight back the tears. "I can't do anything about how you feel."

"No, but you can give her the meds to help her."

Fourteen Years Earlier

"Please pick up, please pick up," I chant as I wait for Bryce to pick up. It's been two weeks since we've spoken, and even then, it was less than five minutes that we talked. Lately it's been the same routine: I call, miss him, he calls, and doesn't reach me.

Around and around we go, never getting close enough. Everything is strained in my life right now. My mother is fading so fast and there's nothing I can do to stop it, my father is so depressed he's not eating, and my grades are the lowest they've ever been.

Mom told me today she was unhappy with the amount of time I was spending with her, that she wants me to have a life, but it's not going to change.

We're losing her.

She is growing sicker and they talked about hospice today.

I'm not ready for her to go and I could really use Bryce right now.

"Hi, this is Bryce, I'm not around so leave a message and I'll call when I can."

Beep.

"Bryce, hey, it's me . . . I've been insanely busy and tried to call, but I guess you're the same. It's been too long since I've heard your voice and I just miss you. Mom isn't doing well," I say as I sit down, my head falling back against the couch. "I'm . . . sad. I'm scared too. It's been so hard dealing with all this without you by my side." I'm rambling, but my heart is breaking and I just want his arms around me. "Just please call me back."

It's six at night and I have no idea what he's doing. Maybe he's studying, maybe he's out drinking, or sleeping for all I know. We've had nothing but a series of missed calls and a random email last week, which I'm pretty sure I forgot to respond to.

I close my eyes and my lip trembles while the sadness takes hold. How did we get here? When did we become this distant? Bryce and I were in sync. We were happy and in love. We had plans, damn it, and now we have nothing.

I don't want to be dramatic, but I feel him drifting away from me.

Each day runs away from us and if we don't do as we promised, we're going to fall apart.

I curl up on the couch, clutching the pillow that used to smell like him and cry myself to sleep, hating how many things are leaving me all at once.

The phone blares in my ear, waking me. I rise up off the couch, searching for it, praying it's Bryce.

"Hello?"

"Ren," Everton's voice fills the other end of the call.

I glance at the clock and see it's one in the morning. Panic fills me because no one calls at this hour unless something is terribly wrong. "What is it?"

"Mom."

I quickly get to my feet, throwing a jacket on, and a pair of shoes. I don't even know if they match. "Where is she?"

"At the house. She couldn't breathe . . . you need to get here."

"I'm on my way!"

I hang up the phone, already halfway down the stairs, and once I get in the car, I push my hair back and release a few breaths. *I can do this.*

For my mother, I will keep it together.

The drive to my childhood home from Chicago seems to take forever. The entire way there, I tell myself I'll be strong. I bargain with God, asking for just a little more time. "I'll study harder," I say as I grip the wheel. "I'll be a better daughter, sister, and I'll save lives. Please, just don't take her yet. I'm not ready."

I believe that He will grant me this. I have to have faith.

As I drive, my phone pings with a voicemail and I push play.

"Chick, it's me, look . . . things are . . . strained, and I think maybe we should just take some time and think about why that is. I still love you, but this is much harder than I thought. I don't know, I'm just feeling lonely and you're busy," Bryce's voice is detached and my throat feels tight. "I'm not saying we break up, I'm saying we take a break and see where we're at in a month. I'm sorry, babe, I really am."

I throw the phone in the car and bang my head on the steering wheel. That's how he breaks up with me? Tonight? On a voicemail?

No, I can't do this. Tomorrow, once I have my mother all

squared away, I'll figure this all out, but right now, I can't deal.

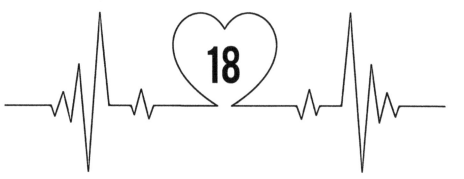

18

"I already told you that I'm doing everything I can for Allison."

"Are you punishing me? Is this because of the way things ended, now you want to make her suffer?"

Another tear falls down my cheek. "You think so little of me?"

Bryce breathes heavily out of his nose, not even able to look at me. "I just know what's happening now isn't her fault. I'm sorry for how things went. I was fucked up and alone. I missed you so much I couldn't breathe. My life was falling apart without you in it. I did the only thing I thought I could . . . let you go."

My heart is broken for the kids we were at that time. Sure, we were in our twenties, but in no way ready to make decisions that would affect the rest of our lives. "I've tried so hard to forget the way you made me feel. I was finally getting there, and then you showed up."

"You weren't the only one who has struggled, Ren. I loved you so deeply, I never thought I could love again," he admits.

"When I left that voicemail, I fucking lost it. I hated myself, and no woman compared to you."

"Until Allison," I finish the statement. "I can't go backward anymore, Bryce. We need to move on, let go of the past. It's going to destroy us both."

He takes a step back, gripping the back of his neck. "I gave you up to save you, not destroy you."

But destruction was all that came from that night. "My mom died the night you left that voicemail." His eyes lift to mine. "I listened to it on the way to her, hearing you say you needed time or whatever it was . . . but I lost everything. I have been trying to find a way back to solid ground since then. Her loss was horrific, but losing you . . . I don't even know how to describe what I felt at that."

"I thought I was doing right by you," he admits, "I knew you were broken up about splitting your time, so I thought if I took myself out of the equation, we'd find our way back to each other. Instead, two weeks later, I got a fucking box with my grandmother's ring in it. No note. No call. Nothing. And I hated you for it, Ren. I swore I'd forget you because remembering, well, it hurt too damn much."

"You have no idea what hurt felt like."

He takes a step closer. "I'm hurting now. I'm watching my wife lose everything and you're the only one who can stop it. Do you understand how hard it is to ask you to do this? How hurting you—again—is killing me? I'm the one who is watching the woman I love drown in cancer and the woman who is half of my fucking soul is with another man and holds the power over it all. I know I'm asking a lot, but *please*, give her the drug."

I turn and look at him as though he's lost his mind. "You

can't ask me to do this, Bryce."

"I know what I'm asking."

"No," I cut him off. "I don't think you have a clue what you're asking me to do."

"It's you who gets to decide our fate. I can't . . . I can't lose another woman because I wasn't able to give her what she needed." Bryce's eyes bore into mine. I see the pain and fear there. "I love her."

My heart races because a part of me wonders if I should help him, but I know it's wrong. It's against everything I took an oath to do.

"And I love you." I regret the words the minute they leave my lips, but I can't take them back. Right or wrong, I've loved him for close to seventeen years. I know he's married. I know I have a future with Westin. These things won't change, but neither will the fact that I will always love him. "You were my first love and that will never change. I love you because I can't unlove you. You're a part of who I am, and for that, you will always be in my heart, but what you're asking me . . ."

Bryce's jaw clenches and he closes his eyes. "You have no idea how much I loved you, Serenity. None. My love for you was dangerous. I learned from that . . ."

"Did you? Because what you're asking me to do is not okay. It's selfish and destructive."

"No, it's asking you to find a way to help someone who is innocent in this story. Allison didn't steal me from you. She healed the broken parts of me. She allowed me to breathe again." He looks up at the sky and then back to me. "If you ever loved me. If I ever meant anything to you, I'm here, begging you to find a way to help Allison with the promise of the medication you sold her on." Bryce takes a step closer.

"This has nothing to do with me caring about you. And I don't want her to suffer either. Believe it or not, I like her, and I'm trying to fix her without destroying everything I've built. But what you want me to do . . . if anyone ever found out, it would ruin my life and my career."

His breathing accelerates and he starts to speak faster. "No one would have to know. You don't even have to say anything, just listen."

No, no, no. It is crazy to even think about switching the medications. "Stop," I beg. "Please, just stop."

He grips me with both hands, holding me so I can't move. "Wouldn't you have done what I'm doing for your mother? Wouldn't you ask the doctor to just give her the medicine if you knew it could heal her?" Bryce's fingers let me go, but he stays close.

"Don't!" I put my hand up, pressing against his chest. "Don't compare this to saving my mother."

The sad part is, he's right. I would've done anything to save her. Asking her doctor would've been the least of the lengths I would've gone to. My mother's cancer tore Bryce and me apart. Am I really willing to be the person who does this to him again?

Life is coming full circle and once again I stand at the crossroads of an impossible situation.

Bryce takes a step back with tears in his eyes. "Just think about it, Ren. You're the only one who can make this right for all of us. If you could heal her, then I could . . ."

"You could what?"

Both hands slide through his hair and he lets out a loud groan. "Then maybe all the pain we've gone through would be for something. You could help Allison and in turn save me.

I just feel like there's a reason we're here—because it wasn't just to torture each other. We're different people, but we were once something pretty amazing, and I loved you with everything I had." He looks away with clenched fists. "This isn't the way I thought this would go. I just wanted to talk, and I was desperate. I can't and I won't ask you to do this. You're right, it's selfish and wrong. Forget I even said anything."

Forget he asked me to switch medication for Allison? Forget that he told me he's torn up too? Forget what? Because all I've been trying to do the last few days is forget. How I'm going to handle weeks of this is beyond me. I keep waiting for it to get easier with time, but each day is a new version of hell.

Bryce looks over my shoulder, closes his eyes, and sighs. "Great. This will go over well."

I turn to see what caught his eye and Westin walks toward us, crossing the street as Bryce and I stand on the sidewalk. Everything inside of me is tense as he approaches.

Both men look at each other, and I can almost taste the spike in testosterone. Westin reaches me, wraps his arm around my side, and kisses my cheek. "Hi, baby."

"Hi," I say with my teeth chattering. If only it was the cold air that was the cause.

Westin, being the sweet man he is, pulls me closer, rubbing his hand up and down my arm to warm me.

"You're her patient's husband, right? We met the other day," Wes extends his hand.

Bryce shakes his hand and nods. "Yeah, you're the doctor."

"Yes," Westin glances at me and then back to Bryce. "Do you guys know each other?" he asks.

"No," I say quickly. "Mr. Peyton happened to find our hidden gem here. I ran into him and we were talking about his wife's condition."

Now, more than ever, Westin can't be suspicious. He's advising and monitoring my trial and if he's tipped off even a little, it'll be all for naught.

His eyes meet mine and then move over to Bryce. "Just funny, this is twice now and both times you two have been pretty heated."

"You know how it is," Bryce says offhandedly. "She's my wife, and when you love someone, you do things you wouldn't dream of in any other circumstance."

His words are meant to be about Allison, but I hear more than that. He's asking me to do what he came here to ask me. To save Allison. To give them the life they're both desperate for.

"I understand, and it's fine." I'm not fooling anyone, but I know the second part of this argument is only going to get worse the longer we stand here.

Westin's arm tightens slightly. "I can't imagine what you're going through, but I'm sure Dr. Adams is doing everything possible."

Bryce's denim colored eyes meet mine and I watch the pain flicker. "I'm sure she is. Excuse me," he ducks his head. "I'm going to check on Allison."

He walks off and now I pray I can find a way to convince Westin it's nothing like it seems.

"Did you eat?" I ask quickly, still shaking from the cold and adrenaline.

"Ren, you can't tell me that isn't weird."

Telling him would be the easiest thing. I could just admit it right here, let him help me fix it, and it would be no harm no foul, but the words are stuck in my throat.

"It is, but he saw me and had questions."

Westin's eyes narrow and he sighs. "I heard part of your fight."

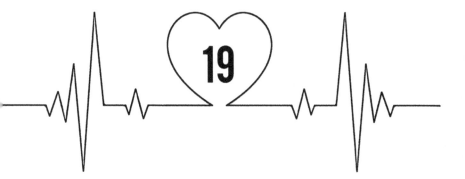

19

MY entire body locks. There's no way out of this, and I'm partially relieved. I'm in over my head and Westin will know what to do.

I open my mouth, but he puts his hand up. "Not now, Ren. We're both exhausted, fought earlier today, and I need a shower. That surgery was intense and I don't know if I even want to know what that was."

The look on his face stops me from fighting back. I've seen him tired, beaten down, defeated, and he's all of those right now.

"Did the surgery go well?" I ask.

"No."

I wrap my arms around him and try to offer a little comfort. "Is the patient all right?"

He pulls back a little, but takes my hands in his. "I'll know more if he makes it through the night."

Those cases are the worst. You have to hope that everything you did will be enough. "Do you want to be alone?" I ask, unsure of where we stand.

I don't know how much he heard, but it's clear he's upset about whatever he knows. He has every right to be. I told him we'd move forward, and it feels like I'm being pulled into the past instead.

His eyes close, but he shakes his head. "No."

"Wes," I say quickly. "What you heard . . ."

"I don't want to know." He drops my hands. "At this point, I overheard something out of context, but if you actually tell me something, I have to report it, do you understand?"

I nod. He's asking me to keep this from him, to protect him and in turn, protect myself. I don't deserve him or his protection. This could cost us both everything.

My work phone pings, and the message states that I need to return due to a patient complication. "Shit," I grumble. "I have to go, something's wrong with a patient. Are we okay?"

"We're good. Go, I'll be at my place if you want to come by after."

I doubt we're good, but I'm not going to push him, either. "Okay, I'm . . ." Sorry is what I want to say, but he takes my face in his hands.

"Just be mine, Ren. That's all I'm asking. I'm sorry I was a dick earlier. I'm just . . . it's you, okay? It's you I want and it's you I need."

My lungs ache and I feel as though I could sob right here. Westin's hands fall as I struggle internally. I want to scream out that I am his, but I don't. I should tell him that whatever he's doubting, he shouldn't, because I know he's who I want. I should say so much but my voice is gone.

Instead, he leans in, presses his lips to mine and then drops his hands.

I'm a fool.

A stupid idiot.

"I'll be over as soon as I get things fixed, and we can talk then."

Westin's face falls at the words I do manage to say. His mask goes up, the same one I wear when I'm done showing emotion, and he gives a fake smile. "Do what you have to do Serenity, but don't be stupid."

I have no idea what that means. Did he hear the part about the trial medication? Does he know what Bryce asked me to do?

Why can't I just go back a few weeks and have never accepted Allison Brown into my damn trial?

None of this would be happening.

He pushes the hair back from my face. "Go."

I'm only two blocks from the hospital and make it there in no time. On my walk over, I didn't allow myself to think about the colossal mess my life is. The things that Bryce and I said don't matter right now, a patient needs me.

The hall feels longer than ever as I make my way to the nurses' station. "Martina," I call her name.

"Oh, Ren, it's Mrs. Whitley," she explains with sadness in her eyes.

No. No. Not today. Please, I'm not strong enough to handle this today.

"How bad?" I ask.

Her face says it all. It's bad, and I won't be able to do anything. "She's asking for you."

I replace my jacket with my white coat, slipping into doctor mode. I won't get through this any other way. She's the bright spot in my dark days, and I'm going to lose her today.

The beeping from the monitor is the only sound in the

room. I make my way to her bedside, and take her hand in mine, relieving the nurse who is here. Mrs. Whitley doesn't stir and the sound of her labored breathing makes my throat constrict. Just a few hours ago she was getting stronger, and now . . . she's dying.

"I'm here, Mrs. Whitley. You're not alone." I push her white hair back with a sad smile. She told me once how she didn't want to die in a room with no one who loved her. I promised I'd be beside her. I just wish it wasn't happening at all. If she were well, I would tell her about my plight, and wait for the guidance she'd give. She was like a mother to me in some ways, always looking out for me.

"I meant to come by more often. You were doing better and I planned to come tomorrow to tell you everything. God, my heart right now is brimming and I have a lot to say and maybe you can help."

She opens her eyes just barely. "Serenity."

My name. I'll miss hearing her say it. "I'm here."

"Tell me what's wrong."

I close my eyes, my head dropping to our entwined hands, which rest on the bed. "The man I've told you about—the one I loved when I was young—he came back. He's asking me to do something that I should never even consider, but my head won't stop spinning. I'm not this girl. This weak woman who would do something so stupid for a man, but why do I want to?" I ask, as she lies here, allowing me my confession. "Love makes you stupid, but why would I even think about hurting myself to give him what he wants? What would you do if it was Leo? Would you sacrifice your own dreams if you knew it would be what made him happy? Isn't that what love is? Would you risk everything for Leo even if you knew he wasn't the one for you anymore?" I glance at her and she smiles a little.

"Yes," she croaks.

"Leo loved you with his whole heart," I tell her. Her lips turn slightly at the sound of his name. "Leo is waiting for you, isn't he?" Once again, her mouth moves.

He's what's giving her peace right now.

"I remember the story you told me about him." I rub her hand as tears fill my eyes.

When my mother passed away, it was the story of my father that she heard as she took her last breath. My brother and I stood on each side of her, recalling their love story. I hope this will give my friend the same peace.

"There was once a beautiful woman who was walking down the street, heading to the market. She was minding her own business, focused only on her task, when a handsome soldier bumped into her, causing her purse to fall to the ground and spill all its contents." Mrs. Whitley sighs and I fight back tears. "Staff Sergeant Whitley was the most handsome man she'd ever seen. He smiled at her and had kind eyes. Immediately, he dropped to his knees, and helped collect all her belongings. When their hands touched, it was as if she'd been burned."

"Leo," she groans.

A tear drifts down my cheek at the sound of her voice calling out to him. "Leo walked her to the store, and then carried her groceries to her home. Unfortunately, her father did not take kindly to the handsome soldier."

I remember watching her as she told the story that made me believe that real love does exist, even if it's eluded me. Her father was not a good man, and he forbid them from being together. He was a high-ranking military officer and would not allow his daughter to be with a soldier.

"He threatened Leo, but Leo loved Dorothy the moment he saw her." Her hand tightens slightly. "She loved him too, so each night, she'd sneak out of the house and meet him at the river bank. After weeks of sneaking around, her father became suspicious. Dorothy and Leo made plans to elope before he was shipped out."

Her eyes open, locking with mine. I gently squeeze her hand and finish the rest. "They met that night, with plans to run away, but her father followed her. He threatened them both, but their love was so strong, it couldn't be severed. Leo put Dorothy in his truck, and took her away, marrying her at first light. They were married for a long time, and loved each other until he took his last breath."

Mrs. Whitley starts to gasp and I sit on the edge of her bed, my tears falling freely. A love like that was worth every risk. "Go to Leo. He's waiting for you, his arms are open, he loves you. Go to him."

The monitor shows that she's in her last moments, and I turn the sound off and repeat Leo's name, his love, and tell her she's not alone.

I hit the call button, then the nurse enters and I shake my head. She stands on the other side of Mrs. Whitley, monitoring her pulse.

Mrs. Whitley's eyes open one last time, and then close. And then she drifts away peacefully and I hope she's with her Leo again.

"Time of death, twenty-forty-three." My voice cracks on the last number and so does a part of me. I wanted to talk to her again, tell her about Westin and me starting to really become serious. She would've smiled when I let her know we were going to go to my father's house.

"I'm sorry, Dr. Adams," Martina says. "I know Mrs. Whitley meant a great deal to you."

I close my eyes, trying to hide my emotions. "She was a great woman who I cared for very much."

"She was like mother and grandmother to the entire staff," she sniffs. "I looked forward to coming in here and visiting."

"Has anyone called her son?"

The nurse's eyes shift down. "Yes, he was on his way."

"I'll notify him when he arrives," I let her know.

I glance over at my friend's still form and another tear falls. She was a part of my day that I'll never have again. She made me smile when I felt like I couldn't because she was just that person. There was so much love in her heart, you couldn't help but feel it when you were around her. I feel as though I've lost my mother all over again.

She loved me in her own way, treated me like her daughter. I saw how proud, and at times how disappointed, she was in me, but she was always kind. Mrs. Whitley was a part of me, and I just lost her.

Fourteen Years Earlier

I turn down the dirt road. The lawn is a beautiful green with little patches of wildflowers. As a little girl, I always loved going out there, picking them and bringing them to my mother. She would gush about how lovely they were and put them in a vase. To the left is the big oak tree where my initials are carved and the tire swing sways. This house is my safe haven, the place I call home.

My brother sits on the porch, his head in his hands. "Everton," I say as I walk toward him. He looks so much older than the carefree kid he was just a year ago. His features are sharper, and he's not a kid, but a man.

His eyes meet mine, filled with unshed tears, and he doesn't have to say anything more. There is only one thing that could bring both of the men in this house to their knees, and I just need some time to set things right.

Everton gets to his feet and pulls me into his arms. "You can save her, Ren. You're almost a doctor, you can do this."

"Is it bad?"

Tears fill his eyes and I feel his chest heave. I can count on one hand the times I've seen Everton cry. He's more like my father than I care to admit. He's over six feet tall, has broad shoulders that carry the weight of the world, and kind eyes, unless you piss him off.

"Serenity," Daddy's voice is soft, but I can hear the sliver of relief when he sees me.

"Dad, where is she?"

"She's in with the doctor, but sweetheart, it's not good."

"No, you're just saying that because you don't know. I'll get in there, look her over, and talk to the doctor."

Everton comes behind me and places his hand on my shoulder. "Ren," he sighs and I look back.

"What?"

A tear falls down my father's cheek and he shakes his head. "Don't make this harder on her."

I won't, I tell myself as I enter the house. I'm just going to do what I can to make her fight. We just need more time for the chemo to work, damn it. They're both giving up and I'm not. My mother never gave up on me, and you'll have to take me with her before I do.

When I push open her bedroom door, the words escape me. I realize that God wasn't willing to heed my request. There are dark purple bags under her beautiful blue eyes, and the word frail almost seems too strong to explain how she looks.

All the hope I was feeling as I stepped through here is gone. My mother is dying.

"Serenity," she croaks and my heart breaks. "You came."

"Mom," my voice shakes. "Please, just . . ."

My thoughts are jumbled.

"Come," her smile is soft. I do as she asks, making my way to her. Her hand rests on mine and the light in her eyes returns just a little. "My sweet girl, it's time."

"I should've been here earlier. I should've left school and been here."

She shakes her head and sighs. "You got here," her words come in soft breaths, "when you could."

"There has to be something we can do. Talk to another oncologist? Maybe we can . . ."

"Shhh," she squeezes my hand. "There's nothing else to do now. I just want my family here."

Losing her will destroy me, my father, and my brother.

"You can't stop fighting, Mom."

"I can't keep going, Serenity. I'm tired now."

I look over and see my father and brother in the doorway. All three of us have tears streaming down our faces. My mother smiles at my dad, and he comes forward. All four of us hold each other in some way, connected around my mom.

Time passes, but none of us care, we just hold my mother's hands, letting her know that we're here.

Most of the time it's quiet, but every now and then someone speaks words of encouragement. My father leaves the room, and Everton and I stand on each side of her. Her breathing is softer, and less frequent. I lean down, press my lips to her cold skin, and whisper, "There was this beautiful woman named Harmony and she met a man named Mick. Mick wasn't the kind of man she envisioned, he was gruff and rode a Harley. He had tattoos and a beard that hung low off his chin." I wipe the tears as I recount the story of their life. "Harmony was soft, sweet, and her outward disposition was the opposite of Mick's, but that was the thing, she saw through to his heart."

Mom grasps at my hands and Everton's. And then my brother begins speaking with silent tears. "Mick was all bluster because on the inside, he knew that Harmony was the woman for him." My brother looks to me with desperation. So I continue.

I tell her about their love and the life they built. How adversity was nothing they couldn't tackle if they had each other. My heart turns over in my chest as I think about how I felt the same before a voicemail. How I believed my love with Bryce was all I needed, and now it's gone.

My mother's chest rises and falls, and I see the struggle. I bring my head back to hers, tears falling, leaving droplets on the pillow beside her, and I know what she needs—permission to stop fighting. "It's okay, Mom. You can let go, we'll take care of Daddy."

She takes two more shallow breaths, and then nothing else comes.

Everton sinks into the chair and I cry quietly, already feeling the loss of the woman who made me who I am.

I vow right now that I will fight cancer and ensure that as few people as possible will ever suffer loss like I just felt.

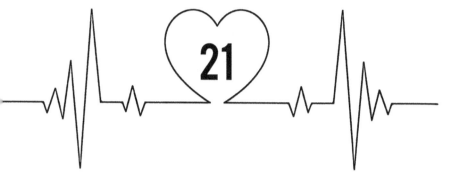

Mrs. Whitley is gone. She's gone and my world feels as though it's crumbling around me. Bryce, Westin, Allison, my family, my beliefs . . . they all seem to dissolve around me as I stare at the woman I cared for so deeply.

If I stand here, I'll break down. I don't say a word as I rush out of the room, feeling disoriented and confused. Patients die. That is my reality. I've spent the greater part of my career keeping them at a distance, but never being cruel. Why did I let her in? Why did I have to lose her today? She should've been surrounded by her son and grandchildren. She was a beautiful woman who should've been loved by everyone. Cancer once again claimed someone and robbed them.

I'm supposed to be the one who stops it.

I'm the doctor that should've saved her. I did everything, and I still failed.

My feet move, but I can't see anything through the tears.

I failed her.

I failed me.

I failed my mother again.

People move around me, but I don't pay any attention, too lost in my own world and drifting away. That's what the last few weeks have felt like. My anchor has broken and I'm lost at sea.

I hear someone laugh and I glance up to see Allison and Bryce huddled together in her room. He's lying on the bed, arms wrapped around her and she's staring up at him like he's the reason she's on this earth. I don't know how long I stand here, watching them, but it's like a movie in front of me.

"You love me?" she asks him.

"A little," Bryce teases her.

It's clear he loves her. His natural smile, the way his eyes are tender and his voice is soft. She means the world to him, and I see it all now. Bryce stares at Allison like my father saw my mother, and I realize it's nothing like how he once looked at me. We were in love, yes, but it was young and wistful. We didn't know the cruelties of life outside of college. Neither of us knew the strains of working, stress, finances, and true trials of the world. We failed our very first test, they haven't.

She is who he is meant to be with.

"You know you love me more than a little," Allison touches his face. "Besides, no one else would put up with your shit."

She loves him the way I never could—enough to fight.

He laughs. "Is that so? Well, how much do you love me?"

He needs her like he never needed me.

Allison pretends to ponder. "I'm not sure. You're kind of a pain in my ass."

They're meant to be together.

"That's part of my charm."

We were kids when we loved, but what they share is a true, honest, and beautiful love. As adults.

She shakes her head, and suddenly her mood shifts. Her fingers move softly against his stubble. "Who will take care of you if I'm gone?"

Bryce's voice is full of determination as he takes her face in his hands. "You're not going anywhere. Do you hear me? Say it. I won't let you because I won't survive it, Ali."

"Okay, okay, I'm not going anywhere. Relax," she smiles. "I love you, and our love will keep us strong. Besides, I'm getting the medication to make it better. I can feel it working."

I take two steps back, hitting the wall and feeling the breath leave my chest in a huff. The remaining parts of my heart shatter and I know I can't watch this. He could lose the happiness and future they deserve and I could be the one to stop that. One less loss in the world.

One less person in pain because of cancer.

Giving a patient what they truly need shouldn't be this difficult of a choice.

I'm a doctor. I took an oath to help people. I'm a woman who has watched the people around me suffer when I didn't have a way to help, but now I have a way. I believe it deep in my bones. It's a risk, but I don't care, because I'll be the only one ruined. Allison will be happy. Bryce will be happy, and by the time anyone finds out, all my patients will have gotten the meds.

I have to do this. It's the right thing.

Without another thought, I walk to the lab, determined to not allow one more person I love to suffer. Fourteen years ago, Bryce made a choice to push me away to save my mother and my schooling. Now, I'm going to help someone he loves.

There's a doctor walking out of the lab as I get there, and I catch the door before it closes so I don't have to put my code in.

"Hello?" I call out.

No one answers.

I walk to the locked cabinet where the trial information is kept, and I dig through the folders. There's one folder that I know has the medication that was meant for Lindsay, the patient that dropped out. This drug is just sitting here while Allison got the placebo. I stand here, holding the one thing in my hand that can destroy me to save another.

All I have to do is change the number on this folder and the number on Allison's.

One swipe of the pen and no one will know except for me.

I close my eyes and hear my mother's voice. *"You have a gift Serenity, a beautiful gift and the ability to heal those around you, don't ever squander that. Push past your own fears my beautiful girl. Don't fear what you know is right."*

But can I do it? Can I actually go through with it? What if this isn't right?

There's no *what if.*

I know what I'm doing is wrong on a professional level. I'll lose my job, respect, Westin, my family, and everything could go up in flames, but . . .

It's wrong to not do it.

I can help someone. I can give them what they want, I know it. I know this trial is the right combination of meds, and while I may lose everything, I can give something to someone else. I can save her. This is the right thing. Allison will die otherwise and I will never forgive myself. Yes, I can do this.

I grip the pen and write the number, grab the vial, and stick it in my pocket. Tomorrow, Allison will be given the next dose of the actual medication and I pray this will be the cure she needs, keeping Bryce from ever feeling the pain of losing anything else. I look back down at the vial, memorizing the numbers so I can adjust her chart, peel the label on the vial she actually received and swap it with this one. It'll look like they were always this way now.

I've . . . done it.

My heart pounds as I rush out of the lab before anyone sees me and head down the hall. I need to change out the scan code on the bag in the machine to match the vial that I'm holding now. That's the only loose end.

Now that I've gone this far, I can't stop. I have to make sure that I do my best to cover my tracks.

My mind is racing, my stomach in knots as I knock on the door to finish the goal I have.

"Dr. Adams," Allison says as I enter the room.

"I just need to check your machine," I say with a strangled smile. My throat is tight and I feel out of control. The ground isn't the same as it always was. Now it has cracks, flaws, and uneven edges that I'm tripping on.

"Are you okay?" she asks as she glances at Bryce.

No. I'm not okay. I'm not even sure what I'm doing, other than following my heart. I've come this far, I can't go back now.

"I'm fine. I just have to make sure there are no errors on the paperwork," I say, looking at Bryce for the first time. I see the panic in his eyes, but I nod, hoping he'll understand to trust me.

I walk over to her chart and look at the code, it's two numbers off. If I make it too obvious, it'll be suspicious. One of the zeroes could be made into a six. It's the easiest to change, and something that could have been a simple mistake. I strike a line through it, initial, and rewrite it with the six as though the new vial is what she received today. If anyone asks, I can say I wrote the wrong number the first time and needed to fix it.

"Everything looks great," I say as I close her chart. "I'll be back tomorrow and then you'll have a few days off."

Allison smiles. "At least I'll have this week before the fun really starts."

"Yeah," I twist my hands as my adrenaline starts to ebb. "Have a good night."

Bryce rises from the chair and extends his hand. "Thank you, Dr. Adams."

I shake his hand and then pull back. "Don't thank me. I'm doing my job."

My legs are like jelly as I walk out the door and I grip the edge of the counter outside to keep myself from falling.

Holy fucking shit, what did I just do?

I open the door to Westin's apartment, unsure how I even got here. I'm in a haze, things are going on around me, but I don't register anything.

I did something potentially stupid, and now I can't undo it. The time on the clock says eleven forty, and I grip the back of the chair for support. Where have I been the last few hours?

I remove my coat and boots, and make my way to the bedroom. Westin lies there, snoring lightly. I strip down to my underwear and climb into bed. He doesn't move, and the tears I've fought back all night finally fall, soaking the pillow.

I miss my mother.

All the years of grief I've stuffed down deep rises to the top, spilling over and leaving me raw. She should be alive right now. If I never lost her, none of this would've happened. The course of my life would have been very different.

How can it hurt so much this many years later?

Westin rolls over, his eyes meet mine and he shifts up on his elbow. "Are you crying?"

I've only cried once in front of him, and it was two years

ago when I thought my father had cancer.

"I lost Mrs. Whitley," I say as a sob escapes my throat. Saying the words out loud brings it all forward. "I lost her, Wes. She died and it was like going back in time."

"What do you mean?"

I look at him, wanting to say everything and nothing at the same time. "My mom. It was like . . . just . . . I-I'm a doctor. I should be used to this. I d-don't know why I'm crying."

Westin doesn't say a word, he just pulls me to his chest. I wrap my arms around him, holding on because he's the only thing I know is safe right now. "You loved her," he says as he rubs his fingers in my hair. "That's why you're crying."

The sounds that fill the air terrify me. I cry for the patients I've lost, for my father, my mother, the mess that is my life, for Bryce and his wife, and for a woman I never should've allowed myself to get so close to. There's no stopping the tears, I have no control over my body in this moment. "I'm so weak," I admit.

"No, baby. You're not weak, you're human and have a lot of shit going on. Mrs. Whitley was a wonderful woman."

I nod. "She was like my mother in so many ways." I turn my head to look at him through the tears.

"Yeah?"

"She met her husband when she was a young girl, like my parents. They struggled to make ends meet, but it never broke them."

He wipes a tear falling down my face. "You've never told me about your family."

How could Westin be so important in my daily life but know nothing about me? Oh, because I wouldn't let him in. I've fought against feeling more than friendship because of fear.

"They were hippies who smoked a lot of pot," I sigh. "A lot. They loved each other more than anything else in the world. We grew up poor, but Everton and I had no idea because we wanted for nothing. Mom had ovarian cancer and her clinical trial helped, but not enough. There are so many things I didn't know that I would've done differently if I was her doctor."

His lips turn up into a sad smile. "You couldn't save her, Ren. I see the look in your eyes, it's the same one I had when my brother died. It's not your fault, and you can't save everyone."

Six years ago, Westin's brother was in a horrible accident, one that left Westin watching another neurosurgeon operating on him, but he was too far gone. We were both interns at the time and I'll never forget the way he looked that day.

"Isn't that my job?" I ask with so much pain in my voice even I can hear it. "Our job is to save everyone! I didn't save Mrs. Whitley!"

He sits up, pulling me with him. "You're not God. You can't save everyone and you'd be a fool to think you can."

"Then I'm a fucking fool!" I scream. "We're supposed to do more."

He takes my face in his hands, holding me so we're nose to nose. "Do you not think you did enough? Seriously? You were there for her when her son wasn't. You made her smile, laugh, and gave her hope. Fuck, Ren, you did more for her than most doctors would. You never gave up on her. You care more about your patients than anyone I know. You don't see it, do you?"

I shake my head.

"You're an exceptional doctor because your patients become a part of you. Watching you, and the way you treat your

patients, has made me a better doctor. You give them everything."

My body is trembling, but Westin holds on tight. He has
no idea what I've given, and it could just take everything I've
worked for. Westin is a far better doctor than me.

"So do you," I say as tears fall. I think about the man he
is, the man who learned to flash mob just for his patient. The
doctor who is so broken down at the end of the day, but gets up
ready to fight the next.

"Which is what makes me drawn to you. I see you, all of
you, and I know that you struggle, but I'm here. I've been here
for two years whether you wanted me or not."

I'm such a mess. I look into his beautiful green eyes, wishing he could repair all that I've done. The wrongs that need to
be righted. But I know he can't. If only I had just been a little
stronger and trusted in him before I went stupid and lost my
mind . . . but I didn't.

I realize how many moments we've lost because I was too
afraid he might leave me.

"I'm so sorry, Westin," my lip trembles.

"For what?" he asks as he moves my hair back.

I'm sorry for much more than I can admit to. I hate that
I'm seeking comfort from the man I just betrayed. He sees the
good in me, but will he still want the ugly?

"I . . . was so . . . stupid," I start to confess. I need to be
honest with him. Give him the truth so he can tell me what to
do.

"Serenity, if this is about before, I don't need to know. Just
don't get involved with a patient's husband."

"No," I cut him off. "It's not like that. I swear, it's not
like that at all, nothing even close to what you're insinuating.

You're the only man I care about in that way."

"Then whatever is going on, I really don't want to know. I trust you and I'm sure it'll be fine."

Guilt slams into me like a freight train, crushing me under its weight. If he ever finds out what I did, he'll suffer as well. Because of Westin's surgery, I was able to switch the medications easily. No one ever saw the original vials or signed off on the trial paperwork. If they look back on the records, someone could figure it out, but since they didn't sign the daily log, their asses are on the line as well.

He trusts me, and I'm a fraud.

I can't do this to him. I was selfish and not thinking.

"Westin," I plead for him to listen to me. "I have to tell you."

"No!" he raises his voice, dropping his hands. "Right now, you're emotional and whatever you say can't ever be taken back. You have to sleep. You have to get through tonight, and then tomorrow you'll understand what I'm telling you. You *have* to shut your mouth. I'm not just your boyfriend, I'm also an advisor and hospital board member, and I will have no choice but to report whatever it is you say. Let me protect you, please."

It's me who has to protect him, I realize. If this comes out, it'll ruin his chances at chief. He's made an error and it's my turn now to protect him. I can't hurt him. I've done enough of that.

"Okay," I acquiesce. Telling him ties his hands and if I can keep him out of it, if anyone ever finds out, I'll be the one to take the fall. Not Westin.

He lies down, pulling me tight against him, and I don't say another word. After a few minutes, Westin's breathing evens out as I stare at the wall. Tomorrow maybe this will all be a dream. I can wake up, realize none of this was real, and relax because I didn't just single-handedly fuck up my entire life. Maybe.

But I know the truth, this was all real, and the nightmare has just begun.

Westin and I walk hand in hand to work. I woke up with a promise to act normal. I made my choice to keep this from him, and now I have to do everything in my power to ensure those around me don't pay the price.

"Do you have surgery planned today?" Westin asks.

"Yeah, I have one early this morning, but after that it's just rounds. I'll check on my trial patients, visit with . . ." I stop myself. I can't visit with Mrs. Whitley, she's gone.

Wes squeezes my hand. "I've got a full caseload today."

"Okay, so maybe we'll see each other later?"

He winks with a grin. "I sure hope so."

Last night was a real turning point for me. I realized just how much Westin means to me. I want him to succeed and become chief, or whatever he wants to be.

Now that I've done something to jeopardize that, it's tearing me up inside.

"I'll text you when I'm done, okay?" I ask.

"Of course, have a good day." He gives me a chaste kiss as we head in opposite directions.

My day is pretty easy. I get through my first surgery without any issues. I'm able to push all my shit down and just focus on what I'm good at. Martina watches me as I lean against the sink with a sigh. I'm exhausted.

"I'm sorry again about Mrs. Whitley," she says as she tosses her surgical gown into the bin.

"I'm glad she's not suffering."

"I'm sure that wasn't easy for you," she notes.

"No, it wasn't," I admit. It made me snap and have a complete lapse in judgment, but I can't tell her that.

She moves toward me, leans in, then pulls back, and repeats the movement again. "What are you doing?" I ask her.

"Deciding whether or not I should hug you."

I laugh and shake my head. "You're insane."

"I just know she became family to you, Ren. I also know how personally you take not being able to save the world."

I shouldn't be allowed to save anyone when I can't even save myself. "I'd rather not talk about it." Honestly, it's making me nervous to think about anything that happened yesterday.

"I understand," Martina says. "So, things are going well with you and Dr. Grant?"

Another topic I'd rather avoid. No doubt Julie and Martina have been gossiping. They're roommates and they don't believe in secrets.

"They are." I nudge her. "He's a good guy."

"Finally!" she giggles.

"Dr. Adams," Dr. Pascoe calls my name as he enters the scrub room. "Can I have a minute?"

"I'll just go check on the OR and make sure it's cleaned up," Martina says looking between us and then hurries out with an apologetic smile.

Panic fills my stomach as the door closes. The air is sucked out of the room while he stands there in silence. This can't be good. He knows something or maybe someone saw me last night. I wasn't thinking clearly and probably fucked something up.

"How are you?" he asks.

Ready to shit myself. "I'm fine. You?"

Keep it cool, Ren. Just breathe and act normal.

"I'm doing well. Is the trial going well?"

"So far," I almost choke on the lie. I need to do better than this. "How's Monica?"

"Good, she's doing good. I wanted to talk to you because I have it on good authority that the current chief of surgery will be stepping down in the next month. Do you think you'll put in for it?"

If I could let out a huge sigh, I would. The tension in my body loosens as I realize this has nothing to do with yesterday.

"I don't think so. I really haven't thought about it." Which is partially true. I had wanted the position years ago. It was what I was working toward, until I realized I'd never get to work on patients other than when I pushed my way into the operating room. There's also an insane amount of paperwork, politics, and listening to doctors bitch, and I'd rather avoid that.

"Really? I figured you would be one of the top candidates."

"Maybe a few months ago I would've been," I explain. Now, though, I don't deserve it. "I think there are others who would thrive in that position. I really like being with patients."

He smiles. "I can see that. It definitely is a game changer in regard to practicing medicine. Well, I wanted to see your interest level before I recommended you."

That throws me back. "Recommended me?"

Dr. Pascoe nods with a grin. "I think you'd make a great chief."

Another wave of guilt hits me. If he ever finds out, he'll be disappointed in the choice I made. While I know it was a grave mistake, it was in the best interest of my patient. Allison and Bryce didn't need to have that drug withheld because of a technicality.

If I had never lost Lindsay from the trial, Allison would've gotten the drug, but since she was cut, the folder with the placebo fell to Allison in the lotto.

At least that's the load of bullshit I'm feeding myself.

"I'm sure there are more qualified people. I think Dr. Grant would be an excellent choice, but I appreciate you thinking of me," I smile. It does mean a lot that he thought enough of me to consider my name.

He nods and then claps his hands, making a loud boom. "Well, I better get back to my stacks of paperwork."

"Sounds fun. Please tell Monica I said hello."

Now, to follow up on my other trial patients. They should've received their next dose, Allison receiving the new vial with the mixture she didn't get yesterday.

I decide to check on her first. Maybe if I get it over with, I won't feel so off balance. I grab my files and head in.

"Good morning," I say as I enter.

"Good morning, Dr. Adams," Allison says with so much happiness, it's infectious.

This woman always has a smile on her face. As much as I was dreading this, being around her instantly makes the traces of regret vanish. She's a warm light you can't help but feel better around.

"How are you feeling?"

"Good, I'm almost done and then we can go to our apartment." She looks over at Bryce. "I haven't gotten to see it yet, but I'm sure it'll be perfect."

His eyes are trained on me, and I focus only on her. "I'm sure it's great."

She nods quickly. "I'm excited to be out of the hospital."

Sometimes I feel like I live in the hospital, so I know the feeling of being sentenced to serve time here.

Bryce grips her hand. "When can we expect to be released?"

It's the first time he's addressed me since all that was said on the street, and I don't know what it is, but I don't feel that flutter in my stomach when I look at him. Instead, there's a sense of—finality. After everything that happened last night, I saw myself clearly for the first time. I'd been holding onto this love that couldn't endure. My heart was refusing to let anyone else in, and I'd been a fool.

I had allowed the wound that was Bryce to fester, and now it's time to heal.

"Tomorrow morning. We'll finish up this round of medication and as long as her vitals are good, we'll release her, and then she's due back in two weeks for the next dose." I turn to Allison who is beaming.

"Did you hear that? We have two whole weeks off!"

You'd think I told her she was pregnant, she's so happy.

"When will we know any kind of results? I need to head back to North Carolina for a short while," Bryce informs us both, and her face falls.

I want to punch him for ruining her mood. Seldom do patients maintain this attitude, and I truly believe a person's will is sometimes stronger than medicine.

"Peyton," she complains.

"It's the reality we face, baby. I have to go to work for a bit and I need to plan around your treatments."

"I know, but can't we just enjoy what we have right now?" she asks him.

I shift my weight a little and they both stop. "It's okay," I reassure them both. "Allison will be monitored with more frequent scans since she's on the trial. She has six doses ahead, and we'll do scans each week, but remember, she's been given a strong dose of chemo, and though she may be feeling okay today, we don't know how she'll respond in the next three days. I would keep an eye on her if you can."

"Yes, that means no going back to North Carolina. Doctor's orders," Allison points at him.

"Okay, I'll call my firm now," he sighs.

"Just don't back down," Allison urges him.

"I won't." Bryce grabs his phone, kisses her forehead, and heads out of the room.

"I know he can be harsh," Allison says.

"Who?" I ask, knowing she means Bryce.

She smiles impishly. "My husband. He's been through a lot, and sometimes his need to save me overrides his sense of diplomacy and reasoning. It's like he can't see what's in front of him, because he's already a mile away."

"Sometimes we're all weak when it comes to certain things," I reply.

Allison shrugs. "I just . . . I wish you knew the man I know."

My chest is tight as I try to scramble for the right thing to say.

"Don't worry about anything, it's my job to make sure everyone is comfortable." It's as close to the truth as I can get. "I want you to promise that you'll keep smiling though, Allison. The more positive you are, the better it will be when things are hard, okay?"

"I promise. I don't know how to be anything but me." She looks up at the bag of chemo and back to me. "This disease has taken enough, I won't let it destroy who I am and what I want."

A part of me wants to wrap my arms around her and tattoo the words on her head, because I feel like that's exactly what I did when my mother got sick. I allowed my grief and anger at cancer to overwhelm me. I let it break me to the point of no return.

But now I know one thing for sure. I won't break again, even if everything crumbles around me.

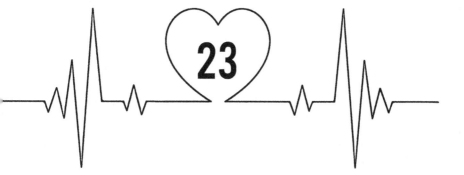

23

"You need all of this to see your dad?" Westin asks as I'm loading the car with cleaning supplies.

My brother called late last night. Apparently, my father locked the cleaning crew out of the house and has basically barricaded himself in his room. God forbid Everton actually manage things. No, he calls me to handle it.

Thankfully my surgery was postponed and my trial patients were all released today. Now I get to drive back out there and try to make my father stop being a stubborn ass.

"You have no idea," I grumble. "You're sure you want to meet them?"

"Are you trying to back out?" Westin asks.

"No, I'm just giving you one last chance to save yourself."

He moves close, pushing a stray of blonde hair from my face, giving me an unfettered view of him. Westin has decided not to shave his beard again, and I like it. He's rugged, a little mischievous, and irresistibly sexy when he doesn't force himself to look perfect all the time.

"I'm not backing out."

I smile. "I'm not either."

He taps my nose. "Then let's go."

"All right," I laugh. "Be ready to see my crazy in all its glory."

We get in the car and make our way south to Normal, Illinois, where nothing about my life was normal. Westin asks questions about my childhood and I do my best to warn him about my father. Daddy is a protective man by nature, but when it comes to me, he's a little past crazy and borders on insanity.

"Scared yet?" I ask as we're entering the county limits.

"I've dealt with you for two years, Ren. Nothing scares me anymore."

I slap his chest and laugh. "Jerk."

"It's fine, once I meet your dad, and he realizes how good I am for you, it'll be just a matter of time." Westin pushes back in the seat with a self-assured smile.

"Until what?" I challenge him.

"Until *you* realize how good I am for you."

"Is that so?"

He looks over, grips my hand in his, and laces our fingers. "Two years of waiting for the perfect moment to make the move has me pretty damn sure. I'm a surgeon who would never make a cut I wasn't sure would heal right."

I roll my eyes and snort. "Surgical talk about relationships?"

"I figured you'd appreciate that one," he laughs.

"You really know the way to my heart. Nothing says romance like scalpels and stitches."

"Let's be real, we both know that the idea of surgery is a turn on for people like us," Westin challenges.

He's not wrong. There's a thrill in knowing you are in control of life and death in that moment. The patient can't advo-cate, you have to make the tough calls, and if things go down a bad road, you fix it. I love the power I feel over myself more than anything. I can't get excited or flustered. I need to be composed and ready to handle whatever gets thrown at me. I'm very good under pressure—well, at least in the operating room.

"So if I talk about the weight of the scalpel and the bright light that hangs above you," I drop my voice to sound seduc-tive. "Does that turn you on?"

He shifts a little. "Nope."

I lean close, taking the tip of my finger and running it around his ear. "Really? You wouldn't want to tear my clothes off if I said something about the way everyone's eyes are on you when you take the blade to someone's skin the first time? How every breath is being held because you're about to start . . . surgery?" My voice is barely a whisper while my lips graze across his skin.

Westin's pupils dilate, but he keeps his eyes on the road. "You really want to play this game as we're getting close to your dad's house?"

I giggle and move back to my seat. "Well, here's one more thing about you to catalog. Surgery turns you on."

We enter the town of Normal and my nerves hit me. I have no idea how bad things are at my father's house. I worry that once Wes sees the real truth about who I am and what I come from, he'll look down on me, or his family will. It won't matter that I'm a doctor now, and don't need their money. I'll still be the white trash girl from Illinois who has more student loans than she can manage. I'll never be good enough because I'm poor, and rich guys don't love poor girls.

Westin grew up in an affluent family. They go to church on Sunday, have big Christmas dinners, and he doesn't know what it's like to struggle. I don't want anyone to judge my family.

"There's an opening in the cornfield right up there, turn right," I direct him.

I wanted to drive up here, but Westin was adamant we take his car. I bet he's regretting it now, based on the sound of rocks clanging against the paint on his very expensive Tesla.

The house comes into view after the bend, and I try to see it through someone else's eyes. It's a small white farmhouse in desperate need of paint. The shutters are missing from the one window, and my brother's motorcycle sits by the front steps. And then there's the washing machine that broke five years ago that currently serves as a lawn ornament. Over on the other side is a scarecrow sculpture I made in high school. And apparently Everton hasn't mowed the lawn in about three years.

We look like hillbillies.

I close my eyes, inhale, and look to Wes for the judgment I'm sure will come.

Instead, Westin just takes my hand. "Let's go meet your dad."

"It wasn't always like this," I say quickly.

His head jerks back. "What?"

"The house," I explain. "It was once beautiful. My mother would've never let it look this run down. She would've kicked their asses until they cleaned it up. I just don't have the time to come up here as much as I should. That's why it looks like we're poor and a mess."

This is just another example of me not being able to hold

it all together.

"Ren," Westin says and waits for me to look at him. I slowly lift my eyes to his. "I don't care about any of this. I care about you, and my first thought when we pulled up was: I bet they had fun growing up on this farm. My house was a museum. We weren't allowed to touch anything or build a tin man." He points to my scarecrow. "I would've sold my left arm to have a place where we could just . . . be."

How is it that he sees the house the way I once saw it? It was my happy place. I could be whoever I wanted to be when I was on this land. I was a grease monkey who loved to sew clothes, equal parts my father and mother. Each day here was an adventure with two loving parents who nurtured whatever it was we were passionate about.

My gaze moves back to the same house and instead of focusing on the washing machine, trash, and overgrown lawn, I see the tire swing in the tree. I'm hit by memories of Everton and me trying to swing each other high enough to make the other puke. A little farther over is the tree my mother and I planted on my fifth birthday. Each year, she'd take me out there for a photo. That tree is huge now, and we grew together.

This land was more than just a place we lived, it's home.

"Thank you." I move in and press my lips to his. "Thank you for reminding me that I was looking at this place I love without seeing it the way it really is. I was so nervous you would judge me, or my family, because you didn't grow up like this. I wore thrift store jeans, and I made my own dresses."

"Just because we grew up different doesn't mean either one was better, babe. Yeah, I had nice things and a new car at sixteen, but I had demands and expectations. There was no tire swing. It was fencing lessons. I didn't get to climb trees, I had to climb to the top of the class with grades. I fucking hated my life."

"I'm sorry I predetermined how you'd see me."

Westin's smile is warm and comforting. "I think we've all been judged enough. With me, you don't have to worry about that." It seems like I've been doing the same in regards to him.

I touch his cheek. "I'm a lucky woman, aren't I?"

"I'm glad you're finally seeing it. Come on, let's get inside," he nudges.

We exit the car and my father steps out onto the porch.

"Hi, Daddy," I say as he studies the both of us.

"Serenity." His expression turns to a smile. "You're back so soon?"

I look to Westin, and he moves toward me. "I told you I would be, but Everton called. Daddy, this is Westin, my . . ." this is so awkward ". . . boyfriend."

Daddy hobbles a little down the stairs. "Well, I'll be," he chuckles. "The girl listened to me for the first time in her life."

"Dad!"

Westin laughs and starts to walk toward him. "Hi, Mr. Adams, it's great to meet you. I'm Westin Grant."

They shake hands and Dad slaps him on the shoulder. "It's great to meet you too, son. Come on in. You must be tired from your drive."

"It's only a little over an hour, Daddy," I scoff.

"One would never know that based on how hard it is for you to get your ass out here and see your old man," my father tosses back.

Touché.

"Here we go," I mutter as we head into the house.

"I like him," Westin whispers.

"Give it time. You'll change your mind."

We enter, and sure enough, the house is trashed. How, in one week, they were able to reverse everything I did baffles me. I take a deep breath, trying to calm myself. I want to scream at him, but it won't help. Instead, I move things off the kitchen table and chairs and take a seat. Westin and Dad follow me and now it's time for the talk.

"Dad, why didn't you let the cleaners in?"

He turns quickly, glaring at me. "I told you before. This is your mother's house and I'm not letting some strangers come in and move her stuff."

Tears fill my eyes, but I shove them down. "I understand that, but the house has to be cleaned. Did you eat the food?"

He curses under his breath. My father and I had an amazing relationship that's been reduced to me having to scold him. This is not what I envisioned. "I eat every damn day, Serenity. I don't need you telling me what to do."

Westin's hand grips my thigh and he clears his throat. "Ren tells me that you fix cars?"

Dad nods once. "Since I can remember, I've been fixing engines."

"My dad has a love for cars. I actually restored my first car." Wes sounds proud.

I glance over at him since he just mentioned getting a new car at sixteen.

"Really?" Pride fills my father's tone. "How about that?"

Dad gets to his feet and heads to the fridge. He grabs a soda for himself and offers one to Westin.

Cars, bikes, and my mother is all anyone needs to talk about to win Dad's heart. So far, Westin is off to a good start and I didn't even tell him what to say.

I lean in, speaking so only he can hear, "I thought you got a new car."

He whispers back, "I got two. One I could drive and one I had to fix."

Two cars for his sixteenth birthday? Who does that?

Westin and my dad start to talk about the car he restored. I expected Westin to be trying to get back to Chicago by now, but instead, he's looking relaxed and carefree in the chair at the kitchen table. My heart, which has been trying so hard to not lose another piece, is pulling away and seeking him out.

I get up and start cleaning a few more things. This place is a mess and I really need to get to work making it livable.

The two of them talk and I lean against the counter with a smile. My father has never done this. I feel horrible for the guy I brought home in high school, when Daddy told him he had a hundred acres and no one would ever find his body. Then, when he met Bryce, he threatened to beat the shit out of him. After that, there was no one else. I never imagined he'd react this way to Westin.

The screen door makes a loud bang and I jump. "You got him to leave his room? Nice," Everton says as he tosses a six-pack on the counter and grabs one.

"Yes, well, it helps when you talk to him."

Everton flips me off and pops the bottle cap off, letting it drop to the floor. "Who is this?" he asks as he tips the bottle-neck at Westin.

"This is your sister's boyfriend," Dad answers.

"Amazing how you have time to be a mediocre doctor and date someone, but not enough to help out up here."

My family is falling apart and there's not a damn thing I can do. Everton is so angry at the world, he can't even see what's around him. I'm aware that everyone deals with grief their own way. I chose to immerse myself in work, but becoming the town drunk isn't exactly the best coping mechanism.

"Go take a shower. You smell like a bar." I cross my arms, refusing to play his game.

"Go save our mother, oh, wait . . ." Everton walks out of the room with the rest of his beer and I want to kill him.

I feel as though he just slapped me across the face.

Everton's insult stings more than I want it to. I have enough guilt over losing my mother the way we did. She trusted me to help her make the right medical decisions. Even though I was only in medical school, she had such faith in my ability to lead her down the right path.

I was the one who convinced her to do the trial. But that drug didn't help the way it promised, and she spent months in pain. Our family watched her struggle through the treatments.

"Don't you dare let him in your head, Serenity Adams." My father's voice is hard as steel. "You did everything you could for your mother. You hear me? She was proud of you. She trusted you because you loved her and would never put her in harm's way."

My head might know that Everton is a drunk asshole, but my heart doesn't care. She wouldn't be proud of the choice to change Allison's medication when I was drowning in my own sea of grief.

Westin gets to his feet as my lip trembles. He wraps his arm around me, tugging me against his chest. I really hate my stupid brother.

"I'm fine," I say after a few seconds.

"I knew you were," Westin says with a light tone. "I just wanted you to hug me. I was feeling lonely."

I burst out laughing. He's so full of it, but I appreciate the gesture. "Well, at least after this, you can't say you didn't see it all." I smile and then look over at my dad, who is grinning.

"You know, I have this car that's giving me problems, would you like to check it out?" Daddy offers to Wes and my jaw drops.

"Sure, it's been a while since I've been under the hood, but I'd love to take a look."

"What?" I ask. Both their heads turn. "You want Westin to go to the shop? To work on the car?" This can't be happening. No one goes in the garage but me and Everton.

"That's what I asked the man." Dad looks at me like I'm crazy.

Is there anyone that Westin can't win over in one minute? It's not normal. The toughest man I know is putty in his hands, inviting him to work on a car. Unbelievable.

"We'll be back in a bit." Westin grins at me.

Then another possibility hits me. Maybe my father is trying to make him think he likes him so he can berate him when I'm not around. Westin will be alone—in the woods—with my father who may be old, but has a gun.

"He could be trying to lure you into a trap," I warn.

Westin's face scrunches. "Are you all right?"

"I'm serious, Wes. Daddy doesn't like men who date his daughter."

He laughs through his nose. "We'll be back in a bit. You're free to make sure your father, who has been nothing but nice, hasn't trapped me, if it makes you feel better."

I tuck my hair behind my ear. "Don't say I didn't warn you. It'll be hard to operate with one hand."

"I'll take my chances," Westin says before giving me a

kiss.

And I'm going to take care of my brother.

When they both leave, I march into his room, throwing the door open. "You don't get to blame me for Mom's death. You want to blame me for living a good life, have at it, but don't you ever imply I didn't do enough for her. It was you who ran away when things got too hard. I was the one who cleaned her up, changed her sheets, and tried to comfort Dad while you were too busy fucking anyone who would open their legs."

I continue on, getting it all out. "I gave up everything for her. I don't live with any regrets about how I cared for her, so don't project your shit on me! Selfish prick!" I pull the door shut, not giving a shit about anything he has to say.

I've had it. For years I've put up with my brother insinuating it was me who was responsible for Mom's death, but my father is right, I did what I could. I walked away from the life I wanted desperately because I hoped it would help her. My brother can't walk away from the bar to help get food for my father.

He frustrates the hell out of me. Life isn't easy, but we make sacrifices for the people we love. Everton, apparently, is above that.

Once again, I clean, while my brother's music blares in the other room. The kitchen is the least destroyed since I cleaned up last week. I get through to the living room, and head to my parents' room.

All of my mother's belongings are still where they were when she died fourteen years ago. I grip the picture frame of the four of us that sits on her dresser. The photo is faded, but our faces are still clear. My father has his arm around my mother, and she's looking up at him, while my brother and I are in front of them sticking our tongues out at each other. We were at a summer barbeque, and I was maybe ten and Everton was eight.

I sink onto the bed with a mixture of sadness and joy. This photo was supposed to be thrown out, but my mother said it was the best picture she'd ever seen. This was who we were and she never wanted to forget it. She did throw away the one we took not even a minute later where we were all standing with smiles. To her, we were the most beautiful when we were the most honest.

"I'm sorry, Mom," I say as I touch her face. "I don't know what I was thinking, but I'm going to make it right somehow. You would be so disappointed in me for lying. I just wanted to stop another person from hurting the way it hurt to lose you."

I don't regret switching the medications, which is what I grapple the most with. I truly believe this will help Allison, and she deserves the best I can give. What I'm struggling with is that if anyone finds out what I've done, I'll never be able to help another woman who's suffering like my mom did. I might have destroyed many more people by making a choice to save one. I've managed to risk so many people, including those who matter most in my life, all because I was weak and didn't truly process the ramifications.

Maybe if I can believe that my mother would forgive me for what I've done, I can start to forgive myself a little.

For now, I just have to find a way to atone. If I tell people what happened, I'll destroy Westin. If I don't, I'll live in this constant state of fear. There's no easy choice, but I know I'll spend the rest of my life trying to make up for what I've done.

My vision blurs and I close my eyes, wanting to feel her with me. So many times, I sat on the edge of this bed, seeking her advice. She'd push my hair back and run her fingers through it as she talked. I imagine this time she'd say I should protect who I can, and do my best to clean up the mess I've made, but I needed to be honest with myself about why I did it.

"Ren," Everton's voice breaks the silence.

"What?" I say with defeat.

"I know you're pissed, but I just miss her. It doesn't help that Dad talks about her nonstop and he's always fucking sad. It's like I can't breathe here." A tear falls down his cheek. "It's not you I'm mad at, it's me. I can't . . . I can't do this . . . I'm drowning here."

Instead of seeing my six-foot-five younger brother, I see a broken man. He loved my mother with everything, and I think maybe he just wasn't able to handle seeing her in pain. Everton started drinking, partying, and doing God knows what with women when Mom died. He struggled with her death just as much as I did, but I went to work to make things better. Everton tried to drown out the pain however he could.

"Why didn't you say something?" I ask.

He sits beside me, taking the photo from my hand. "I tried once, but you're kind of scary."

"Me?"

He pushes his shoulder against mine. "You're a surgeon who was in a damn magazine. I'm a shitty mechanic who works for my father and still lives at home. I hate this town and I'm going nowhere."

I sigh. "I'm also your sister who you used to torment by putting garden snakes in my drawers."

Everton laughs. "That was a long time ago. But now I'm saying I can't do this anymore. I can't live in this house. I swear, sometimes I hear her voice and wait for her to come around the corner. Dad needs help that I'm not able to give. I need to leave."

My head falls forward, and I feel more overwhelmed than ever. Getting my father to leave this house will be impossible. If I asked Everton to stay for him, he probably would, but it's not like what he's doing is helping as it is.

"Where will you go?" I look in my brother's brown eyes, eyes that are filled with sorrow instead of anger.

"I don't know, but I have to get out of here."

And now the million-dollar question. "What about Dad, Ev? What do I do, because he won't come with me, and he can't stay here?"

"I'm not sure, but you're smarter than me."

Helpful as always. "And I guess it's up to me to figure it out," I sigh and get to my feet.

I understand my brother's plight, but my father is the one who will have his life flipped around. I'm not sure what to do, but I'm going to have to figure it out—fast.

"You're the good one between us, Ren. I'm sure you'll think of something." Everton touches my shoulder and strolls out of the room.

The worst part of this is that I'm not surprised. I expect this kind of thing from my brother. He'll do what's best for him and I'll sacrifice what I have to in order to make sure Dad is taken care of.

I hear my brother's bike fire up, and I have no idea if he's leaving for good, but I can't worry about him. He's going to make his choices, and in the end, he will have to live with them.

"I don't know how you did this, Mom." I touch her face in the photo.

I grab the cleaning rag, unwilling to think about the very shitty options ahead of me, and tidy up. Cleaning is mindless and I've done enough thinking for a long time.

Once the bedroom is livable, I head to the worst room in the house, the bathroom. I gag and cut a hole in a plastic garbage bag and pull it on, making myself a hazmat suit. I swear, if anything is dead in here, I'm burning the house down.

For over an hour, I scrub every surface, and manage to keep myself from puking twice. I run the water, washing out the tub that's now been bleached. I feel like I need to do the same to my body, when I hear Westin's voice.

"Hey," I say, wiping the sweat from my brow as I emerge.

He chuckles, looking at my homemade protective suit. "Interesting outfit."

"Don't mock. I was cleaning and needed protection."

Westin shakes his head and looks around. "You did good."

"I know, and look, you're alive."

"Why wouldn't he be?" Dad asks.

"Because you're crazy when it comes to men and me," I remind him.

He waves his hand at me. "I scared off the idiots. Westin is a good one."

"You figured that out in two hours?"

Daddy smiles. "Try two seconds. A man knows when another man isn't worthy."

I forgot, men have a secret radar that's foolproof.

"Exactly, Mick," Westin agrees. "Glad to see I passed the test."

Mick? He called him Mick? What the hell? I think the fumes are sending me into some kind of alternate reality.

"Sure did. Wes and I got that carburetor working again.

He's good with his hands," Dad praises him.

Mick and Wes? I have no idea what to think of this revelation, but at the same time, my heart swells. I've never seen my father like this, and it means the world to me. There's no man in this world I love more than Daddy, and I don't know if I could love someone who he hated.

Westin's eyes are trained on me and I smile. How could I have been so blind? For two years, this amazing man has been right in front of me, and I'm not letting him go now.

"Well, he's a surgeon, Daddy," I grin. "Did you and *Wes* have a good time?"

"We were fixing a car, pumpkin, not braiding each other's hair," Dad scoffs and heads to the fridge.

I raise my hand in surrender and then remove the bags from my body.

Westin laughs. "Your dad had it figured out. I think he was being nice."

"Serenity can tell you, I'm never nice when it comes to cars or my daughter," Dad retorts and I nod.

"He's right," I agree. "He's not even nice to his daughter about cars."

"Well, then I'm glad I could help," he tells Daddy.

Dad yawns and looks around the house. "You cleaned up. Everton will be happy . . . before he trashes it again."

My brother's name reminds me that I have a serious issue I need to handle before I leave. Who is going to help take care of the man who spent his whole life doing just that for me?

"I'm going to show Westin around the property," I inform them both.

Westin raises a brow and I shake my head, hoping he understands not to fight me. I need to talk to him about my brother and his decision to leave. Maybe someone on the outside can see this for what it is and offer guidance.

"Sure, I'll just watch the game," Dad groans as he walks to the living room. "You two have fun."

We walk out the back door, down the dirt path where the tire swing still hangs. His fingers are wrapped around mine, and I rest my head on his arm. This visit didn't exactly go as I thought; it's been so much better.

Seeing Westin fit in with my family has meant everything to me, now I need to see if he can help me deal with them. But right now, I just need to be home, and in the moment.

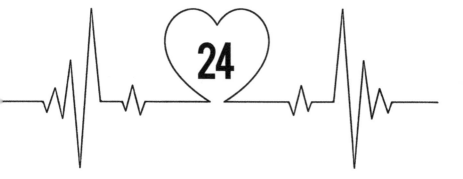

24

"**D**o you think I did the right thing?" I ask Westin as we drive back to Chicago.

"Your father is perfectly lucid. We spent two hours together and I promise, I'd be honest if I thought he couldn't handle it."

Westin told me about their talk, and how Dad mentioned his stress about Everton and his lack of responsibility. Apparently, my brother's drinking is even more out of hand than I knew about. Westin seems to believe it'll actually be a relief to Dad that he's gone.

"But the house . . ."

"You can't fix this, baby. I know that's hard, but believe me, he's going to be fine. It just might require we take a trip up once a month."

I don't miss the fact that he said "we." It also doesn't scare me. In fact, it makes me smile.

"I guess we will." I blush a little and now want to slap myself.

"I meant to ask you," Westin clears his throat. "How is the

trial going?"

Instantly, the good feelings I had about the day are gone. Now the dread of lying to him is all-consuming. What other choice do I have? I can tell him, but then that puts him at risk, and he's repeatedly asked me to keep him in the dark.

"We'll find out more with the scans in a week and a half."

He nods. "Why don't you sound excited?"

"It's just a lot of stress, you know. And losing Mrs. Whitley really threw me for a loop," I explain.

Westin offers me comfort with his touch. "I know, believe me, I know."

"Can we talk about anything else?" I request.

Today has been such a great day, I just want to enjoy it a little more.

"Sure thing," Wes smiles.

We fall silent, but it's not awkward. We just are. For the next twenty minutes, Westin and I hold hands and I close my eyes, enjoying the peace that cocoons us. There's something about being comfortable with someone in the silence.

The car stops in front of my apartment, and I sigh. "Thank you for today."

He cups my cheek and leans forward. "There's not much I wouldn't do for you, Serenity."

I rest my forehead on his. "I know, and I don't deserve you."

Westin tilts his head back so we're eye to eye. "You deserve to be happy. I want to make you happy."

I touch the prickly hair on his cheek. Westin has no idea, but before we went on this trip, I realized my feelings for him are far deeper than I wanted to admit. I'd been lying to myself, protecting my heart by saying it was just sex.

But it's not.

When I think about my normal day to day, I realize he's always been a part of it. When good things happen to me, I share with him.

He's been faithful to me when he didn't have to be. If I could go back in time, I'd slap myself for not seeing how perfect he is for me.

"Wes, you do make me happy. Come inside?"

He smiles against my lips and kisses me. "I'm more than willing to make you happy in that way too."

"Good to know," I laugh.

We get to the front door, and he holds me from behind, rubbing his beard against my neck, causing me to giggle. After a few more tries, I finally get the door open.

"Are you hungry?" he asks as he heads to the kitchen.

"Not really, but I won't say no to wine," I smile. "There's a burger from Rich's in the fridge," I call out.

I went to the store yesterday because there was sour milk and some sort of science experiment that could've been cheese in the refrigerator. On my way back from the market, I stopped in to see Rich and get takeout. While half of what I got needs to be cooked and I'll probably end up throwing it away, it felt nice to buy food that wasn't made in the cafeteria.

"What's this?" Westin asks, holding up the almond milk.

"It's the milk you like," I reply.

"Right, but why is it here?"

Is he crazy? He brings that stupid milk every time he stays here. "Umm, you drink it, right?"

His eyes narrow and then he goes back to the groceries. "Ren?" He holds up the six-pack of beer.

"Wes," I shake my head. "Is that not the right kind? You

drink that weird lager shit, I thought."

He puts the beer down and leans on the counter. "Yes, but again, you got it?"

I'm not sure what the big deal is. "I was at the store so I grabbed it. Why are you looking at me like that?" I ask as his jaw hangs open a little and then turns into a grin.

And then it hits me.

I thought of him when I was stocking *my* home. He watches me as I start to piece together what has made his entire mood shift.

"Two years and you've never bought shit for me," Westin says. "I've wondered when you were going to mess up and let me in."

"Don't make this weird," I warn. "It's milk and beer."

He smiles and leans forward. "I knew it would happen."

Oh Jesus. "Listen, before this goes too far, I also cleaned out a drawer."

"I'm sorry, what?"

Might as well get this all out and done with. Westin stays here or I'm at his place pretty much every night that we have off. Because of our schedules, exchanging a key wasn't really a big thing. It was more for convenience than some momentous moment in our relationship. He gave me a space in his bathroom for my things, but I wasn't as giving. Not that he was surprised, but I was thinking of how to show him that I'm . . . all in . . . to whatever it is we're doing.

Giving him some speech about what we're doing seems silly now, but I thought having *a* drawer was a nice gesture. Now, I'm a little scared.

"You know, a place you can put your stuff."

"I know what a drawer is, but you gave me one? Here?"

"Yes, *one* drawer," I clarify. "One of the small ones."

"In your house?"

"Well, that was the point."

He moves around the island, places his hand on my fore-head and shakes his head. "No fever. So, you're not sick."

"Ass."

"So, if I go in the bedroom, there will be a drawer that's empty?"

Why is he being such a dork? It's just a drawer. "Westin, you're here all the time. I can fill it back up if you want . . ."

"Shut up," he says as his hands hold onto my hips. "How about some closet space since you're so giving?"

"Don't push it." My hands rest on his chest and then he squats down, lifting me into his arms.

Westin smirks as he carries me back to the bedroom. He drops me on the bed, and walks over to the dresser. "This one?"

I nod.

He opens the drawer, finding it empty as promised, and then he stalks toward me. I push back, moving away from him, but he doesn't relent. Westin hovers over me and my heart races. "I've been trying to break down your walls."

"It's milk and a drawer," I clarify.

"No, baby. We both know it's not." Before I can say an-other word, his lips are on mine, kissing me like I'm the air he's gasping for.

My hands are frantic trying to remove as much of his clothing as possible. It's like a light switched off and I'm com-pletely fine being in the dark. This is what Westin does, he lets me forget, pushes me, loves me even when I don't think I'm worthy.

Our tongues slide together, reveling in the wet warmth. His

shirt falls to the floor, and he tears open my buttoned blouse, while our lips stay fused.

God, he kisses like no one else.

Gone is the tender man who held my hand as I cried, explaining to my father what he needed to do to make sure I didn't force him to move from his home. Who didn't cringe when he saw the home I loved as a child in disarray. The sweet man who promised my father we'd come back and work on his car that runs perfectly fine just so we could check in on him more.

This is the Westin I need right now. The dominant man who will force me outside of my mind.

His fingers tangle in my hair and he tugs it to the side, pushing deeper, making me feel him in every part of my body.

"Don't run away anymore, Ren. Stay here with me." His green eyes are full of emotion.

"I'm not going anywhere."

His lips are back where I want them, and then he's moving down my body, kissing my neck, my shoulders, before finding my breast. Westin's eyes meet mine as he takes my nipple into his mouth, I look away and he stops.

"Watch me," he commands, "watch me love you."

"Wes," I say pushing my fingers through his hair.

Westin's eyes are full of some emotion I can't name. "You need to see. You need to see that I'm right here."

My chest tightens as I watch his mouth lower, keeping our eyes locked. With a tenderness that he's never shown, he runs his lips across my skin, leaving a trail of goose bumps in his wake.

The voice in my head that always shuts down when Wes gets too close is screaming at me to stop this. There's another side of me, though. The one that knew how to love someone once upon a time, and that part of me is euphoric right now. For so long, what we've shared in the bedroom has been just sex. This time, I know it's not.

There won't be a rollover and see you at work. I know that when I give myself to him, it's more than just my body he'll take.

Westin will have my heart.

He places his lips on my chest, right where the organ that hasn't been whole resides, and he kisses me. "I'm going to make you forget all the pain you suffered. I don't know what happened to you to make you keep pulling away," he says as he moves back up so we're nose to nose. "Know this, I'm not going anywhere."

My fingers brush against his face. "I'm tired of running, Westin. I'm tired of fighting everything inside of me that wants to feel something more. So, if I fall, are you going to catch me?"

His eyes close, and when he opens them again, there's not a trace of doubt. "Always."

A tear falls down my cheek at the promise in his voice. I really hope it's true because I'm hanging on the edge of a cliff by my fingernails. If I slip at all, I'll plummet.

"Make love to me, Westin," I request.

With our breaths mixing, he moves towards my lips, gazing into my eyes the entire time. I've never uttered those words to him, I've always kept a barrier between us. It worked until my past came back in my life, reminding me why I was this way. Westin isn't my past. He's the man I want to make room in my dresser for, and maybe one day he'll share my home.

When our lips touch, my head spins with recognition of

this new reality. It's the coming together of two people who have been in this bed many times, but never fully. My fingers tangle in his hair and I pull my body against his, obliterating the remaining space between us.

Westin's hands roam my body, hooking under my leg, wrapping it around his hip. Both of us are lost as we grab onto each other.

He moves his lips from mine, and this time I don't take my eyes off him. "You're so beautiful." His voice is husky with desire.

I go to open my mouth to say something about how hot he is, but his lips wrap around my nipple, and I can't remember anything.

He nips, sucks, and licks, driving me crazy. "Westin," I groan, fisting the sheets when his other hand travels down my pants. With just the right amount of pressure, he starts to bring me higher.

"Tell me, baby. Tell me you want this," he pushes.

"Yes! I want this," I reply. "I want us."

I want everything. I want to forget everything around me and be in this moment because I have no idea when my house of cards could crumble. He's the only thing that brings me any kind of solace. I'm done holding back, my walls are down.

Funny that it took being faced with something I thought I wanted to realize that what I already had was all I ever needed.

Now, I don't know if I'll be able to hold onto him, but I pray I can.

Westin pulls my pants off, and removes his. His lips are back on mine and I wrap my hands around his erection. He moans into my mouth as I pump up and down, loving the noises he makes.

"I can't wait, Ren. I need to be inside you," he says and then nips at my ear.

I know exactly how he feels. "Now, please," I pant.

Westin rolls the condom on, and when he's in position, he stops.

"What's wrong?" I ask breathlessly.

"Not a goddamn thing."

Our eyes lock, and my heart races because I can feel the energy shift. It's as though two pieces of a puzzle are finally fitting after trying a hundred wrong ones. There's nerves, excitement, joy, and fear all battling over different things. I worry that after this, losing him will be my demise.

He grips my face in his hands, searching through the myriad of emotions undoubtedly playing in my eyes.

Gently, he enters me and a tear escapes the corner of my eye. Years of locking myself down are over, the shackles are broken, and the past that has weighed me down has been lifted. How stupid I was to hold onto it, thinking it would protect me.

Westin rocks back and forth slowly, loving me in a way I'll never forget. He doesn't have to say the words because I feel them. I've known it for a long time. Westin is in love with me and I've just fallen for him.

I just hope it stays that way if he ever finds out what I've done.

It's been two weeks since I last saw Allison and Bryce. My life since then has been damn near perfect. Westin and I have had a little more time since I'm not bogged down with the trial, and his caseload is light as well. We've enjoyed the slower pace and it couldn't have come at a better time because today, my trial patients come back for their scans, and then tomorrow the doses start again.

I'd like to believe this won't affect the amazing state my life is in, but I'm a realist, and I know this will put another kink in the line. Not because I worry that seeing a man I loved so much will hurt, but because I'm reminded that I'm not the woman I've prided myself on being when he's near.

"Hey, you," Julie says as I sit in the corner of one of the consult rooms. I like to hide here when I need time to chart.

"Hey," I smile.

She enters the room and plops down next to me. "Charting?"

"The one thing they fail to talk about in med school," I laugh. "It's really such a pain in the ass."

"Yet another reason I love my specialty," she smirks.

"Yeah, yeah, whatever. How are you? Sorry I bailed on drinks yesterday," I say while putting the pen down.

"It's fine." She pops a grape into her mouth. "Martina came, we drank, ate an inhuman amount of food, and she went home with some guy. Did you work late?"

I tap the pen against the table. "No, I was with Westin."

She leans forward. "You blew off beer dip for your boyfriend?"

"I did."

"Well," she sinks back with her arms crossed over her chest. "Look who finally got her shit straight." Julie looks all too pleased. "I was hoping this day would come. I feel like my little girl is growing up."

"Whatever."

"So, things are good?" she asks.

"They really are. Thank you, Jules. Seriously, thank you."

She tilts her head and purses her lips. "What for?"

It was after she was a good enough friend to be honest with me that I was able to see my life clearly. She really pushed me out of my head, and that is what helped me truly face my feelings for Westin, and trust him with my heart.

"For being who you are. Even when I don't want to hear things, you're always honest. If you hadn't made me face facts, I would've kept pushing him away because it's all I've ever done." I clasp her hand.

"I'm really happy for you. Westin clearly loves you, and guys like him don't come around often."

I nod. "I know. I'm just trying to hold onto it for as long as I can."

Julie's head turns and she looks confused. "What does that mean?"

Shit. I can't tell her the truth because that would lead to more questions about what I did, and I don't know if Julie could get tangled in the mess since the meds were kept in her lab. Oh, God. I feel sick.

"Just that guys get bored once there's no chase." I try to sound humorous, but it comes out strangled.

"You're an idiot, but I love you anyway. I need to get back to work. Don't flake on me next week." She gets to her feet, pops another grape into her mouth, and walks out the door.

Once I'm alone again, I wipe my sweaty palms on my pants, and close the files. My momentary lapse in judgment could affect so many people. I didn't think, and it's too late to do anything now.

I grab the charts, no longer having the mental capacity to

do them, and drop them off at the nurses' station. I have about twenty minutes before I will get the scan results of my trial patients, and then I'll visit each one.

Deep breaths, Serenity.

As I make my way to the cafeteria, I turn the corner and slam into someone. "Shit!"

"Sorry!" the deep voice says. "I was in a rush . . ."

I look up, knowing who it is, and release a heavy sigh. "It's fine, Bryce."

"Chick, wait," he grabs my wrist as I'm starting to walk away.

"I really need to go," I tug my hand out of his grasp.

My stomach doesn't drop and no butterflies flutter at his touch. Instead, I notice that it's not warm, like Westin. Bryce feels cold and rough, and I don't like the cold anymore.

"I know, it'll just take a minute."

There are a few people milling around the halls, and I know that if Westin were to see us talking, it would send the wrong signal. My feelings for Bryce are dead, just like the love we once shared.

"I'll be in to see Allison soon."

He takes a step closer, not listening to my not so subtle hint. "I'm sorry about that day at the bar. I just want to say . . ."

His apology doesn't change anything. The truth is, all of this is on me. I was the one who allowed his wife to stay in my trial. I knew it wouldn't be good for anyone, and I should've never touched the drugs, no matter what I was grappling with. If Bryce had never put the idea in my head, I never would've done it, but that's like saying someone commits murder because you give them a gun.

I did this.

I chose to risk my career and the man who is beginning to mean more to me than I ever dreamed because I was lost for a bit. I felt as though my world didn't make sense after losing my mother and then Mrs. Whitley. Having Bryce around brought all of that doubt back and I questioned myself. Was I not fighting hard enough for my mother? Was I not doing enough for my patients? Was I willing to let another person lose everything because of me? The weight that rested on my shoulders was too much, and I broke. My morals and ethics were blurred, but they're not now.

I made the choice to change the drugs, and while no one truly knows other than me, I'm going to do the right thing from now on. I'll treat Allison to the best of my ability, and her husband will be like every other spouse.

"Mr. Peyton, you don't owe me any apologies." I take a few steps as he stands there stunned. "I'll be happy to answer any questions when I make my rounds."

"Don't do this," he says.

"I'm sorry, but this is how it should've been all along," I say as I leave him behind me, where he belongs. "Goodbye, Mr. Peyton."

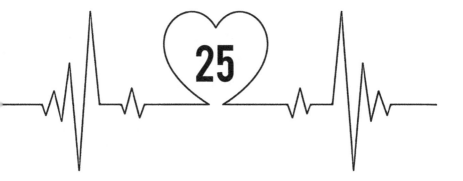

25

"**S**cans look good, Ren," Westin says as he reviews them beside me.

"Yeah, no growth, so that's always good. This one looks like it might have shrunk a little." I compare the two reports side by side.

It's minimal, but I'll take it.

"Good, I have a surgery later, so I'll sign off now." Westin scribbles his signature and kisses the top of my head. "I'll see you later."

"Save a life," I say as he walks away.

"That's the plan," he chuckles and exits.

I gather everything up, and head in to see Allison. Her results showed no growth, but I'm a little concerned with a few of the other tests. When I get to the door, she's yelling on the phone.

Before I can get back out of view, she yells, "Wait! Dr. Adams! Mom, I have to call you back."

"I can come later," I say.

"No, no, it's fine. I was just arguing with my mother about

my wayward brother."

I smile. "I have one of those. When my mother died, he became even worse."

Allison groans. "I'm so sorry. I can't imagine that was easy for you."

I shrug. "It's life, right? We just have to deal with the cards we're dealt. I'm lucky I have my father . . ."

"And your sexy doctor boyfriend," she wiggles her brows.

"And him," I agree.

Allison tells me a little more about her family, and I'm amazed at how many things we have in common. She lost her father a few years ago, whereas I lost my mother. She's a lawyer and a philanthropist and gives a lot of her time now to help her firm with cases that will help better the world.

I'd like to think as a doctor, I do the same.

"My brother is why I chose to become a lawyer. Someone had to be retained for all the illegal things he does," she laughs, but it's not funny. I can see the trouble in her eyes. "Family, right?"

"Yeah, they're something."

"So? We were just chatting away, and I'm sure you came in here for more than a chat, right? Is everything okay?" she asks.

Crap. Yes, that's the point of this, not to be her friend. I'm a little concerned with a few things on her bloodwork. It could be nothing, but I won't run that risk.

"The scans came back good," I say quickly. That's usually the biggest worry. "But your iron is a little low. How are you feeling? Are you dizzy or weak?"

Allison rubs her stomach. "I'm really fine other than the cramping."

Cramping wouldn't be caused by anemia.

I move over to the side of her bed. "Can I take a look?"

She nods.

I press around. Her abdomen is firm, but that's not necessarily abnormal. "I'm going to run a few more tests, order an ultrasound, and just ensure we're seeing the whole picture."

"Okay," she sighs. "I'm not going anywhere."

I pat her shoulder. "It'll be okay, we'll figure out what's going on."

"Thank you," she says and then crumples over, clutching her stomach.

"Allison?"

Her eyes are wide, and she's holding her breath. "Damn it," she cries out and then I watch the color drain from her face. "God, it hurts!"

I hit the button to call the nurse in. Something is wrong.

"Take a deep breath, Allison. I'm right here. Is it your stomach?"

"Yes, it's like stabbing," she huffs.

My training kicks in and I start to assess everything. I pull the sheet back, to find blood everywhere. Fuck. She's hemorrhaging.

A nurse runs in and I point to the door. "Get me an OR. Now."

A few other nurses and Martina come rushing in. Allison's eyes are wide and tears start to form.

"Allison, you're hemorrhaging. It could be just a cyst that the scan missed. I need to go in and get the bleeding to stop, okay?"

"It was just a little," she says and her voice cracks.

"You were bleeding before?" I ask.

"Please," she grabs my hand. "Please don't tell him. It's been days and I didn't want to worry him."

"Who?"

"My husband. I didn't . . . I couldn't tell him . . . please," she begs, and her head falls back.

Right now, none of that is my concern. I need to get her into surgery. My team moves around her, getting everything unhooked so we can move her.

"Let's not worry about that, okay?"

She lifts her hand and then it falls limp. I bark orders at everyone. If her levels weren't so off, it wouldn't be a huge deal, but she can't lose a lot of blood when she's already low.

We start to wheel Allison out and Bryce rushes in the room. "Allison!"

"It's okay," she tries to perk up, but she has no energy.

"What's going on?" The fear is etched into each syllable.

"Your wife has a bleed, and I need to go in and stop it. We're going to prep her for surgery right away," I explain.

He shakes his head as if he can dispel the information I just gave him. "She was fine five minutes ago."

"Peyton, I'll be okay," she holds his hand, and he clutches hers.

"Ali, I love you," Bryce tells her.

"I love you, too."

Martina clears her throat. "I need to get her down there, sir."

He smiles, pulls himself together, and releases her hands. "Okay," his eyes don't leave hers. "You'll be okay."

Allison touches his face. "Go do some work. I'll be back soon."

They kiss, and then she's wheeled out. I start to make my

way behind them, but Bryce moves, blocking my exit.

I see the turmoil in his eyes, the fear and pain, and then resolve.

"I know you're angry with me," he sniffs. "I've been a dick to you. I've asked you to do things I shouldn't have, and I'm sorry. I need you to know that I'm sorry. I'm sorry I didn't love you the way I should have."

My heart races, and I raise my hand. "Allison is my patient. If you're worried that whatever we were will affect how I treat her, you don't have to. I care about her, and I'm going to do everything in my power. This is a routine surgery, okay? You begged me to stay on as her doctor because I'm good at what I do. Now I need to go do it."

He looks at me with a tinge of hope and his lips form a thin line. "Thank you, Serenity. I mean that."

Despite everything, I do care about him. I can imagine this is every fear he can imagine coming to life. His ex-girlfriend, operating on his wife after a huge blow-up. However, I'm not his ex-girlfriend right now, I'm Allison's doctor.

"Go get some coffee, I'll be back in a bit to update you."

"Thank you."

"Don't thank me, I'm doing my job."

I head into the operating room, where Allison is prepped. My mind is moving at light speed, preparing for every possibility and creating an attack plan. Once I'm scrubbed up, I go in to talk to her one more time.

"You doing okay? Any questions?" I ask.

"Can I?" She stops. "Can I talk to you for just a minute? Alone?"

"Now?"

She nods.

"Okay."

My stomach drops a little, but I can't say no. I look around the room and jerk my head to the side. Everyone leaves, and her green eyes start to leak. She's terrified, and I need to calm her down.

I pull my mask down. "I know you're scared, but I promise I'm going to take care of you."

"I need to tell you that I know who you are, Serenity," Allison confesses. "I know that you were once engaged to Bryce."

Oh, God. I can't hide my surprise and I gasp. If she knows, why the hell is she here? Is it just to meet me? Why does it matter, though?

I quickly try to explain, "I don't know what to say. I swear there's nothing between us."

"I found out about you four years ago by accident. I heard his family saying some things about letting go of you, and I got curious. There was this sadistic part of me that needed to see who you were, so I started digging. It wasn't malicious, I just had to know if he ever truly loved me."

"He does," I tell her.

"I know that now. The first few days you two saw each other, I was worried, but when I got to know you, I saw that I was being silly. I realize that what you two shared is different, no less beautiful, but just different. You both let each other go to save the other."

"Why are you telling me this now?" I ask.

She smiles softly. "Because I need you to promise me that if something happens," she starts, but I cut her off.

"Don't say the next words, Allison. Please don't put that out in the universe."

Her lips close, but her eyes tell me the rest. For just a moment, the doctor/patient relationship is gone. Allison is just a woman, and so am I. She's pleading for me to care for something she loves. She needs this peace of mind in order to get through the surgery.

I don't reply verbally, she doesn't need to hear it.

"Thank you," she says and turns her head to the side.

I call everyone back in, and go scrub up again, all the while thinking of the way she begged me with her eyes.

When I get back in the room, everyone is ready and I get in position. "Okay, Allison, we're going to put you to sleep now," I say.

"Okay," she replies with a tear falling down her cheek.

The anesthesia gets turned on, but her eyes are locked on mine. "Until my last breath," she says and then drifts off to sleep.

I take a few seconds, trying to forget the words that make my chest tight. With my eyes closed, I inhale, thinking of the strategic moves I need to make surgically. If I can focus, then it won't feel like the scalpel opened me up.

Two more deep breaths and I'm done being Serenity and back into my doctor persona. All my emotions are shut down, and I no longer care about anything but surgery.

"Ready, Dr. Adams?" Martina asks.

"Yes. Scalpel," I say with my hand out.

It's been an hour, and so far, the surgery has gone flawlessly. I found the bleed easily and was able to stop it, along with getting a good look at her tumor. Scans are one thing, but when you're actually in there, it can be a whole other world. Things are never as they seem, but thankfully, it's nothing that will hinder her progress. The music is playing in the operating room, and I'm in the zone.

Everything looks good. "Okay, let's close her up," I instruct my staff.

I move one of her organs, to ensure the bleed is in fact stopped, which it has. We begin to close her, when suddenly the alarms fill the room.

"Pressure is dropping. She's crashing."

My body's natural fight or flight instinct kicks in, but I can't allow it. Her heart rate is plummeting. "Push some epi," I instruct. "Start compressions."

Fear tries to take over. My muscles are tense as Allison's line continues to stay flat. I need to fix this. I need to stay calm, but my heart is racing, knowing that time isn't on my side.

I move everything back, and the nurse starts CPR so I can close her up. I work quickly, knowing that every second counts. Once I'm done, the people in the room can almost read my mind. They gather the equipment we need to get her heart pumping again. I'm losing her.

I grab the crash cart. "Charge to three-sixty. Clear!" I yell and everyone steps back.

The shock jolts through her, and I watch the screen.

Please come back, please come back. Come on, Allison. Wake up.

Nothing. Her heart is still not responding.

You're not going anywhere. Not on my watch. I won't tell your husband you died.

"Charge again," I command.

Pure determination is all I'm running on. Allison will not die today. I told Bryce it was routine and I can't face him. She was healthy, this is just a tougher case. I've handled tough before, goddammit.

The machine alerts me that it's ready. "Clear!" I yell and

the room stills. The paddles touch her chest, electricity flowing to her heart and her chest lifts.

Again, my eyes move to the monitor. "Come on, Allison," I mumble.

"Dr. Adams," Martina says. "It's been three minutes."

Irrelevant to me right now. She can survive this. I know it, she just has to want it. "Allison, you need to fight," I tell her. "You have to fight for your husband and family. Fight, dammit."

My own heart is pounding so hard that I worry it's going to leave my chest. I watch the monitor, thinking of any idea I haven't tried. A rush of nerves floods me, and I watch the flat line dance across the screen.

If I don't want her to give up, I can't either.

"Ren, you need to call it." Martina touches my arm, but I fling it off.

No.

"Push another round of epi. Someone page Dr. Grant and get cardio in here," I order one of the nurses. I don't know why she's not responding, it could be anything. "Charge it again," I say, desperate to get her back.

My breathing is erratic as I press the panels to her chest again. "Clear!"

Allison's body jerks, and I close my eyes as the beep continues to echo in the room. The last shred of hope I had is gone. A tear forms as I wait for God or someone to intervene. I need a miracle.

"Dr. Adams?" Westin's voice penetrates through the eerie silence in the room.

Our eyes meet, and then I look back to Allison.

"Push another round!" I command.

"We've given her the max," the anesthesiologist says.

"I don't care!"

How could this happen? The surgery went great, she was perfectly okay and then everything went crazy. I stand here, staring at her lifeless body, and I know people are talking around me, but I don't hear them. Allison is dead. She's really dead.

How?

No.

I can't think. This isn't real. I didn't just kill her, right?

She was . . . she was fine.

I shake my head, trying to make this scene disappear.

"Serenity," Westin's voice breaks my fog. "You need to call it. She can't have any more drugs. She's been gone for too long now."

"No," I say. "No, try again!"

He grips my shoulders, stopping me from getting to her.

Westin looks over my shoulder and sighs. "Time of death. Seventeen twenty-two."

I push the air in and out of my lungs, but they're burning. Tears fill my eyes and I can't see. She's gone. That sweet, caring woman who I promised would be okay, isn't. She died on my table while I was singing along to some pop song. My heart is beating and hers isn't.

These are facts.

My eyes meet Westin's and I start to panic. I can't breathe. I open my mouth, but no sound will come out.

He pulls me from the room as I begin to break down. "Easy, easy," he tries to calm me.

"I don't know what happened." I shake against his body and a sob breaks out. "I don't understand."

Westin's hands cup my face and he watches me. "You have to calm down. Explain it to me."

I go over the surgery to him, clarifying the details, and revealing how quickly everything happened. He listens without interrupting me, and nods along. There was nothing that occurred that was out of the ordinary. Each step was handled, until her heart just . . . failed. After that, no matter what I tried, nothing brought her back.

"From what you explained, it wasn't anything you could've done," he tries to comfort me, but I push back.

"I was her doctor! She was fine!"

"Serenity," he touches my cheek, but I flinch. "She was bleeding, you stopped it, but there was something else that caused her heart to fail. You didn't do anything wrong."

"You don't know that!" I scream at him. "It could've been anything. What if the medication reacted with her heart?"

Westin moves toward me, but I lift my hand to stop him. "Then that will all come to light, but you couldn't control that. You know as well as I do that her body was already under an extreme amount of stress."

I shake my head as he speaks. He doesn't get it, there's so much more to this. "None of that matters, Westin. I did this to her. *I* did this!"

"Stop!" Westin steps closer. "Stop it, you did your best to save her."

That doesn't matter. She's dead and I have to tell him.

"Well, I guess my best just wasn't good enough. If it was my best, then I need to rethink my life because I suck."

I glance through the window at her still form, remembering the words she uttered as she went to sleep.

A single tear rolls down my cheek as my heart splinters

into a million pieces.

She loved him, and now I have to break him—again.

26

The walk to the waiting room feels like trying to escape quicksand. Each step I sink deeper into the abyss. Westin walks beside me, and I don't try to stop him, even knowing that whatever Bryce might say could be the end.

I don't even care about me anymore. Let everyone find out, and I'll go down in flames because I fucked it all up. I destroyed everything, and I killed my patient. A healthy, wonderful woman who did nothing wrong.

Westin touches my shoulder, stopping me.

I look up at him, devoid of any emotion. I feel too much and I can't possibly prepare for what will happen next.

"Can you do this?" he asks.

"She was my patient," I say. "I have to be the one to tell her husband."

"I can tell him," Westin offers.

"No, I was her surgeon, her doctor, and he deserves to hear it from me."

Westin shakes his head. "You can barely speak. You're in no state to do this."

I'm never in a good place to deliver news like this. No one wants to be the bearer of bad news, but I think of how brave Allison was. She trusted me without reservation. She knew who I was to her husband at one time, and still allowed me to be a part of her medical care. I don't know that I've ever met anyone stronger than her. Now I need to be strong too. I have to waltz through those doors and tell him the truth.

"Then maybe I shouldn't have killed my patient," I scoff.

"Fucking hell, Ren. Don't say shit like that," he grips my arms. "You didn't kill her. She could've had a heart attack or a stroke. You fixed her bleed, you tried everything you could to save her. There is no evidence that any of this is your fault. Do not walk in that room and say something like that, you know better."

There are no assurances when we operate, I know this, but it doesn't make the reality any easier to handle. I know he's worried about a lawsuit, but I'm not. I'm worried about destroying Bryce's life.

"Can we please stop?" I ask.

Westin runs his hands down his face and nods. "Fine, I'll be here with you the entire time."

I'm grateful he is. Westin is holding me up because I'm crumbling, but it's nothing compared to the break I'm about to cause.

When we get to the door, I take a deep breath, and push through. If I pause, I'll never walk forward because there's never a right time to tell a family you lost their loved one.

Bryce gets to his feet as soon as he sees me. I pull my cap off and move toward him. His gaze moves to Westin, back to me, and I watch the hope and happiness drain from his face.

I stand in front of him, and I can't speak. Words fail me as

I see him start to break. My chest grows tight and my limbs become ice cold. I have to say something, I know I do, but there's nothing to say to help him. Bryce shakes his head as tears start to form, and he looks to me to stop them, but I can't. He knows, and instead of me saying the words, I just freeze.

"Mr. Peyton," Westin starts. "There was a complication during the surgery . . ."

"No, no, no," Bryce chants and then sinks to the ground. "Please, no."

The look in his eyes tears me in two. He's desperate for me to refute the words Westin spoke.

"Every effort was made," Westin says, but Bryce's cry stops him.

"No! Not her! God, no."

The agony in his voice breaks me in two. "Her heart," I croak. "I was able to stop the bleed, but as we were finishing," my voice is filled with remorse, and I pray he hears it. "When we . . . she suffered what we believe was a heart attack. I'm so sorry."

"No," he says again. "Ren, tell me this isn't true. Please. Please tell me she's okay."

I squat, wishing more than anything it was a lie. My lip trembles and I hold onto the very last shred of strength I have, knowing that if I break down, I won't get back up. "I wish I could. I'm sorry. I tried everything. I wouldn't give up, but I couldn't bring her back. I'm so, so sorry."

"Mr. Peyton." Westin crouches down and helps him into the chair. "We're very sorry for your loss."

We both flank him in the chairs as he starts to cry.

"Is there anyone we can call?" Westin asks.

He shakes his head, wipes his nose, and gets to his feet.

"No, I think you've done enough."

Both Wes and I stand as Bryce marches out the door without another word.

I've broken him.

Westin places his hand on my back and guides me back to the locker room. I sit on the bench, staring at the floor, wondering how my day went so out of control. Another part of me worries what will happen now.

The idea of my career being over was sort of a possibility, but now it's not so abstract. There will be an autopsy, I'll go before the board, and there's the possibility of a lawsuit.

Fuck.

I'm completely screwed. If they look into this, they'll find the switch. How could I be so stupid?

Another tear falls and I turn my head to hide it.

"You should go get cleaned up and go home," Westin says after a few seconds pass.

"No," I refute.

"I'm not asking you. I'm telling you to go home, don't talk to anyone, and I'll be there when I can."

I look up at Westin and there's an edge to his words that cause a shiver to run up my spine. "Wes?"

"Listen to me on this," he says as he sits beside me. "You're a mess and you can't see patients, but you also need to get your head straight before you talk to anyone, understand?"

Always protecting me.

"I need to follow protocol," I sigh.

"No, you need to do as I say." Westin touches my knee.

I glance at him through wet eyelashes. "How do I get through this?"

He pulls me into his arms, kisses the top of my head, and

squeezes. "With time, you'll see that you didn't do anything wrong. Sometimes people die and sometimes we can prevent it, but you tried. I'll come to your place later, okay? I need to check in on another patient before I can leave."

It feels like I'm crying, but there are no tears, just shame. I can sit here and let people see me fall apart or I can go home and hate myself there. I need to listen to Westin. When his trial went to hell, it was the whispers of the staff that were the worst. People gossiping about the doctor who'd lost his mind. I don't need that. He's right to force me to leave.

"Okay," I finally agree.

Westin helps me get ready like a father dressing a child. He holds my coat out, pushing my arms through the holes, and then zips it closed.

His lips part as though he's going to say something, but whatever he sees in my eyes stops him.

He holds my hand as we walk through the halls toward the hospital entrance. Just a few hours ago, I stood in this same spot, ready to be epic. I wasn't epic, though. Unless you count epic failure.

"I'll see you soon?" I ask.

"Yeah," he kisses my lips and then walks away.

The warmth I was feeling is gone and dread fills me. Does he think I'm a failure too? Or worse?

I walk the few blocks to my house, open the door, and sink to the floor. My head rests on the cool wood floors and I cry. I cry for all the hell I've endured and caused the last few weeks. I let my sobs out and fall apart, because what else can I do?

A loud bang on the door startles me awake. Disoriented, I push myself up. I look around, trying to see what time it is.

The knock comes again and I get to my feet, hoping it's Westin.

When I open it, I stumble back.

"Bryce?"

He looks as bad as I probably do. His eyes are red rimmed, hair disheveled, and I can smell the alcohol on his breath.

"I didn't know where else to go," he confesses.

"How did you find me?"

His eyes are haunted. "I followed you one day, I wanted to talk, and then I thought better of it. I didn't want to cross that line and make Allison think . . . but . . . I guess that doesn't matter now, does it? I'm alone. Where do I go, Chick? What do I do now?"

My stomach drops and I don't know the right thing to do. Should I offer him comfort or send him away? Then I remember I killed his wife, and the least I can do is listen to him.

"Do you want to come in?"

He nods.

We walk into my living room and he sits on the couch, head in his hands. "I don't know what to do now. I don't understand."

I move in front of him, and sit on the coffee table. "I don't know what to tell you. There's nothing I can say to make this better."

His head jerks up. "I lost her. She was taken from me."

The accusation in his voice is louder than the words spoken. He means to say, *you took her from me.*

"She was," I agree.

"You don't know what we were like. You don't know how

perfect she is . . . was. Fuck, she was. She's isn't anything any-more. I need to know what happened in there."

I close my eyes in sadness. "It doesn't matter."

He gets to his feet. "I need answers, Ren. You're the only one that has them."

Apologizing isn't going to bring her back, and I remember when my mother died, I wanted to punch everyone who said it. Things like 'they're in a better place,' or 'at least she's not suf-fering anymore' don't make the person in agonizing grief feel any solace in their loss. Those words only comfort the speaker, and I won't do that to him.

The best thing I can do is let him know something real about her final moments.

"You should sit down," I tell him and he listens.

We sit here, and I recount the surgery in a clinical way. As each moment, decision, and adjustment I made come back to me. I relay them, hoping he'll see how hard I tried. He lis-tens with tears streaming down his face when I get to the part where her heart rate dropped. I work hard to keep myself to-gether and just give him the facts.

When I'm finished, we both sit here in silence, letting it fall around us as soundless tears fall from my eyes. Bryce's hand touches mine, and I rest my head on his shoulder. I'm grieving the loss of Allison Brown, not just my patient, but a beautiful woman who, even though the circumstances brought us together in the most bizarre way, I am sad to have lost. She was graceful, kind, and in the short time I knew her, learned more about me than many patients do in years.

I lift my head and give him something I hadn't planned on, but think he should know. "She knew," I tell him.

"Knew what?"

I pull my hand back. "About us. About who I am and what we were."

He jerks upright. "No, she didn't."

"Yeah, she did, Bryce. She knew from the day she walked into that hospital."

"She never said a word."

"That doesn't mean it isn't true. Right before we put her under, she told me. She said she was curious about me, found the trial, and came. She told me about her love for you as opposed to what we shared and," I start to cry again. "She said, 'until my last breath.'"

He moves toward me, gripping my arms and shaking me. "Don't lie to me."

The tears fall and I push away. "I'm not lying. She said that if something happened to her . . ." I don't know how to finish it. I have no idea what she really wanted me to do.

Did she want me to look out for him? Love him? Marry him? None of these questions were supposed to need answers.

"To do what?" he asks as he gets to his feet.

"I don't know, I really don't."

Bryce's chest puffs in and out as he struggles for breath. "I'm so lost, Chick."

"I can't imagine," I say as I stand before him.

"I thought losing you was the worst pain I'd ever been in." He laughs once. "I had no idea."

I'm the one who has inflicted this on him—twice. "I never wanted to hurt you."

He looks down at me with tears in his blue eyes. "I know that."

"Do you?"

He nods.

"I'm so sorry," I tell him.

Bryce starts to break down and I pull him into my arms. He's someone I once cared very deeply about and it hurts me to see him like this. I think about how I felt when my mother passed, and I had family to lean on, but he has no one here but me.

He pulls back, his eyes glistening, and then he leans in, pressing his lips to mine. He grips my face, holding me to him, kissing me hard, and I completely freeze.

What is he doing? I know he's grieving, but he can't kiss me.

I push against his chest, my fingers rest against my lips, and I take a step back.

We both look at each other.

"Fuck!" He grips his hair, pulling, and begins to lose it. "I just . . . I wasn't thinking. It wasn't like . . . I just . . ."

He doesn't know what to think or feel. He doesn't have to explain it, I understand. He's desperate for something to make it hurt less, but that doesn't exist. I tried for years to find something to replace him, thinking if I could just find a substitute, the pain would end. Once I realized there was no such thing, I decided to never feel again. Both choices were dumb, but when your heart and soul are being torn apart, you don't give a shit.

"You're in pain, Bryce. You're hurting and lost," I tell him. I take a step closer, but he retreats. "You should go home, get some rest, and grieve."

He looks at me, another tear falls. "I will never be the same again," he says.

I shake my head. "No, you won't, and neither will I."

27

I walk back into the bathroom and turn on the shower. Maybe I can scrub myself clean and not feel like this. I step into the scalding water and wait for it to wash away my pain. I watch the water swirl down the drain, thinking that's exactly what my life is doing, funneling downward.

All I wanted was to make things better, but I ended up fucking everything up.

I sit on the ground, curled up in a ball, and let the water wash over me, drowning out my tears. After the water starts to turn cold, I climb out, and wrap my robe around me.

How did I get here?

At what point did my life go so far off the rails that this is who I am now? For so long I've blamed it on losing my mother, but now I wonder.

The girl in the mirror doesn't even look like me. My eyes are red, puffy, and dull. I was once vibrant, happy, and ready to tackle the world.

Maybe tomorrow I'll feel human again, because right now, I'm dead inside.

I step into my room, and Westin sits on the bed.

Relief floods me that he's here. He always comforts me and gives me hope, and if there's anyone that can reach me, it's him. "Wes," I breathe. I head toward him, but he gets to his feet and shifts away from me. "What's wrong?"

"Do you think I'm a fool?" he asks softly.

"What?"

"Maybe you think I'm willing to look the other way," he mutters. "Maybe you just hope that I'm so in love with you I don't know what you're doing."

Oh, God. He's figured out that I know Bryce. I don't know how this is going to go, but maybe if I can explain it, he'll understand. We're both doctors who want to help others. Plus, we're in a great place so maybe we can weather this storm.

"I'm not doing anything," I say.

"No? Let's stop pretending now. I didn't want to know, but now, there's no denying it."

"It's not what you think," I say quickly. "We just—"

He holds up a file in his hand and slaps it on the bed, causing me to jump. "Why were you in the shower then, huh? Were you cleaning yourself after you fucked him, thinking I wouldn't know?"

I jerk back, confused. He thinks I just had sex with someone? "What? I took a shower to try to feel anything other than numb. I wasn't with anyone."

"I saw him!" he yells. "I saw him leaving fifteen minutes ago! Don't play stupid. I watched another man walk out of your front door. The same man who we just told that his wife died. The same man that was at the bar. What the hell do you take me for?"

"I'm not playing at anything. It's nothing sexual at all. He was here because he was lost. He didn't know who else to talk to, Westin, please!" I try to explain. "Nothing happened!"

"A patient's husband happened to know where you live?" He shakes his head.

"We knew each other years ago, but listen to me," I grab his hand. "Nothing happened."

I'm not going to tell him about the kiss because it's irrelevant. That wasn't Bryce kissing me because he loves me, it was him searching for comfort. It wasn't sexual, and at this point, it's only going to make matters worse.

Westin's eyes narrow and he pulls his hand back. "I thought we were on the same page. I thought we were building a life together. I fucking love you and you do this!"

"We are! We are building a life. It's you I want. It's you I choose, Westin! It's you I love!"

He scoffs and moves around the room. "You don't know what love is!"

"Don't," I beg. "Please don't."

Don't leave.

Don't say that.

Don't give up on me.

"Fuck this. You want to screw your life up, fine." Westin jerks the drawer open and removes his things. My chest is aching with each item he removes. "I'm not going to let you take me down with you. I tried for years and I thought you were changing."

"What are you doing? You're leaving?" I start to panic. "Please, believe me, I didn't do anything like that. He just lost his wife and he's alone."

"You're fucking your dead patient's husband!" he screams at me.

He has it all wrong.

"I never slept with anyone! Stop!" I grab the shirt from his hand to stop him, but he rips it from my grasp. "Westin!"

"No, I can't believe you. I came here thinking there had to be a mistake because the Serenity I'm in love with wouldn't do something so fucking stupid, she wouldn't, but then it was all there, right in my face, but I wouldn't believe it."

My head is spinning, trying to figure out what led him to assume I slept with anyone. "You're not making sense!"

"Look at the fucking file." He rolls his eyes.

I move over there, and it clicks. Allison Brown's file sits on my bed. He put the pieces together, but they're the wrong ones if he's concluded that I cheated on him. I did something worse.

"I didn't sleep with anyone." I move in front of him. "Stop, damn it!" He tries to shift around me, but I can't lose him too. I can't handle it. I need him. "Please, just talk to me, please let me explain!"

"Explain?" he rages. "Explain what? That you have some kind of relationship with your patient's husband! The same patient that died in your surgery? Not to mention, whatever the hell you did to the medications. I haven't figured that part out, but I *will*. You know . . ." His jaw is tight and hands shake. "I thought something was up, but I was trusting. Then, when he called you Ren, I knew it. The way he looked at you, the way you were so broken. Was I just some game to you?"

I stand in front of him, his hot breath blows on my face, and I start to cry again. How many more tears do I have inside of me? "No! God, no."

"You used me to cover up whatever it was that was happening, didn't you?"

"Westin, please," I sob. "Stop. It's not like that. I dated Bryce when I was in college, but I haven't done anything inappropriate with him. I hadn't even seen him until he showed up at the hospital with his wife."

"Do you know how much I wish that were true?" There is defeat laced in each word. "But coupled with the damning evidence that is in that file, I don't believe a word that you're saying."

Even if that's the case, I'm not stopping now. If he wants to crucify me then it's going to be for the real crime. I never betrayed him. I'll lose him tonight, but at least he'll know it all and if he walks away, I won't blame him.

"There was nothing between him and me. Yes, I was in love with him for a long time. His wife was selected for my trial, and I tried to walk away. I knew that it was a mistake to treat her, but he begged me to help her. So, against my better judgment, I decided to keep her on," I sniff and wipe my tears. "If I hadn't, the trial would've been stopped because I lost that first patient."

He shakes his head. "I don't want to hear any more of this."

I push against his chest, my heart racing, desperate to get the rest out. "Bryce figured out that Allison was given the placebo. He saw it in my eyes or something. The day you saw us outside the bar, he confronted me, begged me to change the medication, but I said no. I wouldn't do it because of everything it would mean." Westin looks down at me with disappointment, but I continue on. "Did you see the letter in her file?" I ask.

"The one stating her wishes about treatment?"

I nod. Good, maybe now he'll grasp the gravity of what I was facing. "Yes. That night, I got the call that Mrs. Whitley was dying and I lost her. I was out of my mind, I know this, Wes. I know I was wrong and stupid and everything else, but after that, I saw Allison. She was happy, in love, smiling, and I knew I had to give her the best medical care possible. I knew that her having the placebo wasn't giving her that care. She was going to die if I didn't . . . she would let herself die just for a chance at the life she was desperate for. When I looked at them, at Allison and her husband, I saw my father and mother cuddled up on that bed, and I snapped."

His mouth falls open and he rubs his temple. "Serenity, please tell me you didn't!"

"I went into the lab and changed the folders. I altered the paperwork and gave her the trial drug that day."

"Are you fucking insane?" he bellows. "You doctored the trial? Are you kidding me?"

I shake my head quickly, knowing how bad this is. "I wasn't thinking!"

"Clearly! Jesus Christ! You put all of us at risk! Do you realize that?"

"I know and I hate myself!" I scream at him. "I hate myself and I don't know what to do anymore, Westin!"

He continues on. "When did you do this?"

"That day," I admit.

"Weeks ago?"

"Yes."

Westin's body locks and the veins on his neck enlarge. "I'm one of the advising doctors on this. My signature is all over the paperwork," he moves his hands like he wants to grab me, but drops them. "You didn't just fuck yourself, Serenity, you fucked every doctor that touched this!"

I've never seen him like this. I've seen him angry before,

but never on the edge of losing it. "I'm sorry! I know I was wrong! Believe me, I know. I came to you that night. I begged you to let me tell you!"

He blows his breath through his nose and I can feel the anger radiating off him. "Don't you dare put this on me! You changed the medication on a clinical trial. Do you even know what this means? Do you understand you're going to lose your medical license? Do you?"

"Yes." I drop my head. "I know, and I deserve it."

"Yeah," he agrees. "You do. How could you do this?"

"I was broken, okay? I was broken, sad, and feeling like I couldn't do anything right. There was so much life in that woman's eyes and I couldn't watch it go out because of the luck of the draw. She was going to *die*! I needed to help her and it all happened so fast."

My breathing is frantic once the truth is finally out. It's all too much. I've spent years bottling things up—and those bottles have finally started to explode.

"You just, what? Walked into the lab and decided you knew best? What were you thinking? And what about the person without the medication you took from them!" he screams. "So you're okay with helping Allison, because you're in love with her husband, but not some other patient?" Westin gets in my face, his anger is palpable, and I see the hate in his eyes.

He really thinks that I would take the medication from someone else to give to another?

"I took Lindsay's drugs, she was the patient who was dismissed from the trial before it began, but her file hadn't been removed yet. I switched the numbers," I explain. "I didn't take a drug from another patient to give to her. How could you even think I would ever do that? And, I'm not in love with him," I say as a tear falls. "I love you."

There was no harm done to another to benefit Allison. To give her the chance I thought she deserved while we tossed aside the actual trial drug that no one would get.

"Oh, please, if you didn't love him, you wouldn't have done that."

"You don't have to believe me, but it's the truth!"

I'm watching him pull away with each second, taking a part of me with him. It's killing me to see him look at me this way. He always respected me at the very least, and it's clear that's gone.

Westin's head shakes and then he runs his hands down his face. "I don't even know who you are anymore."

"That makes two of us. I lost Mrs. Whitley. I lost Allison. I lost myself."

He moves closer to me as my tears fall. "And you lost me."

I try to hold it together, but I can't. A loud, agonizing sob breaks from my chest. I knew it would happen, but hearing it breaks the very last shred of control I have. He touches my cheek, watching the tears fall and then his hand drops.

Westin grabs his bag, the file, and then starts to walk away.

"This is why I didn't want to love you. This is why I kept you at a distance. I knew if I fell for you, I'd lose you."

He stops, and his shoulders slump. "I guess we both learned our lesson. I should've let you keep pushing me away." Westin turns back. "Then I wouldn't feel like I was just stabbed in the heart. No matter what happened, you betrayed me, Serenity. And for that, I'm done."

Without another word, Westin walks out the door with my heart, leaving me with nothing.

I fell in love again.

I lost him.

And this time, I may never get him back.

I pick up my phone and dial the number of the only person who will never abandon me. It rings twice, and then I croak into the phone. "Daddy, I need you."

"How long has she been like this?" I hear a soft voice, maybe Julie's, ask someone.

"It's been a day now and she won't eat, talk, or stay awake for longer than a few minutes," my father's deep gravelly voice sounds worried.

"Ren?" Julie sits beside me, pushing my hair back. "Ren, what happened?"

I turn my head to look at her, not sure if my mind is playing tricks on me, since just a few minutes ago, I swear Allison was here.

Sure enough, it's Julie.

I don't answer. There's nothing to say, so I roll back over and close my eyes. I just want to sleep. Sleep is peace, where there are no dreams. I don't feel the enormous hole in my chest or the pain of knowing I lost everything again.

"Serenity," Julie tries again.

I continue to ignore her. Westin has probably gone to the board by now. My life, my career, and the man that I love are gone. I don't feel the need to rehash it. The news will be all around the hospital by the end of the day.

"Okay, I'll come back when you're awake," I hear her sigh in resignation.

She can come back, but I'll still be like this. When I met Westin, he figured out that I wasn't whole. And piece by piece, Westin found a way to put me back together. He showed me that I was never really gone, supporting me through times when I didn't even know he was doing it. All along, he was there, but I was too stupid to see it.

For years I neglected him, and now I've really screwed up. The fact that I changed the trial drug would have changed everything if I had been able to tell him that night, but it still would've been better than this.

Now, there's no going back.

Julie and my father talk a little in the other room, far enough away that I can't make out what they're saying, but I hear their voices.

It's too much energy to focus, so I grab the shirt Westin left behind, clutch it to my chest, and drift back to sleep.

"You have to eat." My father is standing in front of me as I try to head back to my bedroom.

"I'm not hungry."

"This isn't normal, Serenity. You need to tell me what happened." He cups my face. "Please."

My father looks like he's ready to fall apart, and guilt assaults me again. Will I ever stop hurting the people I love? He came, even though I couldn't say why I needed him. He got in a car, drove to the city he hates, and has been here for three days. Daddy hasn't pushed me much, but I've basically become a shell of a person.

I can't eat. The smell of food makes me nauseous. I just lie in my bed, looking at the wall, and wallowing in my self-pity.

It's ridiculous, I know, but I have nothing.

"I fucked up, Dad. I lost everything!" Yelling at him takes energy from my already drained body, and I start to sag. "Just . . . I need to sleep."

"No, you need to start talking and go back to work." He stands in front of me with his arms crossed. "Where is Westin?"

I look away, unwilling to see whatever emotion he displays. "Gone."

"A man like him doesn't walk away willingly," he ponders. "What happened?"

No, guys like him don't, but a woman like me forced his hand. I can't do this right now. I know I'm being unreasonable, but for my entire life, I've held it together and I can't anymore.

My father stands there, waiting for an answer. "I broke his heart."

He purses his lips and nods. "And then you just gave up?"

I let out a half-laugh. "No. There's no way to change what I did."

"You cheated on him?"

"No." I shake my head. "It's not like that."

"I'm going out on a limb and going to assume it has something to do with Bryce Peyton being back in your life," he challenges.

I'd love to blame him, but it's not Bryce's fault that I lied to Westin. It's not Bryce's fault that I changed the medication.

Those were my choices.

"No, Dad. This time it wasn't because of Bryce. It was my choices that made Westin leave. I did this." I push past him and curl up on the bed.

An hour later I hear people talking again. Why the hell is everyone coming here? Who cares that I'm sad and broken? Why can't people allow me a few days of sulking?

I climb out of bed to slam the door, but the voice halts me.

"I understand, Mick, but her phone is off and she needs to come into the hospital this week," Westin's voice fills the room. "Just tell her, please."

For the first time in days, my heart starts to beat again. I grip the door handle, not wanting anyone to hear me and him leave. He came, maybe . . . maybe nothing, the hope that began to fill me deflates.

"Son, I just want to know what is going on."

Westin pauses. "It's up to her to talk to you about it."

"She won't get out of bed," Daddy tells him. "She won't talk to anyone or eat. I've never seen her like this." I hear the worry in my father's voice. "Even when her mother died, she was the strong one. I'm asking you to just talk to her."

I hear a sigh and I peek around the door to see him with his head down. "I wish I could, but I can't right now."

And the hope is gone, just as it should be.

"Do you love her?" my father questions.

"It's not about love, Mick."

My father shakes his head. "Love is all that matters. It's worth it if she's the right girl for you."

Westin closes his eyes and takes a step back. When he disappears from view, I know that he doesn't love me anymore. I've hurt him, and there's no coming back. "Just tell her she needs to come in. It's important."

"All right," Daddy resigns himself. "I'll let her know."

"Thank you, I'll talk to you soon," Westin says.

The door shuts, and I climb back into bed, feeling the loss of Westin all over again.

"That's it," Julie yells. "Get up!"

"Go to hell," I say and pull the covers up.

She rips them off and tosses cold water across my face. "What the fuck?" I scream as my bed is wet now.

"You are Serenity Adams, world-renowned gynecological oncologist. You've had your three days of self-pity, now it's time to get out of bed and grow up."

I shoot daggers at her in my head. "Grow up?"

"Yeah, grow up!"

Julie raises a brow in challenge. I don't need this shit. I'm old enough to live however the hell I want to. I'm not a child.

"You're telling me to grow up and you just threw water in my face," I spit the words.

She shrugs. "You're lying in your bed, neglecting the other patients who need you, because you lost one? That's not you. They *need* you, damn it. You need to help them! Whatever happened with you and Westin, I'm sorry, but he's not missing work, clutching your shirt in bed. Now, get in the shower." She points toward the bathroom.

Hearing her talk about my patients needing me forces me to move. When I get up, Julie's relief is all over her face.

"I'll be in the kitchen with food, once you're done being

an idiot."

I flip her off.

"If you take more than twenty minutes, I'm coming in there, so don't do anything stupid!" she says as I slam the bathroom door.

There's no denying she's right. I'm acting like a child and the idea that others are suffering because I'm upset with myself makes me even more disappointed in how I'm behaving.

As I shower, I start to think about the events and how they unraveled. We're all victims in some way. Bryce just wanted to save his wife. Westin loved me and wanted to protect me. Allison paid the ultimate price. And I was at the center of it all, thinking I had it all handled.

Well, no more.

I didn't handle it right, and that changes now.

It's time to pick myself up and do the right thing.

I get dressed with a newfound sense of purpose, and move forward to clean up the messes and face the consequences of my choices. I can't continue the way I have, and I will never be at peace with any of this if I don't stop acting like the martyr.

When I head into the kitchen, Julie and Daddy are sitting there.

"I want to talk to you both," I say as I sit.

They look at each other and then back to me. "Okay?"

As much as I want to shut down, the way my father's eyes hold tenderness breaks me. He should know the things I did to get to this point. The way I was stupid and put Westin's career, our relationship, and my integrity aside needs to be explained.

I go over the ugly details with tears streaming down my face. I don't leave anything out from start to finish, and ignore the reactions of shock, disappointment, and even a little sadness on the faces of my audience.

"Ren," Julie clears her throat. "Why didn't you talk to me?"

I shake my head. "I was protecting you. If you knew, you'd have to turn me in. We both know that and I didn't want to put you in that position."

"But, you're telling me now?"

I nod. "Yeah, because tomorrow, I'm going to talk to Dr. Pascoe. I screwed up, Jules. I know this, and I need to take responsibility for it. That's the only way I'm going to ever make amends with myself and the people who trusted me."

Julie just stares at me. "Are you sure? I mean, there's no going back."

I nod. "I'm sure. No matter what, I have to own my mistakes."

She stands and touches my shoulder. "I would've never turned you in, Ren. I don't agree, hell, I can't even pretend to understand why you did that, but I know you . . . I've known you a long time," she says and squeezes. "You're an amazing doctor, don't forget the lives you've saved."

I get to my feet and pull her in for a hug. "Thank you."

"I'm here for you." She leans back. "No matter what. I'm the girl you call to help you bury the body, remember that."

Julie has always had my back, and I've had hers. I should've gone to her, but I thought keeping my mistake from her was the right thing.

She leaves, and Daddy stands there looking at me. "You're doing the right thing."

I start to cry again, hating that I failed people, and my father gathers me in his arms. It doesn't matter how old I am, he's the man I can always count on. I soak his shirt, crying over the mistakes I've made.

"I'm so sorry if I disappointed you, Daddy."

He rubs my back as I fall apart.

"Never. You could never disappoint me."

I cry harder, thanking God that I have him in my life. When the tears ebb, he pushes my hair back and stares into my eyes. "I raised you to be a strong, independent woman who cares for others. You've devoted your entire life to make things better and you take care of everyone else. I can't pretend to understand what it's like to watch people die around you all the time. You're doing the right thing. It won't be easy, but you'll get through it."

I nod. "I'm going to lose my job," I choke on the words. "I won't have money, a place to live, and I don't know if I'll lose my license. I'm probably going to need to move back home, but I won't be able to help financially."

"Is that what you're worried about?" he asks.

"Dad, I've been sending Everton a lot of money each month," I confess.

He nods. "I know, but I've come into a bit of money myself. You don't need to worry about taking care of me."

"What do you mean, a bit of money?"

He smiles impishly and we sit at the table, where my father tells me something that leaves me completely stunned.

29

sit on the cold, dirty floor outside Westin's apartment. I spent twenty minutes debating whether or not I should go in. I have a key, but then I thought better of it. Westin and I are over, and I promised myself from this point forward, I'm going to remember who I was before I lost my damn mind. Respect and honesty are at my core, and I'm not going to breach that trust.

It's been over an hour now, but I couldn't exactly call him. So, I wait.

And wait.

I think about all the things we've shared. The first time he brought me back to his apartment, and how we laughed despite the days we had. Westin was able to transport me to a place outside my past without me even knowing it.

"What are you doing here?" his deep voice fills the hallway while he stands in front of me.

I stand, and my nerves go crazy. I'm not sure if it's a mistake that I came here, but I wanted to talk to him about my plan, and also find out what the hell is going on regarding my father.

"I came to talk to you."

He sighs. "I don't have anything to say."

"I know," I say quickly. "I don't blame you, but I'd like it if you could just listen. I'd appreciate it. Just a few minutes, Wes, that's all I'm asking for."

My heart races as he stares me down. I plead with my eyes and then I see the answer I was hoping for in his. He's going to give me a chance—reluctantly, but it's something.

Westin unlocks the door and holds it open for me. It's only been a few days since I've seen him, but he looks different. His eyes are tired and his facial hair has grown out more. I try not to focus on how good it is to see him and how much it's killing me to stay away, but I need to focus.

"So?" Westin pushes.

"Right. Sorry." I release a deep breath. "My father said that you came by, and . . ."

"I didn't turn you in," he says quickly. "If you're here to beg, save it, I haven't and I'm not sure if I can. I guess that's the funny thing about loving someone. It doesn't go away that easily."

Well, that's unexpected. I wasn't sure if he would. Honestly, I don't know why he didn't, but that's neither here nor there. "I'm planning to confess everything," I tell him.

"You're what?"

"I'm going to admit to what I've done, and face whatever comes." He opens his mouth, but I keep going before a word can be said. If I don't get this out now, I have no idea if I'll be able to later. "I did this on my own, and I won't let you or anyone else have any disciplinary action brought against them. More than that, it's the right thing to do, and it's what I should've done from the beginning," I sigh. "It's what I would've done a month ago. No, that's not even true, I wouldn't have done it."

"Ren," he starts.

Westin was absolutely right when he said he didn't know who I was, because I'm not that person. "No, please don't say anything, just listen," I say and continue before he can answer. "I lost myself when Mrs. Whitley died. I don't know what it was, but I felt as though I'd lost my mother all over again. It broke me in a very real way. My life spun so far out of control and I couldn't right the car, no matter how hard I tried. I did try to tell you, so many times, but then you asked me to stop and so I thought maybe I should protect you instead."

"I had no idea that's what it was. I thought," he runs his hand down his face. "I don't fucking know, but not that you altered the trial."

"I know. But I did, and I'm going to have to pay the price."

"You're sure?" Westin asks.

"Yes. I'm sure. I can't live with this and I can't ask you to lie, either. Not for me, not when it's not who you are. You're a good doctor who cares, and who prides himself on integrity, Westin, and I won't make you someone else. That's not fair. That's not what love means."

I stop talking, trying to get my heart to settle, but it's beating so loud I worry I'll pass out. Being open and honest isn't my thing. I've spent so many years mastering being closed off that being vulnerable is terrifying. However, this may be the last time I ever talk to Westin like this and I won't waste it. He needs to know how I feel, and how sorry I am for hurting him.

"The thing is, Wes." I take a step closer. "I fell in love with you at the same time my entire life imploded. You don't have to believe me, and I don't blame you, but I do love you," my voice cracks.

I turn around quickly so he doesn't see the tears that form in my eyes. I promised myself I wouldn't cry. I've done enough of that and it's time to put the pieces back together.

"I know you think what I did is because of Bryce," I continue on. "A long time ago I would've done anything for him, but me changing the medications was about me. For years, I've been closed off to feeling, I thought it made me a better doctor. If I didn't love, then loss wouldn't break me, and that bled into our relationship." I look back at him. "If I felt nothing but friendship, when you left, I wouldn't fall apart. I was starting to let my walls down with you, and then Bryce came back, sending them to the ground."

"Ren," he tries to stop me.

"It wasn't about him, it was about fourteen years of grief, anger, resentment, and loss, all coming to the forefront at once. I never dealt with my mother's death, I just took care of people, fixing them because it was the only thing I could do. There's no excuse. It was so wrong, stupid, and what I'm the sorriest for," I step closer to him, needing him to hear me, "is that I lost you in the process. My entire life I've run away when things hurt too much. I didn't want to feel love because losing it was worse, but you got to me. I saw that we had this beautiful relationship that meant more to me than I could ever imagine. You found a way so deep into my heart, and even though it hurts like hell now that you're gone, I don't regret loving you."

Westin shakes his head and rubs his eyes. "I don't know what you want from me."

"Nothing," I say without hesitation. "I don't want or expect anything. I came here so that when I go in there tomorrow, you'll know what is happening. I don't want you to be blind-sided—again. You loved me once, and I hope that some-day, you find someone worthy of all you have to give."

All I want is for him to love me, but I had that and threw it away.

"So you're going to walk through that door tomorrow and ruin your career?" he asks.

"No," I correct him. "I'm going to make this right."

He comes closer to me, almost like he can't stop himself, and my heart races. He had a surgery today, I can smell his cologne mixed with sweat and soap. So many nights we'd stand just like this and the pull I felt then is still here now.

His eyes are trained on me, and I can't breathe. I can see the conflict swirl, but I've known Westin long enough that this is unforgivable to him, and what he's fighting himself over won't end in my favor.

I take a few steps back, breaking the connection before either of us gets hurt. The tightness in my chest starts to ease the farther I get from him.

"I have one question," I push the words out.

"Which is?" his voice is thick with emotion.

"You bought my farmhouse?"

Westin looks down at the floor and then back to me. "It was between your father and me."

That's great, but now I know. "Okay, but why? Why would you buy my house? Why would you and my father have some kind of agreement without me knowing?"

"Want a drink?" he asks.

I'll do anything if it means he'll talk to me. "Sure."

He heads toward the kitchen and grabs a beer. The same beer that is sitting in my fridge that will go untouched. Westin pours me a glass of wine that he keeps—kept—here for when

I'd spend the night, and hands me the glass.

We both stand at the island in silence, taking small sips of our drinks.

I wonder if he notices the puffiness in my eyes or the red splotches that stay on my face for days after I've cried like this. Does he see the pain I'm in, the way I see how this is wearing on him? Westin may not have spent days in bed, but the bags under his eyes tell me he's not sleeping, and the dishes in the sink are completely out of character.

After another minute, he finally begins.

"The day we went to visit your dad, we went out to the garage. He told me about a lot of things, your brother's gambling debt, how your mother had some outstanding medical bills, and that he was having money problems."

My stomach drops. Everton was gambling the money? I'm going to kill him if I find him. God, I've been taking care of nothing all this time.

"I didn't know."

"He was going to lose the farm if he couldn't get his taxes current. He didn't know how much money I have, so it was just a man asking how to shield the daughter he loves from the pain of losing her childhood home. I can't imagine it was easy for him, but he knew I loved you and would be there for you."

I close my eyes with a low sigh. I had no idea. My brother was getting over two thousand dollars a month from me, which was more than enough to pay the taxes. "Why didn't you tell me?" I ask.

"Because you already worry about everyone else so damn much, I wanted to take something off your plate. It's what you do when you love someone, you ease their burdens, or try to at least," Westin explains and I crumble.

He watches me as he drains his beer. I thought I was angry at myself before, but it's nothing compared to now. I lost the best man I've ever known. "Westin," I say his name as a plea. I want to say so much.

"Anyway," he says as he places the beer down. "I talked to him about his options, and then I told him I would help. He fought me, he's a very proud man, but I bought the farm, asked him to stay on and care for it."

"Care for it?"

Westin nods. "I don't want your family's farm. I wanted to help Mick. So we drew up a very clear contract stating that he lives on the farm for free until he chooses not to, and then you take over the agreement. At any point, you can buy me out, but the farm stays in your family until the sixty-year lease is up."

"I . . . how?" I say, words failing me.

"It doesn't matter, but I won't go back on that, no matter what we are or aren't anymore. You don't have to worry about your father or the land."

That's the craziest part, I wasn't worried he'd ever do that to my family. Westin isn't vindictive or cruel. He wouldn't throw my father out because he could. No, this is the guy who learns to flash mob for a kid, buys family farms, and loses his mind when he loses a patient.

Only when Westin lost his mind, he didn't make ethical, medical, and legal violations. That's just my thing.

"I never thought you would, Wes."

He spins the bottle on the counter. "I can't seem to hurt you, even though I want to. I just can't do it."

There's a mix of anger and resentment, but underlying all that, there is still love. "You have every right to hate me."

"If I could, it would make things easier."

"I should go," I say.

A sadness washes around us and I garner the self-restraint I have to hold it together. I want to fall into his arms, beg him to love me and forgive me, but I won't. He deserves a chance to be happy, and I've done enough damage.

"Tomorrow is the review board, I told your father. You have to go over Allison's case file, so I'll be there."

I nod. "Well, you'll get to see it firsthand then." I push the wine glass to the center of the island.

I can't help it, I need to say goodbye to him. I move around the counter so there's nothing between us, waiting to see if he'll push me away, but he doesn't.

When I'm close enough, I lift up on my toes, take his face in my hands, and press my lips to his. It's a sweet kiss filled with everything I have. I want him to know I love him, I'm sorry, I'm in pain, and I would do anything for him, but most of all, it's goodbye.

I release him, drop back down, and the tear I fought back falls down my face.

"I will love you, until my last breath," I say and then rush out of the apartment.

I stand outside the hospital, staring up just like I did the day before my trial started, only this time, I'm filled with dread. This will be the last time I enter those doors as a doctor. There's no way I won't be fired.

"Hey," Julie says as she comes up next to me. "You okay?"

"No," I reply honestly. "But I will be."

She takes my hand in hers. "Yeah, you will. You have a lot of people who love you."

"Are you one of them?"

Julie squeezes. "Of course I am. I know you're hurting and I can't imagine what having Bryce back around was like, either. He was the one that got away, and we all have one. They have this innate ability to screw with our heads and make us do incredibly stupid things. Welcome to the club."

I smile and rest my head on her shoulder. "I told Westin last night."

"Yeah? How did that go?"

"I kissed him, started crying, and ran out." I shrug.

"So, it went great?" she laughs.

"I wish you would've kicked my ass earlier when it came to him," I tell her. "I could've known I loved him a lot longer and cherished it."

Julie wraps her arm around my shoulder. "Isn't that the way life is? We don't know what we have until it's gone."

It's the truth. So many things I've taken for granted, expecting they'd always be there, but nothing is guaranteed, and I knew better than to think Westin was permanent in any way. Julie walks with me down the halls and toward the boardroom. We talk a little about Westin buying my farm, which still blows my mind.

"Well, my train stops here," she says as we come to the fork. I have to go right and face the music. "I'll come by after work, okay?"

"Okay," my voice trembles.

My God, I'm going to do this. All the years that I've built my career—they're all going to come down to this moment where it disappears. I won't be the doctor who has saved countless lives, I'm going to be the disgraced woman who doctored a trial.

It doesn't matter, though. This is the right thing and it's the only way to make sure no one I love gets hurt.

I take a few deep breaths, standing outside the boardroom where I've sat on the other side, listening to doctors go over each step, rolling my eyes at the choices they made at the time.

Now, it's my turn.

I push my nerves down, square my shoulders, and march in.

"Dr. Adams, please take a seat," Dr. Pascoe instructs.

"I'd rather stand, if that's okay."

No point in delaying this. I scan the room, where some of the colleagues I respect are staring at me. I give them small smiles back, nods, and other forms of acknowledgement, looking for the one who matters most.

Westin isn't here though.

I keep scanning and gasp when I see Bryce sitting there. He looks at me with sad eyes, and then gazes back down to his feet.

"Mr. Peyton asked to be here for the reading of the autopsy. He was adamant that he have the opportunity to speak, and so we'll change things up," Dr. Pascoe begins.

My eyes shoot to Bryce because that's never the order in which we've done it, but I'd like to hear what he has to say, for my own sanity.

Dr. Pascoe clears his throat. "Once I read this, Mr. Peyton has agreed to let the review board meet without him, so, let's begin with the autopsy."

The slide shows up on the screen and it's all there. "The official cause of death is a pulmonary embolism. The embolus was seen in the left main pulmonary artery with extension into the lower lobe," he explains. "The autopsy reports that her iron was low, but the surgery was not the cause of death."

There's a swell of relief inside me, but even as it floods through me, it ebbs back out because Allison is still dead.

Bryce clears his throat and gets to his feet. "I'd like to speak on be—"

The door opens and Westin comes in with his hand up. "Sorry, had a difficult case."

I fight back the urge to fall to the floor. They're both here, and both can destroy me in so many ways.

"Please continue, Mr. Peyton." Dr. Pascoe looks unamused.

"I'd like to speak on behalf of Dr. Adams. She treated my wife with humility, respect, and became a friend to her. Upon Allison's death, I found a letter that was addressed to me, as well as one for Se—Dr. Adams. I'd like to read it, if that's okay?"

I can't handle this. My throat is dry and now I wish I had sat down.

"Dr. Adams, if you're reading this, well, I died. I hope you know that your friendship, no matter how short it was, meant everything to me. You were warm, kind, and caring through a difficult time in my life. It's the reason I was willing to fight. I want you to know that it's doctors like you that give people like me hope, and whether we make it or not, it's what carries us through our darkest days.

"I know that I placed a great burden on you in asking you to keep my secret, but it was what I truly felt was right. If I couldn't have a baby, I didn't want the cancer to rob me of anything else, even if it meant I would die. I was desperate, sad, and on the borderline of giving up, until your trial was offered. Then, suddenly, there was a glimmer of possibility again. I was faced with the renewed hope that this could give me the chance to have the life I desired.

"I know that my family won't understand the risk I took. The only thing that gives me peace is that I was given the chance that soon, hopefully, every woman will be afforded. Those slivers of hope reminded me that sometimes, the smallest things can make the greatest difference for someone else. Because of you, I found a man who made my days full of laughter and smiles. Thank you."

Even in her death, she's a bright ray of sunshine in a dreary place.

Bryce puts the paper down and then looks to me. "I'm leaving to head back to North Carolina in a bit, but I wanted to read that to you all, especially you, Dr. Adams. Thank you for giving her peace when she was battling something that was far deeper than cancer."

I smile at him softly, knowing that this is the end of the road for us. There's nothing left to say and we both know we're not the people we once were. Our love may have been all-consuming once, but we had our chance and lost it. "Thank you. I appreciate you reading that."

"Goodbye, Dr. Adams."

"Goodbye, Mr. Peyton."

He looks to the group, his eyes staying on Westin for a beat longer, and then he folds the letter up, and walks out of the room.

The closure we probably both needed has come, and now it's time to set things right.

"Let's go over the surgery," Dr. Pascoe says as the door closes.

"First," I cut him off. "I'd like to talk."

"Dr. Adams—"

"Please," I say.

If I were any other doctor, he probably would argue, but like Bryce, Dr. Pascoe knows what it's like to watch a spouse suffer. I'm sure hearing that has broken him a tiny bit, since it could've been him sitting in that chair.

I look around the room, my eyes landing on Westin, and I begin as if it were just him and me in the room.

"There is a problem with the medication that Allison Brown received," I admit the truth, and there's no going back now.

30

"**W**hat do you mean a problem?" Dr. Pascoe asks.

I steel myself for the disappointment that will shine in his eyes. Dr. Pascoe has supported me, believed in me, and been a mentor. I'm going to prove that he was wrong in all of that. I've spent the last twelve hours playing this out. All of the endings are the same, and none of them are good.

"If you look at her file," I start, but Westin stands, stopping me from speaking.

"Dr. Adams," he clears his throat. "Sorry to interrupt and I don't like doing this to a fellow doctor, but I feel like I have to speak up. There is, in fact, a problem with Allison Brown's file. I was going over it last night, to prepare for the line of questioning today, and I noticed there was a very important piece of paper missing."

I look at him, wondering what the hell he's doing. There's no paper missing. "I'm sorry? I don't understand . . ."

He looks around the room, taps his fingers on the table, and then starts speaking again. "I wanted to see where the sign-offs were regarding the trial drugs and then compare them with the toxicology report," Westin says.

He's going to take me down himself. The very last shred of hope I had regarding us is gone. I guess he needs to be the one to bring it to light to prove that he had nothing to do with it. I watch him walk toward the front, where I stand, and begin to shake.

"Is this your signature?" he asks.

I take the paper from him, holding back any outward show of emotion. After spending years pretending not to feel, you'd think this would be easier, but it's not. Having someone I love be the one to drive the knife through my heart hurts more than I could've imagined.

I look over the paperwork I forged, changing the number on the folder. "Yes," I agree. "That's mine."

He takes the paper back and nods. "Right. I got curious as to the line that was crossed off. And then I noticed that the next thing signed by Dr. Adams was the daily sheet which verified each coordinating number with the vial given." Westin holds the paper for everyone to see.

"Correct, and that's—" I begin.

He keeps going, cutting me off again. "That's when I noticed that the correction form was missing."

"Yes," I sigh.

There's no point, he's out for blood and I'm hemorrhaging right now. Might as well let him save himself. It's all going to come out eventually.

"Now, I conferred with Dr. Ney and she said she didn't sign off on anything. The same with Dr. Wells and the other advisors."

Of course, no one signed off because I fucking did it myself. He knows this. He's just digging the damn hole deeper and then covering me with the soil. Westin stops, looks at me with a disappointed look, and I want to stab him with a pencil.

"I'm aware of this," my voice is so detached it doesn't sound like me.

"I wasn't sure why this would be missing from a trial run by a doctor who has impeccable organizational skills. So, I started digging further," Westin continues. "I looked into the other trial patients as well, wondering how many more errors I might find. I was looking for files that were missing the other advisor's signature or mine. It wasn't until I opened Lindsay Dunphy's file, the patient who was dismissed the day the trial began, that I found the unsigned document," he gives me a pointed stare.

What is he doing? He's lying because there is no paper that was in a file. I look at him, begging him to stop this before there's no way out, not wanting to let him get even more tangled in this mess.

Westin continues. "You see, Dr. Adams made a clerical error. The document would've been signed had it not have been placed in the wrong patient file. Which is why it's unsigned," he says while looking around the room. "While I know following procedure is a priority here, I'm sure we wouldn't want to crucify a doctor who has always given her patients the best medical care possible over a lost paper. More than that, punishing Dr. Adams would be a great disservice to the patients she's saved and could save."

"Dr. Grant," I interrupt.

His eyes meet mine and I can't breathe. "There are things that we do that are forgivable when it's in the best interest of the patient, Dr. Adams. Things that are foolish, but come from a place of caring. That day, you'd suffered the loss of a patient, along with a lot of other things that clearly led to you being out of sorts."

Every muscle locks, and I don't want to think he's found some way to forgive me because if he's just covering his ass, it'll decimate me. But Westin is standing in front of the room, commanding it, and eliminating any chance of me telling the truth now. If I do, it'll make him look like a fool and a liar.

I had a plan. I was going to do this the right way, and maybe a small part of me hoped that Westin would see that and find a way to at least not hate me. Now I don't know what to do, but my judgment hasn't been the best in the last few weeks, so I stay quiet.

I'll follow his lead and hope he's not leading me into the fire.

Dr. Pascoe clears his throat. "So the paper was filled out, but put in the wrong file, which resulted in it not being signed by the auditing and advising doctors?"

"It appears that it was," I say, corroborating Westin's story.

"Well," he sighs.

"Since the medication wasn't the cause of Allison Brown's death, Dr. Adams clearly wasn't at fault. We've read and reviewed the reports along with the surgical notes. Dr. Adams handled things exactly as she should've, so I don't believe that the review board should take any drastic measures."

Dr. Ney speaks now. "I agree, this was clearly an oversight of a very prestigious doctor." She gives me a sad smile.

I feel worse than I did thinking I'd lose my job. Westin put his entire career on the line and lied on my behalf. He covered for me when he never should have.

Dr. Pascoe looks around. "But still, we can't allow doctors

not to have major forms signed. If the FDA or NIH were to look at this, the hospital would face serious repercussions. We could lose our research hospital status, making it difficult to run further trials."

Westin still doesn't look at me, but he nods slowly, seeming to process what he says. "I would suggest a probationary period of three months, a two-week suspension, and a formal reprimand," Westin suggests. "It's a message that these things can't happen, but we also understand it wasn't malicious."

Basically, a slap on the wrist, but it will go on my record. I came in here ready to lose my job and no longer practice medicine, and instead, he's talking about a much more lenient punishment.

The question remains, why would he defend me? After we spoke, it was clear he couldn't forgive me, so why now?

"I would agree," Dr. Pascoe says. "Does the board have any further questions?"

Everyone's head shakes and then they start to get out of their seats.

In all of my imagined versions of how this would go, never in a million years was this it. I could never have hoped I would still be a doctor here or that Westin would defend me. I'm not sure how to process it.

A part of me wanted to be punished. Punished much more severely than the consequences I'm looking at now.

The guilt was all-consuming, and now there's a new wave of it.

I stand here, as they file out. Dr. Pascoe walks over. He smiles, touches my shoulder, and squeezes. "This hospital needs you. I think maybe you should take a few weeks and allow Dr. Ney to work on the trial in your absence, okay?"

I've never known him to advise doctors to take time off. "Okay?"

His hand drops and he sighs. "When my top doctor needs to take days off after a patient loss, it's something deeper. Take the time, Serenity. Recharge and then come back to work. The two weeks wasn't because of the patient, but for you."

Westin walks over and shakes Dr. Pascoe's hand. "I'll be by your office in a few minutes. I just need to handle something," he explains.

They share a look and Dr. Pascoe nods and leaves.

"Hi," Wes says after the room is cleared.

I don't want to exchange pleasantries. I want to know what the hell is wrong with him. "Why?" is all I'm able to get out.

He moves in front of me, resting against the table. "I'm not a hundred percent sure I know why. When you started to go down that route, I couldn't let you. Everything inside of me was screaming to stop you."

"It wasn't supposed to happen that way."

"Which is why it didn't," he says.

Westin is no longer the controlled man from the boardroom. I can see that he's grappling with what just happened.

"I wish you hadn't." I look down at the floor. "I was willing to take the fall and deal with the choice I made."

His finger tucks under my chin and he lifts it so we're eye to eye. "I couldn't watch you destroy yourself any more than you already have. Her death wasn't caused by you changing the medications. Her heart was weak, and she died. It was tragic, but you're not a bad person, Serenity. You just did a dumb thing. If you didn't think there was anything wrong with it, that would be one thing, but you know you fucked up, and you were going to lose it all to save your colleagues."

I step back and shake my head. "No, I was just making sure I paid for what I did."

"Let someone else save you for once." He moves closer.

My eyes meet his with my heart racing. "You can't say things like that," I warn him.

"Why not?"

For so many reasons. My emotions are all over the place and I can't seem to stop myself from saying them. Westin is—was—my safe place. He's the person I wanted to be able to say anything to, and now it comes out too easily.

"Because you don't love me. Because people don't save me, it's never been that way. Because it will make getting over you harder."

Westin's eyes close and he runs his hands through his hair. "I'm telling you to let someone take care of you, love you, and protect you for a change."

"And are you going to be that person, Wes?"

We both know he won't. He made it clear that we're done, and I don't blame him. He did what he did to save me, but on a strictly professional level.

He moves another step closer, and I tilt my head to look into his eyes, needing to see confirmation that he means what he says. "If you'll let me, I want to be."

"But," I start to say and move away. I can't think like this and all I want to do is believe this is real, but I'm afraid. "You said all those things, but how can you possibly feel that way? I screwed up so bad, I hurt you, lied to you, and now you, what, forgive me?"

I don't know why I'm trying to talk him out of this, but I don't want to feel this way ever again. Loving Westin was a leap I wasn't entirely prepared for and then to fall without a net damn near broke me.

Westin grips my arm, stopping me from getting away. "I was angry and felt betrayed. I'm not saying I'm over it or that it'll be easy. But I've spent a long time waiting for you, and the fact you were willing to come in here and lose your career for me . . . I don't know, it shows who you are. You might be lost right now, but I'm holding out my hand, asking you to let me pull you back."

I gaze up into his soulful green eyes, looking for a sign to tell me this is a dream. "I don't want to screw this up."

He runs his fingers down my arm, taking my hand in his. "The only mistake we'll make is to walk away at the first sign of struggle. I love you, Ren. That means even when you fuck up, I'm going to be here to help you back up."

Tears form and my lip trembles. I wanted to hear this. I prayed for another chance to prove to him that I was the girl he loved all along, I just got off track.

"I'm so sorry," I say as a tear falls.

"I know," he sighs and wipes my face. "I know you are, and I am too. I should've let you tell me when you were in trouble."

I shake my head. "I put your entire career in jeopardy, you don't owe me any apologies."

He wraps his arms around my waist, and I melt. I don't care that people could see us as tears stream down my face. I couldn't stop myself from crying if I wanted to. Right now, he's holding me. Westin's arms are around me, keeping me from falling, and I feel at home.

For so long, I thought I had to close myself down in order to find my center, but I was so wrong. Being open to him is what made me face everything and see how destructive I was being.

"Can you forgive me anyway?" Westin asks.

I touch his cheek. "If it makes you feel better."

"It does, and we're going to spend the next two weeks figuring things out," he says. I tilt my head, not sure how that's going to happen. I'm off for two weeks on suspension. "I put in for vacation this morning. I had an early meeting with the board, where I was offered the chief position."

"Wes!" I squeal and he holds me tight against him. "That's amazing!"

He grins. "I told them that I would accept as long as I could take a few weeks to get some personal things in order."

He planned this? "Is that why I got the suspension?"

"No. That was just a lucky coincidence. However," he brushes my hair back while touching my face, "I've decided that we've spent enough time apart, waiting for one of us to be ready. And we need this."

He doesn't have to convince me. I want to rebuild what's been broken. It's clear that with Westin is where I belong, and I'll spend the rest of my life fighting to hold onto him. Nothing is easy, but he's worth the struggle.

"All I need is you."

Westin leans down, presses his lips to mine, and kisses me with so much love, I feel it in my toes.

EPILOGUE

Five years later

"**M**ick, you have to help me out here, man." Westin passes my dad a beer. "There's no way the Cubs are going to win the World Series back to back."

"This conversation is lame," I reply as I rest my head on my father's shoulder.

"Babe, you have to tell your brother he's wrong!" Westin urges.

I look at Everton, who just returned home for leave before he reports to his duty station. Then I back Westin up. "You're stupid and wrong."

Everton shrugs. "I'm telling you, it's going to happen."

They continue their argument as I nestle closer to Daddy. We're up at the farm for a few days. My father suffered a stroke about six months ago and he's now living with us in Chicago. Twice a month, we ride out here, and let him enjoy being in his space.

I never understood that being at home could affect huge physical difference in patients until I began taking care of my father daily. I feel as though both Westin and I have become better doctors for it as well. We see the whole picture and have both adjusted our treatment plans because of it.

"What do you think, Daddy?"

He jerks his head up and tries to speak. "Idiots." Thankfully, Westin and I can understand most of what he says. He's been getting stronger with Westin's help.

Westin scoffs and then drains his beer. "Am not."

"Yeah, that's debatable." I roll my eyes at all of them and get to my feet. I look at my brother. "And you're definitely an idiot."

Everton flips me off and I laugh as I walk into the kitchen.

Three Christmases ago, Westin signed the house over to me. I cried, hugged him, made love to him, and took it as the first real sign that he had one hundred percent moved past everything that happened with Allison Brown-Peyton.

The house has been mostly redone, but in a way that it's in line with its roots. I stand in front of the sink, looking out at the grass and think about my mother. She would've loved the changes to the house, and she'd be happy with how we're all doing now. Daddy has been doing well, minus the residual speech issues, and it's been nice having him around. I think he likes the company as well.

My brother joined the Marines a few years ago, and is shipping off to Japan for three years. It wasn't until he finished boot camp that we even found out he was in the military, but the look of pride on my father's face said it all. As much as him taking off changed the dynamics, I think it was the best thing possible for everyone.

I can only hope my mother is at peace with how I'm living as well. The first year after my giant mistake was rocky, but we found our way. I struggled with the guilt, secrets, and trying to build a new foundation with Westin. He grappled with trusting me, but through a lot of talking, we were able to learn the power of forgiveness.

The more I held onto my past, the more it was dragging me down. It wasn't until my first trial patient's tumor shrunk and I saw that I could do good things, that I was able to heal a little.

Arms wrap around me from behind, and Westin's chin rests on my shoulder. "What are you smiling about?"

"My family, work, you." I lean my head against his.

"Me?"

"Yeah, I guess I like you."

His arms tighten and he kisses my cheek. "I guess that's a good thing, huh?"

"I tend to think so." I smile a little bigger.

He turns me around and I wrap my arms around his neck.

I more than like him. I'm so madly in love with this man I can't see straight. Westin saved me in so many ways, and I'll never be able to thank him for it. He loved me when I didn't even realize I needed to be loved. He was always supportive, emboldened me, and then, when I fell from grace, he lifted me back up. Each time I ran, he chased me until it was my turn to stand and face life.

"Let's go for a walk," he suggests.

"Okay?"

He kisses my nose, and takes my hand, leading me outside. I wrap my arms around his middle as we stroll down the little dirt path that goes to the tire swing.

"You know I fall in love with you a little more each day?" he says it as both a statement and a question.

"Is that a good thing?"

He laughs. "I tend to think so," Westin repeats the words I used a few minutes ago.

"Are you happy, Wes?"

His green eyes stare down at me and his grin is warm. "Yes. I'm happy."

"Good."

"You make me happy," he adds on.

I'm glad, because I'm not the easiest person in the world. We work together, live together, and take care of my father; it's not always sunshine and roses. Which is why the farm trips are never missed. When we're here, it's like life slows down. We're able to breathe, and not be two insanely busy doctors, trying to save the world. We're two people.

Life is simpler here.

Love lives here.

My parents built this place with their hearts and souls. You can feel it as soon as you step in the door. It's like taking a breath, and when you exhale, all the bad things leave your body.

"I love you very much," I tell him.

"I know and I love you," he says before kissing me.

We make it to the swing, and he gets behind it as I climb up.

"Did you want to talk?"

Westin lets out a short laugh. "You can't handle the quiet, can you?"

"You usually want to talk when we come out here," I remind him.

Over the last few years, this has been what he does. We come here, go for a walk, and he reveals something that's on his mind. I'm just wondering what it could be this time.

"I'm getting that predictable?"

"No, I just can see there's something going on in that head

of yours."

I look back from over my shoulder and he holds the tire still and then comes around to face me. Westin squats down in front of me, caging me in.

"Do you still love being a doctor?" he asks.

"Most days. Do you?"

"If I was one, I would say yes," he sighs.

In the last few months, he's pulled back a bit. As chief, his days are filled with paperwork, complaints, and cleaning up messes. He's almost never in the operating room, and for a surgeon, that's home. It's where you feel alive, and it feeds your soul.

"You are a doctor, Westin," I remind him.

"What if I asked you to move out here? Would you give it up? We could come live on the farm with your dad, work a little less, and just relax more."

I won't lie and say I haven't thought about it. Especially each time we drive away from here. I find myself looking forward to the next visit.

"Would you really be happy with that?" My hand touches his cheek, and he leans into my touch.

"I'd be happy with you no matter where we were."

I can't stop the smile that forms at how sweet he is. Westin says what he feels, no matter what, when it comes to me. I've learned over time to do the same. I show him, but sometimes, it's nice for him to hear the words as well.

"I feel the same way, but I don't know that we could go from living a life at a hundred miles per hour down to ten and be happy. What happens when all the projects we do every other week here are done? How would you fill your time?"

He wiggles his brows with a mischievous grin. "I can think

of one."

I shake my head with a laugh. "You're ridiculous."

"I want to marry you, Serenity. I want to live the rest of our days together and not just passing each other in the hallways. I want to wrap my arms around you at night and know you'll be there when I wake up. We've lived our lives for everyone else, now it's time for us to live for ourselves."

My heart races as he reaches into his pocket, drops to one knee, and looks into my eyes.

He's going to propose. All this time we've kind of swept it under the rug because we've been happy.

He removes a diamond ring, holding it between his fingers, and takes my hand.

"I know we've said we didn't need a ring, a wedding, and all of that, but I need you. I don't want any regrets, and not making you my wife would be one of them. I'm asking you to be my partner all the days of our lives. Will you do me the honor of becoming my wife?"

The butterflies in my belly flutter, making me feel dizzy. I nod quickly, tears falling down my cheeks.

"Yes, yes, I'll marry you!"

He stands, lifting me in his arms and spinning me around. I take his face in my hands and kiss him.

"She said yes!" he yells behind me, and my father and brother come out of the house.

He pulls me to his chest. "Thank you for being my reason for living."

I rub his cheek. "No, you're mine. You gave me everything and then somehow managed to give me even more."

I'll never get back the time I spent pushing Wes away, but I'll spend the rest of my life cherishing each day we have from now until forever.

Thank you for reading this book and I hope you enjoyed it. I wish I could sit here and tell you the adventure it was to publish it, but that would be an entire new story. Serenity was a voice I heard back in 2014. I was going to write this book back then, instead I put it aside. I wrote it, believed in it, and kept thinking it wasn't good enough. I don't know how it's actually in your hands right now. Honestly, I don't. I swore it would be that book that just sat on my computer, never to be seen.

A good friend believed in it. She urged me to push forward. So, here we are. Thank you for coming along this ride with me.

ACKNOWLEDGMENTS

To my husband and children. You sacrifice so much for me to continue to live out my dream. Days and nights of me being absent even when I'm here. I'm working on it. I promise. I love you more than my own life.

My readers. There's no way I can thank you enough. It still blows me away that you read my words. You guys have become a part of my heart and soul.

Bloggers: I don't think you guys understand what you do for the book world. It's not a job you get paid for. It's something you love and you do because of that. Thank you from the bottom of my heart.

My beta reader Melissa Saneholtz: All I can say with this one is . . . THANK GOD it's over. LOL.

My assistant, Christy Peckham: How many times can one person be fired and keep coming back? I think we're running out of times. No, but for real, I couldn't imagine my life without you. You're a pain in my ass but it's because of you that I haven't fallen apart.

Sommer Stein for once again making this cover perfect and still loving me after we fight because I change my mind a bajillion times.

My editor, Nancy Smay, thank you for caring for me through this.

Julia Griffis for always finding all the typos and crazy mistakes.

Melanie Harlow, thank you for being the Glinda to my Elphaba or Ethel to my Lucy. Your friendship means the world to me and I love writing with you. I feel so blessed to have you in my life.

Bait, Crew, and Corinne Michaels Books—I love you more than you'll ever know.

My agent, Kimberly Brower, I am so happy to have you on my team. Thank you for your guidance and support. Especially with this story.

Melissa Erickson, you're amazing. I love your face. Thank you for always talking me off the ledge that is mighty high.

To my narrator, Julia Whelan. You. Are a goddess. Thank you so much. I am so blessed to know you and even more so that you were so willing to come on this story with me.

Vi, Claire, Chelle, Mandi, Amy, Kristy, Penelope, Kyla, Rachel, Tijan, Alessandra, Laurelin, Devney, Jessica, Carrie Ann, Kennedy, Lauren, Susan, Sarina, Beth, Julia, and Natasha—Thank you for keeping me striving to be better and loving me unconditionally. There are no better sister authors than you all.

BOOKS BY CORINNE MICHAELS

The Salvation Series
Beloved
Beholden
Consolation
Conviction
Defenseless
Evermore: A 1001 Dark Night Novella
Indefinite
Infinite

Hennington Brothers Series
Say You'll Stay
Say You Want Me
Say I'm Yours
Say You Won't Let Go: A Return to Me/Masters and Mercenaries Novella

Second Time Around Series
We Own Tonight
One Last Time
Not Until You
If I Only Knew

The Arrowood Brothers
Come Back for Me
Fight for Me
The One for Me
Stay for Me

Willow Creek Valley Series
Return to Us
Could Have Been Us
A Moment for Us

A Chance for Us
Truth Between Us

Standalones
All I Ask
You Loved Me Once

Co-Written with Melanie Harlow
Hold You Close
Imperfect Match

ABOUT THE AUTHOR

Corinne Michaels is a *New York Times*, *USA Today*, *and Wall Street Journal* bestselling author of romance novels. Her stories are chock full of emotion, humor, and unrelenting love, and she enjoys putting her characters through intense heartbreak before finding a way to heal them through their struggles.

Corinne is a former Navy wife and happily married to the man of her dreams. She began her writing career after spending months away from her husband while he was deployed—reading and writing were her escape from the loneliness. Corinne now lives in Virginia with her husband and is the emotional, witty, sarcastic, and fun-loving mom of two beautiful children.